HOLLOW EARTH

HOLLOW EARTH

JOHN BARROWMAN &
CAROLE E. BARROWMAN

Aladdin New York London Toronto Sydney New Delhi

This book is a work of fiction. Any references to historical events, real people, or real places are used fictitiously. Other names, characters, places, and events are products of the author's imagination, and any resemblance to actual events or places or persons, living or dead, is entirely coincidental.

ALADDIN

An imprint of Simon & Schuster Children's Publishing Division
1230 Avenue of the Americas, New York, NY 10020
First Aladdin paperback edition July 2013
Text copyright © 2012 by John Barrowman and Carole E. Barrowman
Illustrations copyright © 2012 by Buster Books
Illustrations by Andrew Pinder
This work was originally published in Great Britain in 2012 by Buster Books,
an imprint of Michael O'Mara Books Limited.
All rights reserved, including the right of reproduction in whole or in part in any form.
ALADDIN is a trademark of Simon & Schuster, Inc., and related logo is
a registered trademark of Simon & Schuster, Inc.
Also available in an Aladdin hardcover edition.
For information about special discounts for bulk purchases, please contact
Simon & Schuster Special Sales at 1-866-506-1949 or business@simonandschuster.com.
The Simon & Schuster Speakers Bureau can bring authors to your live event.
For more information or to book an event contact the Simon & Schuster Speakers Bureau
at 1-866-248-3049 or visit our website at www.simonspeakers.com.
Designed by Mike Rosamilia
The text of this book was set in Goudy Old Style.
Manufactured in the United States of America 0613 OFF
2 4 6 8 10 9 7 5 3 1
The Library of Congress has cataloged the hardcover edition as follows:
Barrowman, John, 1968–
Hollow Earth / by John and Carole E. Barrowman. — 1st Aladdin hardcover ed.
p. cm.
Summary: Possessing extraordinary powers, including the ability to bring artwork to life,
twelve-year-old twins Matt and Emily are sought by villains trying to access the terrors of
Hollow Earth, a place where demons and mythological beasts lie trapped for eternity.
ISBN 978-1-4424-5852-9 (hc)
[1. Magic—Fiction. 2. Art—Fiction. 3. Twins—Fiction. 4. Brothers and sisters—Fiction.
5. Scotland—Fiction.] I. Barrowman, Carole E. II. Title.
PZ7.B275679Ho 2012
[Fic]—dc23
2012020116
ISBN 978-1-4424-5853-6 (pbk)
ISBN 978-1-4424-5855-0 (eBook)

To Clare and Turner, Kevin and Scott,
Marion and John, with love and thanks

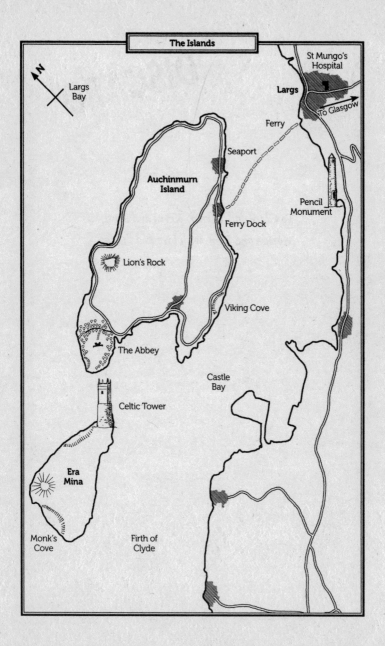

The Islands

N

Largs Bay

St Mungo's Hospital

Largs

To Glasgow

Ferry

Seaport

Auchinmurn Island

Ferry Dock

Pencil Monument

Lion's Rock

Viking Cove

The Abbey

Castle Bay

Celtic Tower

Era Mina

Monk's Cove

Firth of Clyde

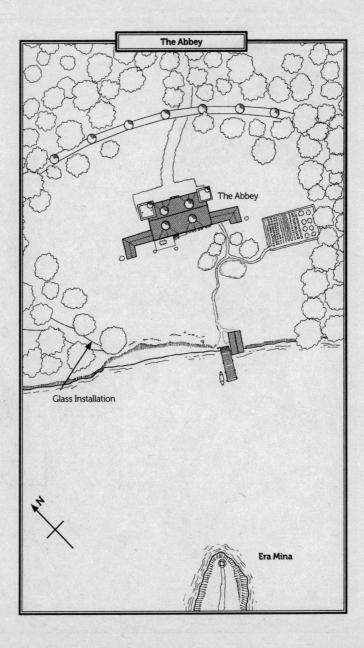

The Abbey

The Abbey

Glass Installation

N

Era Mina

The Abbey and Era Mina beyond

In the universe, there are things that are known, and things that are unknown, and in between, there are doors. —William Blake

PART ONE

ONE

The book the old monk was illuminating began with these words:

> THIS Book is about the nature of beasts. Gaze
> upon these pages at your peril,

The old monk yawned, his chin dropped to his chest, and his eyes fluttered shut. The quill dropped from his fingers, leaving a trail of ink like tiny teardrops across the folio. He was working on one of the book's later pages, a miniature of a majestic griffin with talons clutching an imposing capital G. As the old monk nodded off, the griffin leaped from its place at the corner of the page and darted across the parchment. In its haste to flee, the beast brushed its coarse wings across the old monk's fingers.

The monk's eyes snapped open. In an instant, he thumped his gnarled fist onto the griffin's slashing tail, pinning the beast to the page. He glared at it. The griffin snorted angrily and scratched its talons deep into the thin vellum of the page. The monk shook off his exhaustion and focused his mind, and in a rush of color and light the griffin was once again gripping the G at the top of the page.

Glancing behind him, the old monk spotted the bare feet of his young apprentice poking out from under the wooden frame that held the drying skins to make parchment.

Something will have to be done, the monk thought.

When he was sure the image was settled on the page, the old monk crouched to retrieve his quill. He was angry with himself. He would have to be punished for this terrible lapse in concentration and go without his evening meal. He patted his soft, round belly. He'd survive the loss.

But the boy. What to do about the boy now, given what he'd witnessed? That loss would hurt. The old monk did not relish having to train another apprentice. He had neither the strength nor the inclination for such a task. Not only that, but this boy had already demonstrated a great deal of skill as a parchment maker, and was a natural at knowing how long to soak the skins in lime and how to carefully clean and scrape them. And, at such a young age, he was already an elegant calligrapher and a brilliant alchemist with inks. Between the two of them these past months, they'd almost completed the final pages for *The Book of Beasts*. The boy and his talents would be sorely missed.

The boy sensed that the old monk was debating his future. He could hear the weight of the monk's ideas in his head, like a drumming deep inside his mind. He associated the sound with the monk because at its loudest, when the monk was concentrating hardest, the drumming was deep and full and round, much like the monk himself.

The boy's mother was the only other person the boy could sense in his head: a feeling not unwanted, although often peculiar. Not because he missed her. Far from it. His mother and his brothers and sisters still lived in the village outside the monastery gates. But his mother's echo in his head had helped him escape her wrath, warranted or not, many times. Quickly the boy lifted his pestle and mortar and finished crushing the iron salts and acorns for his next batch of ink.

The old monk straightened himself against his desk. What should he do? What if he were to fall asleep again while illuminating, only the next time his dozing was too sound? He didn't dare think about the consequences of such a terrible slip. Only once before had he let such a thing happen, with tragic results. He'd been a young man and had not had the benefit of his training yet. In his nightmares, he could still hear the apprentice's screams. Oh, and there had been so much blood.

No, something would definitely have to be done about the boy.

He stared at his apprentice across the workroom now in much the same manner as he had stared down the griffin.

But the boy was courageous and smart. He knew this was an

important moment in his short life. He loved everything about the monastery and didn't want to leave. He was genuinely fond of the old monk, with whom he'd worked since his father had given him to the service of the monks in return for grazing rights on a prime piece of church land outside the village.

The boy knew how much such a trade was worth to his family. It was worth everything to him, too. This was a time when men, women, and children believed in miracles and magic with equal faith. It was a time when kings and queens fought for their crowns with armadas and armies whose allegiance they bought with land and crops and even bigger armies. And it was a time when hope and happiness had everything to do with where you were born and who was protecting you.

Yes, indeed, the boy knew better than anything else that he had to stay with the old monk and remain part of this ancient holy order. So he did the only thing he knew how to do in the circumstances. He stood up and stared directly back at the old monk without flinching and with an equal measure of concentration.

The monk glared.

The boy's heart was pounding in his chest. The drumming in his skull was so loud, it felt as if a vise was tightening across his ears. He was sure his head was going to burst. His nose started to bleed, dripping into the mortar he was gripping in his hands. Behind the monk, the boy could see the griffin's tail thumping against the page. But still he held his gaze.

After what seemed—to the boy, anyway—to be forever, the

vise around his skull loosened, the pulsing of the old monk's thoughts stopped, and the boy thought he heard a sigh inside his head. The monk's shoulders drooped, and he turned away. The boy let out his breath and wiped his sleeve across his nose.

Ah, thought the monk, *I have neither the strength nor the inclination to challenge this boy's fortitude. Something else will have to be done to ensure that he honors the monastery's secrets.*

He turned away, his focus back on the beast.

With great relief, the boy returned his attention to the pot and his mixtures. When he'd finished creating the ink, he filled the monk's inkwell and stored the rest for another day. Then he turned to the goatskin stretched across the rack. Gently the boy ran the tips of his fingers across the surface, making sure the skin was drying smooth and thin enough to absorb the inks. He looked again at the old monk, his body draped across his tall desk, his quill dipping in and out of the inkwell. The monk's concentration was so intense, the boy knew nothing would shift him until the final touches had been put to the page.

Soon the light was fading from the room, and the old monk could feel his mind drifting again. After cleaning the tip of his quill, he set it inside his leather pouch along with his other tools. Then he sealed the inkwell with a wax plug before covering the page he was illustrating with two thin layers of vellum. Lifting the pages, he set them on a rack inside the cabinet next to his desk, weighing down the corners with polished stones. The pages he'd been working on for the past month were similarly laid out across the cabinet's broad shelves. Tomorrow, he'd begin the process of illuminating the final beast, the most terrifying of them all—the grendel.

The monk locked the cabinet, dropping the key into the pocket of his robes. Before closing the shutters, he peered out through the wide slits in the thick stone walls, stunned for a moment by the sight of an owl and one of its young lifting off from a nearby tree. *A sign*, the old monk thought. *An omen, to be sure.* Of good, he trusted.

"Time for prayers, and then perhaps you and I should discuss the matter lingering before us."

"Yes, master."

The boy echoed his master's ritual, cleaning his tools, wrapping them in their soft leather pouches, and setting them on his workbench.

The old monk dampened the peat in the hearth and pulled on his fur cloak. Grabbing his cap and scarf from the floor, the boy tied his leather soles onto his feet and followed his master to the heavy oak door.

"Solon, you would do well to forget what you believe you saw earlier. It was only a trick of your youthful imagination."

The boy stepped in front of the old monk and held the door for him.

"Beg pardon, master, but weren't it really a trick of yours?"

TWO

Twelve-year-old twins Matt and Em Calder were sitting on a hard wooden bench. The gallery was quiet and not yet open to the public, but they were not happy. Their mom had made promises that morning about their plans for this sweltering day, and they didn't remember having to stop to look at paintings being one of them. Setting their backpacks on the floor in front of them, the twins glared at their mother.

"Behave yourselves," Sandie warned. "Do not leave this bench. Do not even *think* about it. I mean it. I'll only be gone ten minutes at the most. I'll be right over there."

She pointed to the tall, yellow-haired man in a dark suit holding a stack of books in his arms. The man dipped his head toward them in his usual acknowledgment. Em smiled politely, but Matt turned away, more interested in a woman wheeling a cart with a wooden crate the size and shape of a painting strapped to it through the next gallery. A museum guard followed close behind her. At the elevator, the guard swiped a key card across the security pad. The doors opened. Dismissing the guard's help with a wave of her hand, the woman eased the cart into the elevator. The guard backed away, but as the doors were closing he changed his mind, shoved his foot between them, and ducked inside with the woman and the painting.

"Matt! Are you even listening to me?"

Matt slumped on the bench, shoving his sister to the edge as he did so.

"This is a lovely painting to look at while you wait," Sandie went on. "It's by Georges Seurat. He often painted using tiny dots instead of brushstrokes."

The twins frowned at her. In unison.

"We know," said Em.

Sandie soldiered on. "I appreciate this isn't what we'd got planned, but I need to take care of some business with—" She cut herself off mid-sentence and changed tack. "How about when I'm finished with this meeting, we go swimming just like the boy in the painting?" She put her leather messenger bag over her shoulder. "What do you say? Deal?"

"Deal," said Em, who, in these situations at least, was always the first to agree.

Matt shrugged. "Whatever."

They watched their mom walk over to the yellow-haired man

and settle on a similar bench in the next gallery. The man leaned close to their mother as if about to share a secret with her; in response, Sandie flipped open the sketchbook she always carried, handing the man a sheet of paper she had tucked into one of the pages. Boring. Turning her attention back to the painting, Em leaned forward and squinted hard, trying to see all the dots without leaving the bench, while Matt emptied his backpack into the space between them—the pens, chalk, and charcoal he always carried in a bashed cookie tin, his iPod, earbuds, two *Captain America* comics, assorted candy wrappers, a pack of bubble gum, an empty Coke can, and a sketch pad. Tearing a sheet of paper from the pad, he handed Em a pen. She shook her head.

"Swimming would be a lot of fun," he said. "No one's paying any attention to us."

Em accepted the pen, and they began to draw. The next thing the twins knew, they were in the painting, splashing in the cool, blue water of the River Seine with a boy in a red hat. He said his name was Pierre and spoke to them in French. The twins understood. He said he had only a few minutes to bathe before he had to get back to his work.

"Is that your dog?" Matt asked Pierre, worried that the dog would have nowhere to go when Pierre returned to his job. But Pierre didn't answer the question, so Matt gave up and began splashing water onto the men lounging on the bank. They ignored him. Matt floated on his back for a while. He could feel Em splashing next to him. He looked up at the sky, but it wasn't there, and he thought he knew why—and then he and Em were suddenly sopping wet and lying in a big puddle on the floor in front of the painting in the National Gallery. Two very angry guards were rushing toward them with Sandie close on their heels. The yellow-haired man was gone. Quickly gathering up the twins' things, Sandie apologized to the guards. "I'm so sorry. They must have dumped their bottles of water on each other. It is really warm today."

She glared at the twins. "All I asked was ten minutes. Ten minutes!" She yanked both of them upright. "Oh God, you've no idea what you've done."

Feeling some sympathy for the twins, one of the guards told them that since the museum was not yet open to the general public for the day, no real harm was done. The staff could get the mess cleaned up quickly before anyone else came through. He wasn't planning to take any chances though, and quickly escorted the three of them outside to the morning heat of Trafalgar Square.

A member of the National Gallery's cleaning staff was called to the Postimpressionist room, where she soaked up the water with her mop. She had to smile to herself. Her own boys might have done much worse than a water fight if it had been them sitting there feeling hot and bored.

As she was wringing her mop out into the bucket, something on the floor under the bench caught her eye. Reaching down, she snagged a folded sheet of paper torn from a drawing pad. The drawing had to belong to one of those children because she'd cleaned this particular gallery earlier that morning and she knew she hadn't missed a thing.

Unfolding the paper, she was surprised to see a recognizable sketch of *Bathers at Asnières*. There was something off in the dots of color around the boy in the red hat, the men languishing on the shore were distorted in their dimensions, and the little brown dog had a kind of smudged-sausage look to him, but it was a very good copy indeed.

She glanced at the sketch one more time. The water of the Seine was dashed in thick blue strokes across the bottom of the paper, but the top half of the drawing was a complete blank.

No sky.

She gathered up her mop and bucket, rolled her cart toward the exit, and crumpled the paper into a ball. On her way out of the gallery, she chucked it into a nearby bin.

She could have sworn she heard a splash.

THREE

Arthur Summers couldn't believe what he'd just witnessed. When Sandie, the twins' mother, had sprinted across the gallery to her children, Arthur had moved with haste in the other direction. At the staff elevator, he swiped his key card on the security pad. The elevator doors opened immediately, and he darted inside, pressing the button to the basement three, four times, hoping more jabs would speed up his descent.

His pulse was racing. Sweat was beading under his shirt, and his straw-blond hair felt damp with perspiration. He'd known the twins since they were toddlers. He was supposed to monitor their development and ensure the Society heard of any evolution in their powers before the Council of Guardians did. But he'd never imagined they would reach this level while the children were still so young. It—changed things.

He squeezed out before the doors had fully opened and quickly headed for the National Gallery's restoration lab. To most employees at the National, this floor was nicknamed "the morgue" because it had been created from the catacombs that ran beneath Charing Cross Road from the church of St. Martin-in-the-Fields. Arthur had always thought the enormous basement lab should really have been called "purgatory" because, although it was the place where paintings were resurrected to new life, working down here always felt like punishment. Unfortunately, no one at the National cared what Arthur thought, which was why he was so successful at keeping his secrets.

At the lab doors, Arthur used his key card again. This time he waited for the pad to flip open and reveal a fingerprint sensor. When it did, he wiped his sweating thumb across his trousers before pressing it to the pad.

The doors slid open with a hiss, and he stepped into an enclosed glass chamber, an anteroom, where he waited for the first doors to seal and the air to be calibrated before a second set of doors opened.

Just as the first doors locked, Arthur saw a cloaked and hooded person move from the stairwell and into the shadows of the hallway. When the second set of doors slid open, Arthur's heart was pounding so fast, he thought he might hyperventilate.

He dashed into his purgatory, the doors sealing behind him. The figure wouldn't follow. It *couldn't*. Could it?

The lab was the size of a school gym. Despite the high-tech equipment spread around the room—portable imaging machines, scanners, microscopes, copiers, and computers with huge flat-screen monitors—the worktables of the men and women who restored and repaired paintings in this room were covered in the more traditional media of paintbrushes and palettes. Row upon row of easels stood like sentinels against the walls. As Arthur marched down the aisle bisecting the room, he noticed a row of paintings being readied for the exhibition he was curating: "The Horror in Art."

When Arthur was about ten steps from his office door, the lights went out. Cursing under his breath, hands trembling, he fished a penlight from his inside pocket and continued onward, glancing back now and again.

He stopped short at the last painting in the room, his breath catching in his throat.

Despite the relevance of the image, Arthur had most certainly not requested *Witch with Changeling Child* for his exhibition. In the painting, only the witch's large pocked nose was visible from the shadows of a shabby woolen shawl. Seated on her bony lap was a dwarfish demon child with a misshapen head; a bulbous nose; pale, waxy skin; and eyes like tiny yellow marbles sunk into its fleshy forehead.

What disturbed Arthur even more than the repulsive subject matter was the painting's history. It had been linked to a number of grisly deaths that had occurred at the gallery when the painting had first been exhibited to the public. As a result, *Witch with Changeling Child* was said to be cursed and had been locked in storage, never to be displayed again.

Until now. Who had put it here?

Arthur swept his penlight across the witch's gnarled hands and up and over to the horrible creature perched on her lap. When he reached the changeling's face with his penlight, he froze in terror. He knew it wasn't his imagination.

The dwarfish demon was grinning at him.

FOUR

The twins had not been in a taxi in ages—they always traveled on the Tube with their mom. But as soon as the security guard had hustled them from the National Gallery and out onto Trafalgar Square, Sandie hurried them into a taxi. Giving the driver their address, she settled herself on one of the flip-down seats facing the twins. She was so angry with them, she was almost speechless.

"Seat belts fastened. *Right now*."

"Why are you so mad?" asked Matt. "We didn't do anything wrong."

"You know the rules! You know that what you did was dangerous."

"Your rules, not ours!" Matt shouted back.

"We're sorry, Mom. We didn't mean to make you angry," Em

interjected before the two of them started fighting for real. Matt and their mom seemed to be doing more and more of that lately, ever since their dad had missed another of their birthdays without a call or an e-mail. With every passing year, Matt was becoming more and more convinced that their mom had driven their dad away. Em could hardly remember what their dad looked like. She wasn't sure she missed him at all.

"Really, Mom," continued Em. "We're not stupid. We know we're not supposed to draw in public. But we were so hot. We won't do it again. Promise."

Sandie sighed. Sometimes her terror made her lose control. She patted Em's leg. "I know you're not stupid. Far from it."

She tried to ruffle Matt's hair. He pulled away and slouched against the seat. "It's just that you're getting older, and things are becoming complicated—"

"We were hot and wanted to go swimming," Matt snapped. "And you promised no more meetings. Two days in a row you've dragged us to that stupid gallery."

Sandie leaned forward, fear tightening the knot already in her stomach. "Are you saying you *knew* you were putting yourselves into the painting?" She turned to Em. "Please tell me you've never done that before."

Don't say a word, Em.

Em hesitated as Matt's words echoed in her head. "We didn't know we could do that—until it happened with a painting yesterday," she said at last.

The color drained from Sandie's face. Things were worse than she had thought. Much worse. "What painting?"

Be quiet, Em!

"A painting . . . of Roman ruins. It was easy to copy." Seeing the sudden panic in her mom's eyes, Em blurted, "No one saw us. Honest. We were careful, Mom. I promise we were."

Shut up, Em, or I'll pound you.

I don't like telling lies . . . and you couldn't pound me if you tried.

Em whacked Matt across his chest with her backpack. He yelped, reached across the seat, and swatted his sister back.

"Emily Anne Calder! What was that for?"

Not for the first time, Sandie sensed something strange going on between her son and daughter. She knew twins were connected to each other in ways that science was only beginning to understand—Matt was able to sense when Em was sad; Em was able to know when Matt was angry or hurt. And she knew that twins often had unique ways of communicating with each other. But what was beginning to scare her was that—given who the twins were, given what they were becoming—this was something much more significant.

Sandie tugged the offending backpack from Em's hands and set it down on her own lap. She needed to think. She needed to plan. "We'll talk more about this when we get home."

Matt fiddled with his earbuds and cranked up his music. Em did the same.

Sandie leaned her head against the cool glass of the taxi

window. At the entrance to St. James's Park, she watched a family waiting for the pedestrian signal. A mom pushing her baby in a carriage, a dad with a toddler gripping his hand.

Everything was so much easier when they held my hands, she thought.

Not for the last time that day, Sandie wondered if her children were becoming more than she could handle—a prediction their grandfather, Renard, had thrown at her the day she bundled up her twin toddlers and ran for their lives.

FIVE

Arthur fled from the grinning demon. He didn't have much time. Someone else had witnessed his failure to keep an eye on the twins and their developing powers—and now the Society would know that Arthur was dispensable. He knew too much. He had done too much. At the door to his office, he fumbled for his key card and dropped it. When he bent to retrieve it, he heard footsteps pitter-pattering across the floor in the lab behind him. Snatching up the card, he swiped his office door open, then slammed and locked it behind him. Leaning against the cold metal, he attempted to calm himself. The noises in the lab were louder now, as if someone was scampering across the tables.

"You have time. You have time," Arthur chanted aloud, trying to quell his terror. His nerves were frayed, and he was having difficulty keeping his fear at bay. Sandie couldn't possibly control or change what was in the future for the twins, and yet he felt a deep sadness that he was unable to prepare her for what was to come. He'd grown fond of her over the years. Despite the nature of their work together, they had made a good team. He knew she trusted him—at least, as far as anyone can trust their jailer. Arthur sighed. Sandie Calder really should not have trusted him at all. What a fool he'd been, to think that the Society's plan would go forward without further violence. Arthur was nothing more than a pawn in a murderous chess game that had been going on for centuries. As he sat at his cluttered desk with his head in his hands, an amazing thing happened. Arthur found a little compassion and just enough courage to free Sandie from the chains that bound her. It was time to break his allegiance to the Hollow Earth Society and let Sir Charles and the Council of Guardians decide the twins' fate after all. He lifted the phone and dialed a number. After a few seconds, he punched in a code, then hung up. Within seconds, his phone rang. The receiver almost slid from his clammy hand as he grabbed it.

"What has happened, Arthur?"

"Sir Charles, it's the twins. They . . . they animated themselves into a painting. I've never seen anything like it before. I knew it was possible, but witnessing it for the first time was quite shocking. One minute they were drawing on the bench, then the next minute they were—"

"Arthur, I'm a Guardian. I know what animating looks like."

There was silence on the line for a beat, just long enough for Arthur to hear scurrying outside his door.

"Thank you, Arthur," said Sir Charles Wren. "The Council will take charge of the twins from here on. Something we should have done years ago, if I'd had my way."

Arthur hung up the phone, his nerves frayed but his conscience stilled. Even if the Council of Guardians decided to bind the children, Arthur hoped they would not do so until they were of age—sixteen. If nothing else, he hoped he had given the twins, and Sandie, a little more time. There was just one more call to make. Arthur was reaching across his desk for the phone again when it rang. Startled, Arthur knocked the receiver from the desk. Bending to pick it up, he saw a dark shadow choking the space between the floor outside and his door.

"Does Sandie know of the Society's plans for the twins?"

It wasn't Sir Charles.

"I don't . . . don't think so," said Arthur faintly.

"Good. Good. Oh, and Arthur?"

"Yes?"

"Don't open your office door."

SIX

The taxi turned into Raphael Terrace, a narrow street on the cusp of Knightsbridge, where the houses were clinging with quiet dignity to their wealthy pasts even as their paint peeled and their roofs leaked. Sandie and the twins got out in front of a three-story Victorian mansion that had been the home of the Kitten family since the 1850s. In the 1960s, the Kitten sisters, Violet and Anthea, had turned their mansion into a residence for modern artists. They had leased the top floor, converted into an apartment years ago, to Sandie when she and the twins had first arrived in London. Violet and Anthea were in the hallway with their shopping when the twins burst through the front door, so they helped the two women with the bags. That way they figured they could postpone, if not avoid, more of their mom's wrath upstairs.

Sandie's mobile rang. Sprinting up the stairs, she answered as she unlocked the door to the apartment.

"They're coming for you," said Arthur without any preamble. Sandie leaned against the wall for support.

"The Council of Guardians? But they can't take them now. They're too young. Sir Charles promised me when I came to London he wouldn't take them if I . . . if . . ."

The twins' voices carried up to her from downstairs. She couldn't let them overhear how she'd protected them all these years. "Matt and Em didn't know what they were doing, Arthur," she whispered instead. "Truly, they didn't. How much time do we have?"

"Not enough. Not enough. I'm so sorry, Sandie. For everything."

Sandie flipped her phone closed and stood paralyzed. Tears welled up in her eyes. She loved this apartment and she didn't want to leave. But for several months she'd been trying to ignore signs that this day was coming—and now it was here.

If the Council reached the twins first, they were sure to vote to bind their powers. Terrifying as this was, it was not the worst threat that faced her children. She'd heard rumors that the Hollow Earth Society had once again crawled from its catacombs.

There was only one thing she could think to do. But first she needed to get the twins to safety.

She made a swift phone call, then glanced at her watch. They could get out in ten minutes. She had rehearsed. She hoped it would be enough.

Darting into her bedroom, she pulled a suitcase from under her bed. Quickly she unzipped it to check it held everything she needed. Tossing a couple of extra books into the suitcase, she grabbed her toiletries from the bathroom. Her extra sketchbook sat on her bedside table, so she shoved that into her bag too. Then she wheeled the suitcase out to the main room at the same time as the twins, sandwiches in hands, came into the apartment with Violet trailing behind them.

Seven minutes left.

From the door, Matt stared in shock at his mom. "You can't leave us too!"

Em dashed across the room, throwing herself around Sandie's waist and bursting into tears. "Mom, we won't draw again, I promise. We promise. Don't we, Matt?"

Sandie let go of the suitcase and scooped up both children. "I'm not leaving you. Ever." After a couple of beats, she pulled away from the embrace and checked her watch. Six minutes.

"But we do have to go. Right now. I'll explain everything soon, but I need each of you to get your travel backpacks."

"But where are we going?" sniffled Em.

Sandie glanced at Violet, whose disheveled air made her look her sixty-plus years. "They're coming, Violet."

On the street outside the apartment, tires squealed and car doors slammed. The twins ran to the window.

Violet squeezed Sandie's hand. "When you're safe, let us know. Anthea and I will have everything sent to you. Take our car. Go out through the garden." She fished some keys out of her cardigan pocket and handed them to Sandie.

"Wait," Sandie said, dashing back to her bedroom. She returned with an aluminum cylinder, the kind artists use to protect unframed canvases, and handed the tube to Violet.

Violet's hand instinctively went to her mouth as she gasped. "Is this . . . ?"

Em and Matt turned from the window and watched Violet take hold of the cylinder as if she were accepting explosives.

"Of course it's not," answered Sandie. "But I want them to think that it is. Use it to stall them, but if they take it from you, don't let them think you're giving it up easily."

Violet tucked the tube under her arm. "I can do that, my dear. Now be safe. We'll keep them occupied for as long as we can."

"Thank you." The two women embraced. "For everything, Vi. We couldn't have survived here without you and Anthea." Sandie glanced at the kitchen clock.

Five minutes left.

At the window, Matt and Em watched as a man dressed in dark jeans, a white collared shirt, and dark glasses halted traffic on the street while a woman about their mom's age, with short blond hair and in a bright red dress, opened the rear car door for another man. He was older, and from his demeanor it was clear that he was the one in charge. As he climbed out of the car, apparently arguing with the woman, he turned and stared up at the windows. Matt and Em ducked instinctively, both letting out a yelp.

Did you feel that?

Matt rubbed his temple. *Like someone nipped my brain.*

Who are they?

Dunno.

Sandie set their backpacks against the front door.

"Why do we have to go?" Matt demanded.

"Who are these people?" asked Em, still watching outside.

Why was nothing ever easy? Sandie sighed and pulled her bag over her shoulder. The truthful answers to their questions were frightening ones. But, for Matt especially, having a mom with secrets was perhaps worse than knowing what was really going on. Sandie was exhausted and she really needed their cooperation. She hoped fear would motivate them both.

"We have to go because those people aren't coming to see us. They're coming to hurt you."

Em looked horrified. Matt glared at his mom. One more thing she was making up, to get him to do something he didn't want to do.

"Em, Matt—*now*. We have to reach Vi and Anthea's car before they get inside the building."

The twins turned back to the window and watched the two men and the woman climb the front steps. Grabbing their arms, Sandie pulled the twins away. Matt shook himself loose and ran back.

Three minutes left.

"Em, get your backpack. Please." Sandie stood in front of

Matt, imploring. "I know you're angry with me for all sorts of things these days, but this isn't the time, Matt. There are very dangerous people coming here, and I don't have time to explain why, but *we have to go*."

Matt had hardly ever seen his mom cry except maybe when watching a really sad movie or looking at a painting she was working on, but he didn't think he'd ever done anything to actually *make* her cry. He was mad at her—she was right about that—but he didn't want to make her sad. Not really. Plus, as he watched her eyes fill with tears, he suddenly had a feeling, like a deep kind of drumming in his head, that she was telling them the truth. They were in danger.

"Does it have something to do with our drawing?"

"Yes," she replied, brushing her sleeve across her eyes, "and I promise that once we're safe, I'll tell you more. But please, please, just this once, do what I'm asking without an argument."

One minute left.

The downstairs doorbell rang.

SEVEN

Arthur slammed down the phone and rushed out from behind his desk. He leaned against the door, listening. The lab was strangely quiet, but Arthur was under no illusion that this was anything but a momentary respite from the horror to come. Quickly he unlocked a cabinet behind his desk and lifted out a flat wooden box the size of a notebook. He shivered as he opened the lid. Inside was a page torn from a sketchbook, the paper scored and bruised with age. The drawing spilled off the edges in overlapping swirls of yellows, blacks, and greens, with an angry gaping hole like the mouth of a cave in the center.

The scratching at his office door had started again. It sounded like tiny talons tearing into the metal frame. Mopping his brow with his handkerchief, Arthur thought about Sandie. In his own way, he had come to love her like a daughter, and betraying the Society so she might escape was the least he could do. He took the drawing from the box and turned it over, running his fingers across the inscription inked on the back.

To our sons and daughters,
May you never forget imagination is the real and the eternal.
This is Hollow Earth.
Duncan Fox, Edinburgh, 1848

Arthur returned the drawing to the box and closed the lid.

Without thinking too long about his decision, he tore a sheet of paper from his desk pad and began to write:

Dear Matt and Em,

A high-pitched shriek erupted from the still-deserted lab. Terrified, Arthur watched the edges of his office door begin to melt into light. With no time to waste, he finished the note, grabbed a large padded envelope from his desk drawer, and put the note and the box containing the drawing inside.

The perimeter of his door was now a halo of white heat. Through the gaps between the door and the jamb, Arthur glimpsed the hooded monklike figure he'd seen in the hallway. He snatched a postage label, filled it out, and forced the package into a vacuum tube that ran across the ceiling and disappeared into the bowels of the building to the mailroom.

Arthur's office door had now liquefied into a silver puddle on the floor. The tall figure slid a drawing pad into the wide sleeve of its robes and stepped into Arthur's office.

"I didn't think you'd be alone," said Arthur.

"I'm not alone."

Something sprinted through the doorway, darted past the hooded figure's legs, and shot under Arthur's desk. Arthur looked down just in time to see the grinning demon from the painting tearing through his trouser leg with its needlelike teeth. The changeling child worked on Arthur for a very long time, finally reaching the desktop, where it knocked over the dregs of Arthur's morning coffee. The liquid splashed across the desk like dark tears.

EIGHT

Pacing outside the Kitten house, the leader of the group rang the doorbell once again. No need to hurry. Not yet. He could sense the children were still on the top floor. Although Sandie was more difficult to track, he knew she'd be near the twins.

Upstairs, Matt and Em, backpacks on, were taking one last look around the apartment.

"We can't carry anything else," insisted Sandie, unlocking a dusty door on the landing and beckoning to the children. "We must go!"

The three of them dashed down the old servants' stairs at the rear of the house. With the twins close at her heels, Sandie pushed open the terrace doors to the garden—and crashed directly into the man in the sunglasses, sent to guard the rear of the house.

Sandie's momentum gave her the advantage when they col-
lided. They both went flying against the garden wall. The man's
head bounced off the bricks as he landed with Sandie on top of
him, winded but unhurt.

"Get back up to the apartment," Sandie screamed at the twins.

This time the twins didn't hesitate. They scrambled as fast as
they could, back up the servants' stairs. In an adrenaline-fueled
panic, Sandie followed her children. They could hear Violet and
Anthea in the hall downstairs, yelling that they were not opening
the front door and that the police were on the way.

Sandie locked the apartment front door behind them, ran
into the kitchen, and swept everything off one of her worktables,
sending paint supplies and tools crashing to the floor. Climbing
on top of the table and standing on tiptoe, she stretched up to
unlock one of the skylights.

She couldn't reach the latch.

"Matt, Em—bring me a chair."

From downstairs they could hear glass breaking, wood snapping, and more yelling from Anthea and Violet.

"Mom, I think Auntie Violet and Auntie Anthea are getting
hurt," sobbed Em.

"They'll be fine, sweetie," Sandie assured her, trying to stop
her voice from shaking. "Vi and Anthea are tough."

The twins each took an end of a sturdy wooden kitchen
chair and passed it up to their mom. Sandie climbed on top and
unlocked the skylight, scattering a family of doves roosting near

the window. She pulled herself up and looked across the roof. The pitch was steeper than she'd hoped, but if they were careful, they could crawl across to the roof next door, then head on to the roof of the mews apartments that were once the Kitten stables. From the stable roof, the jump down to Violet and Anthea's car parked in the courtyard in front of the mews would be difficult, but not impossible.

She dropped back down into the kitchen. The twins were gone.

Frantic, Sandie scrambled off the table. "Matt! Em!"

"Under here!"

Sandie was so relieved to see the twins safely huddled under the table that it took her an extra beat to observe that they'd spread their pens on the floor and were drawing on a sketch pad between them. She hauled Em out from under the table and scrambled onto the table with her.

"No," screamed Em, stiffening her body and digging her heels in. "I need to help!"

Em's backpack and flailing limbs were making it impossible for Sandie to make any progress.

Stop fighting, Em. I think I can finish it myself.

But what if you can't?

I can climb faster than you, anyway.

In an instant, Em stopped resisting and climbed willingly onto the chair. No sooner had Sandie joined her than their would-be captors were at the door to the apartment.

"It'll be much easier on everyone, Sandie, if you open this door," came a voice.

"Use my hands as a step, Em," Sandie ordered. When Em's foot was in place, Sandie hoisted her up and out through the skylight onto the roof.

"Don't move!"

Em sat on the roof and stared in through the skylight as Sandie backed down onto the table again.

A bloodcurdling scream exploded from the door. The noise was so full of pain and horror, Em screamed in response: "Oh God, Mom, they've got Matt!"

But Matt was climbing up on the table next to Sandie. Shocked and relieved, Sandie hauled him up onto the kitchen chair, preparing to hoist him outside with his sister. The entire apartment was shaking with each terrible *thump* from the men at the door. Then Sandie noticed.

The wall was trembling. Not the door.

She tore the sketchbook from Matt's hand. When she looked at it, she couldn't help herself. She burst into laughter. Matt grinned at her.

The twins had sketched the apartment's front wall without a door, trapping the visitors out in the hall with no access to the apartment. The intruders were pounding furiously on a wall where the door should have been.

"Mom, we should go," urged Matt.

Sandie cupped her hands and hefted Matt out onto the roof

to join Em. Another searing howl of pain filled the house. Before climbing after her children, Sandie stared at the wall more closely. Her laughter died in her throat. Sticking through the middle of the plaster where the door should have been was a man's left hand and forearm. The fingers were limp, and the hand was already turning a mottled blue-gray.

Feeling sick, Sandie heaved herself outside. Ushering the children forward on their hands and knees, she leaned back in, pushed the chair off the table, and dropped the skylight closed behind them.

The howls of the man trapped in the wall followed them across the roof.

NINE

When Matt and Em were safely on the cobbled courtyard in front of the mews, with only minor scrapes on their hands and knees to show for their escape, Sandie shredded the drawing from Matt's sketch pad into little pieces, tossing them into a neighbor's garbage can.

"What are you doing?" said Matt, trying to stop her. "Ripping it up will make the wall go back to normal!"

"We can't leave Violet and Anthea's wall like that, Mattie, it wouldn't be right." *To say nothing of freeing the man whose arm was trapped,* Sandie added to herself. She trusted his injury would slow the hunt down.

"When we're far enough away, our drawings stop working anyway," added Em without thinking.

"Shut up, Em!" hissed Matt.

"Exactly how many times have you done something like this?" Sandie demanded.

Em looked sheepish; Matt was still scowling. Sandie collapsed on the neighbor's garden wall. Oh, she really didn't want to know the answer to that question. Suddenly, she was overwhelmed by how much Matt and Em needed to learn about who they were. She was paralyzed by how truly unprepared she was to teach them.

In her head, she'd rehearsed over and over again what she'd say when the time came. She'd even started to explain to them about their special abilities—their supernatural powers—when they were only toddlers and their dad was still a part of their lives. The lesson hadn't gone as planned. Sandie hadn't been able to bring herself to use the word "Animare": the ancient and more accurate term that defined them.

"When you're older," she had started, as the twins had scribbled at the abbey's long kitchen table, "your imaginations, your drawings, will be able to alter reality. You'll have the power to change things in the real world."

"Can you hear yourself?" Malcolm had chided. "They're just babies. They don't have a clue what you're saying to them."

He had then reached across to the fruit bowl on the kitchen counter and grabbed an orange.

"What are you doing?" Sandie had asked.

"An experiment. Something harmless."

Malcolm had placed the orange on the roll of paper in front

of the twins. "Em, Mattie, can you draw Daddy a picture of this orange?"

"They're too young, Malcolm," Sandie had said. "Most of us can't animate until we're close to nine or ten."

At first nothing had happened. The children hadn't moved, and the orange had remained an orange. Then Em had begun to draw. She had drawn an orange that looked like a square with legs, and Matt's orange, although mostly round, had a pointy top and a tail.

The real orange had remained a real orange.

Until, that is, Em had grabbed her chewed pink crayon and begun to color Matt's pointy orange thing, and Matt, not liking what Em was doing to his creation, had snatched the pink crayon from her and begun to scribble across all the parts that Em had colored.

Within seconds, the orange had exploded, showering wet slivers of pulp all over the twins.

Sandie stared in exhaustion at her two children standing anxiously in the mews courtyard in front of her. Matt was wearing a frayed concert T-shirt—the only thing of Malcolm's that she'd kept. He'd been wearing it for most of the year. His black hair was too long and curled loosely at his neck, and his blue eyes challenged her at every opportunity. Em was a softer version of her brother, with the same coloring. The twins were both of average height for their age, although Matt was a little taller than his sister after a spring growth spurt.

Sandie pulled out her phone and made another call. The news on the other end made her gasp.

"Okay," she said, whirling back to the twins. "We need to leave London, but I have something I must do before we go. Can you please promise me some cooperation?" She eyed them both. "And no more drawing?"

"We promise," answered Em.

Matt grabbed his sketchbook and shoved it deep into his backpack.

That'll have to do for now, thought Sandie.

They jogged out of the courtyard to the far end of Raphael Terrace. Looking behind them as they ran, Matt and Em noted the big black car still blocking one side of the street in front of the Kitten house, and a police car with flashing lights blocking the other side. A small crowd of curious neighbors mingled on the pavement.

When the three of them were away from Raphael Terrace and far enough along Kensington High Street, they slowed to a smart walk, trying not to call attention to themselves as they headed to the Underground.

"Why didn't we just take Violet and Anthea's car?" asked Matt.

"They'd have expected that. We'll be safer on the Tube. If there are lots of people, they won't try to hurt us."

"But why do they want to hurt us?" asked Em.

"Because you two are very special children—"

"Every mom says her children are special," Matt interrupted, stubbornly ignoring the extraordinary differences between them and other children.

The high street was a cacophony of city noises—angry car horns, screaming brakes from buses, a construction crew drilling the pavement, music blaring from a bustling boutique, a troubled musician on a saxophone, and the all-encompassing din of afternoon shoppers and curious tourists. Sandie let the sounds of the city mask her mumbled and inadequate response to her son. Explanations, rehearsed or not, would have to wait a little longer.

She maneuvered the twins through the traffic to the entrance of the station.

"Where are you taking us?" growled Matt.

"We're going to Scotland to stay with your grandfather."

Matt stopped dead in the middle of the rush of people charging up and down the stairs to the Tube. Em looked at her mom in shock.

"*Grandfather?*" said Matt furiously. "What grandfather?"

TEN

The man with the tattered brown doctor's satchel sat under a canopy at a café in the heart of Covent Garden. The surrounding tables teemed with office workers toasting Friday, while the surrounding cobbled square and narrow lanes swarmed with tourists and teenagers enjoying the pleasures of the West End. A bedraggled street musician in a porkpie hat, carrying a small instrument resembling a violin, passed near the man's table, pausing at the one next to it to offer his services to a couple having lunch.

Doffing his hat and bowing slightly when the couple turned down his musical talents, the musician shuffled across the stones with a barely perceptible glance back at the man with the brown satchel.

Vaughn Grant had noticed the hurdy-gurdy player's surreptitious glance. He kept his eye on the musician as he shuffled across the bustling square. Working for Sir Charles Wren meant Vaughn's ever-present paranoia had ratcheted up a few notches since the events at the National Gallery that morning. The Council of Guardians had learned quickly of the incident with the twins and now Arthur Summers's brutal murder was all over the news. Vaughn knew this meant Sandie and the twins were fleeing once again.

He wanted to be sure they could get away from the city safely. When the hurdy-gurdy man accepted a request from a family eating at the restaurant across the way, Vaughn let himself relax a little. The old musician was pretty good, the playful circus sounds of his instrument drawing a crowd of enthusiastic revelers.

Vaughn nudged the satchel farther under the table, making sure it was hidden, clamping it firmly between his feet. If something were to happen to the satchel after all these years, he thought, the results would be unimaginable. He smiled ironically to himself. Given who he was waiting for, perhaps not so unimaginable.

He signaled to his waitress for a refill of his cider. When she brought it, he smiled and flirted with her for a while, trying to inject a little normality into his situation. He'd prepared himself for this day for years, ever since Sandie and Malcolm had announced Sandie was expecting twins.

Sipping his drink, Vaughn allowed himself to wallow in a

moment of regret and recollection. It seemed so long ago, that summer after university when he and his best friends, Malcolm and Simon, had gone to Scotland to live at the abbey. Sandie and her friend Mara had already been there. Vaughn sipped his cider, remembering how close they all had been, and how quickly all that had changed with the birth of the twins. If only he'd dealt with Malcolm back then when he'd had the chance. Sandie might have been able to make different choices in her life.

If only.

The sounds of the hurdy-gurdy drifted across the square. Vaughn let its childish melody fill his head. He reminded himself how lucky he was to be in a position to help Sandie and her children, and he intended to do just that.

He roused himself from his self-pity when he spotted the three of them hurrying toward the café from the direction of Covent Garden Tube station. Rather than join the line of customers waiting to be seated, Sandie and the twins ducked under the velvet rope bordering the café's perimeter.

Vaughn stood and greeted Sandie with a warm embrace, holding her in his arms. The twins dropped their backpacks onto the ground and perched on a couple of empty chairs.

"Em, Matt, say hi to Vaughn. You won't remember him, but he was . . . is an old friend of your dad's and mine."

Before Em had a chance to say anything, Matt blurted out, "Do you still see my dad, then?"

Vaughn glanced at Sandie. "I'm sorry, Matt. I haven't seen him in a long time."

"Does my dad even know we're leaving?" Matt demanded.

"Matt, that's enough." Sandie sat close to Vaughn, pulling her bag off her shoulder and setting it on her lap. Matt began playing with the salt and pepper shakers at the center of the table, pouring salt into the napkin holder. Em was paying attention to the man. She thought she remembered his face. He was kind of cool for a grown-up. Plus he had amazing blue eyes. He was tall and dressed nicely in a suit. His fingertips brushed along her mom's arm and rested lightly on the back of her hand. She let them rest there.

I think Mom likes him.

She likes everyone.

I mean she like likes him, idiot.

That's sick.

"Do you want to order something to eat? Drink?" Vaughn asked, as the waitress worked her way through the throng to their table.

Sandie shook her head. "We'll eat on the train." She snatched the salt from Matt, and he threw himself back in his chair, sulking. Vaughn waved off the waitress.

"I'll feel safer when we get out of their reach," Sandie added.

"They'll know you've returned to Renard."

"I'm counting on it," Sandie said, standing. "With Renard's protection and your position here with the Council, we should be safe there for a while."

Vaughn stood too, and pulled Sandie close to him. "It's not too late. I can come with you."

"But I need you here," said Sandie, nestling into his embrace. "I need to know how deep the split in the Council has become. Renard was always the voice of reason when it came to binding. Now I'm afraid Sir Charles and those who support his more traditional ways will no longer be so . . . accommodating."

Scowling at the sight of Vaughn and his mother, Matt ducked under the rope and turned his back to the table. He spotted the musician across the square passing his porkpie hat into the crowd and nodding gratefully as the appreciative audience tossed coins into it. When the hat was returned, the musician emptied the change into his tattered coat pocket, set his hat on his head, slung his funny-looking instrument over his shoulder, and began to shuffle back across the square.

Brushing a strand of hair from Vaughn's forehead, Sandie said, "Maybe someday. But right now I need to help Matt and Em learn about who they are . . . and I need you to help keep the others at bay until Matt and Em know more."

"I'll do what I can for as long as I can, but you know as well as I do that the divide is growing," said Vaughn quietly. "The Council knows that it will have to decide whether to support Renard's more relaxed views on binding or stay with Sir Charles's medieval ones. But Sandie, when word spreads that the twins can move in and out of paintings, I don't think it'll help Renard's cause. The Council will feel far too threatened by them."

Sandie flinched.

Vaughn reached for her hand. "You know what else this means as much as anyone. If the Hollow Earth Society really has re-formed, then they may try to get the twins."

"What's Hollow Earth?" Em asked.

The adults both jumped, as if they had forgotten she was there. Sandie didn't know what to say.

"Hollow Earth is an ancient legend, Em. A myth, the stuff of fairy tales and bedtime stories," Vaughn explained. "It's said to be a supernatural space in the Earth, a shadowy home for all the demons and monsters ever imagined.

"But there are some who believe it to be real, and not a legend at all. About a hundred and fifty years ago, there was a group of believers led by a Scottish artist named Duncan Fox. They founded the Hollow Earth Society, whose aim was to protect and guard Hollow Earth, so the monsters and demons trapped there would never escape into the real world."

Em laughed in disbelief. "That's mad," she said.

"Exactly," said Sandie firmly. "Completely mad, and nothing that you should worry about." She turned back to Vaughn. "As long as Renard's alive, he's still the most powerful among us. The abbey and the island are impenetrable when they need to be. Renard will know what to do."

"Does he know you're coming?" Vaughn asked.

"I called as we left the apartment." Sandie paused for a beat, her voice breaking when she spoke again. "He told me about

Arthur. I know you didn't approve of what we were doing, but if it hadn't been for Arthur—"

"Arthur used you, Sandie," Vaughn cut in angrily. "He may have kept your big secret, whatever it is, but he used you to make himself and those he worked for a great deal of money."

Sandie suddenly grabbed Em's arm. "Where's your brother?"

"I don't know," Em said. "He was right here a minute ago."

Sandie darted under the rope and through the crowd into the square, panic tightening her chest and adrenaline spiking every nerve in her body. *Matt, please, please—where are you?*

There were too many people to spot one child. She stifled a sob. Her panic was quickly morphing to terror. She didn't care about consequences anymore. Reaching into her bag, she pulled out her sketch pad. She had to find Matt.

"Sandie, don't!" Vaughn warned. "There are too many people. We'll find him."

The two adults began to call Matt's name, asking anyone and everyone if they'd seen a boy in a tattered T-shirt. No one had. Em watched, concentrated.

Where are you? Mom's really scared.

Over by the musician.

"The last I saw him," said Em, improvising as best she could without giving away how she knew, "he said . . . I mean, he was listening to the man with something that looked like a violin."

"The hurdy-gurdy man," gasped Vaughn.

Sandie darted into the crowd in the direction Em was pointing.

Vaughn pushed back through the crowd to the café, dragging Em with him, two terrible realizations crashing through his brain at the same time. He'd left the satchel under the table, and his instincts had been right—the musician was dangerous.

Relief flooded Vaughn's entire being when his hands reached under the café table and gripped the satchel's hard leather handles.

"Stay there and hold this tight, Em."

He handed her the bag, then stepped up onto the wrought iron chair, his shins banging against the table and knocking over the mounds of salt Matt had left behind. Patrons at nearby tables stared at him angrily. The couple having lunch cursed at him. The manager and the waitress hollered from the front of the café.

Vaughn ignored them. Scanning the crowd, he spotted the hurdy-gurdy player in the middle of the square. Matt was at his side.

Vaughn whistled to Sandie and pointed. His heart still pounding, he jumped down from the chair, grabbed Em's hand and the satchel, and darted back through the crowd. Sandie had already caught up with Matt, who was squirming under her firm grip and obvious fury.

The hurdy-gurdy man was nowhere to be seen.

"Let me go!" Matt spat. "I wasn't lost, and nobody was taking me!"

"You know we're in trouble and you wandered off anyway?" Sandie shouted.

"Like you even noticed."

Vaughn intervened. "Look, Matt, your mom needs to get you all to Scotland in one piece. Tonight. As a favor to me and to your dad, will you help her?"

Yanking himself from Sandie's grip, Matt shifted his backpack on his shoulders, pulling himself taller. That was as much as he was going to give any of them.

Vaughn took the satchel from Em. But before releasing it to Sandie, he asked, "You sure you really want to take this? If its contents fall into the wrong hands, they could destroy us all."

"When the time comes," Sandie said, accepting the satchel, "what's inside may be my only leverage."

ELEVEN

Sandie had left her suitcase at the apartment, so while they waited for the Glasgow train at Euston Station, she bought some extra supplies. Exhausted, the twins slouched behind her. She hoped as soon as the train left and Matt and Em had a late dinner, they'd settle comfortably and be far too tired for explanations and much too exhausted for any more squabbles.

For once, Sandie's high hopes were rewarded. Matt and Em were asleep before the overnight train whizzed past Watford. Sandie was asleep by Milton Keynes.

Surprisingly, given the chaos and the trauma of the day, they all slept soundly until a few minutes before the train pulled into Glasgow Central. Sandie had decided to take the bus to Largs instead of renting a car. Until the twins were safely under their grandfather's protection, Sandie believed that traveling in public among lots of people was her safest strategy.

However, she hadn't bargained on the August heat. Every Glaswegian in the city appeared to be packing into buses and heading to the seaside.

After the first bus of the morning filled without them, Sandie finally managed to get seats upstairs on the second bus. Matt picked the back row, curled himself into the corner, shoved his earbuds in his ears, and cranked up his iPod.

"Do you think your brother will be angry with me his whole life?"

"Maybe till he's twenty," Em said, snuggling against her mom. "Will our grandfather be happy to see us?"

"He'll be thrilled, Em."

"How do you know?"

"Because he was very sad when we left."

Sad and very, very angry, added Sandie to herself. Angry because she was taking the twins from him against his wishes as their grandfather, and very angry because she was acting against his authority as a Guardian.

"What's he like?" asked Em.

"Your grandfather? He's a lovely man."

"Then why did we leave?"

Sandie wasn't sure where to start. "Something happened when you were both very young, and it resulted in your grandfather and I having a big fight."

"Worse than your fights with Matt?"

"Much, much worse. I said things to your grandfather that I'm now really sorry I said. I just hope he's forgiven me."

"Did you tell him you were sorry?"

"Not yet, Em." Sandie closed her eyes. "But I plan to."

The trip west was blessedly uneventful. When the bus crested the Haylie Brae, and the panorama of the Ayrshire coastline unfolded in front of them, Em leaped from her seat, roused Matt from his music, and leaned her face against the window next to him.

"Wow! It's like a painting, Mom," she exclaimed.

She was right.

In the midday sun, the Firth of Clyde was a ribbon of brilliant blue laced with white sailing boats, the western isles of Arran, Kintyre, and Bute bordering its far horizon. Nestled in Largs Bay, like a jigsaw piece broken off from the mainland, was Auchinmurn Isle—craggy and green and soon to be their new home. Matt turned off his iPod and wrapped the earbuds around it. He glanced out at the stunning sight of sea and islands.

"Looks boring."

Sandie couldn't help herself. She burst out laughing.

Two ferries carried passengers and vehicles back and forth to Auchinmurn on the half hour, their paths crossing in the middle of the bay. While they waited to board in the pedestrian line, Matt and Em checked out the Largs beachfront, noting the kiosks spread across the sand topped with brilliant colored beach balls, huge kites, and oversize sand toys, as well as lots of displays of delicious-looking cones and summer treats on every surface. Main Street was lined with souvenir shops and cafés bursting with customers in shorts and sandals.

Matt really wanted an ice cream. "I can get us one and be back before this line moves."

Sandie looked at him anxiously.

"Look, Mom, the kiosk's right there," Matt said. "You can keep your eye on me the entire time."

"Please, Mom. They do look . . . refreshing," added Em.

"You just read that on the sign! Okay. But my eyes will be glued to you, and if you as much as veer off in another direction, I'll be onto you so fast—"

Matt grabbed the coins from his mom's hand and backed up through the queue. Vaulting over the seawall, he jogged across the sand to the closest kiosk.

Sandie didn't blink.

The curve of the street in front of the ferry dock was blocked to through traffic to allow tour buses to off-load their passengers quickly and pedestrians to gather safely for the ferry. When Matt made his way back to his mom and Em with the ice creams, he wanted to avoid walking directly through a family with toddlers, bikes, and carriages so he cut into the queuing traffic waiting to board the ferry—at the same moment that the crew lifted the ferry's security arm and waved the traffic on board.

Matt's move forced a delivery driver to hit his brakes and stall his truck, allowing a Peugeot and a Mini Cooper to cut in front of him. The truck driver was not happy. He leaned on his horn for so long, Matt thought it had stuck.

Matt handed the ice creams over. Clutching their dripping cones, the three of them climbed to the top deck of the ferry and found an open spot with a clear view of the crossing. Auchinmurn Isle stretched before them.

"Do people other than our grandfather live on this island?" asked Em.

"Oh, yes. And it gets lots of visitors in the summer. This side of the island is mostly biking and hiking trails, lots of them with amazing animal and bird habitats." Sandie felt like an estate agent selling her children on the attributes of what she hoped would be their home for a long time. She didn't want them to know that this island was also to become their prison.

"One paved road runs the perimeter of the island and one cuts across its middle," she continued, as the ferry lifted its ramp like a giant jaw clamping shut. "There's a lovely little town—Seaport—directly on the other side from the abbey. But the coolest thing about the island is that it has a sister, a smaller island that actually belongs to your grandfather, and is full of all kinds of secret caves and ancient ruins."

"What's the small island called?" asked Em.

"Locals call it 'wee Auchinmurn,' but its real name is Era Mina, after the abbey and the monastery that used to be spread across both islands." Sandie pointed to a jut of land that peeked from behind the southern tip of Auchinmurn, an ancient Celtic tower visible on the horizon. "Your grandfather's place is on the far side of Auchinmurn, facing Era Mina."

Matt and Em looked nervous and not nearly as excited as Sandie had hoped. Still, the circumstances were far from ideal for a homecoming.

Seconds after the ferry lurched from the dock, the irate truck driver marched toward them. "That wean needs a good smacking, he does," he yelled at Sandie, jabbing his fingers angrily in the air above Matt's head. "Now 'cos of him ah'm stuck at the back of this tug. Ye should keep a better eye on yer weans!" Then he stomped off down to the parking deck.

A well-dressed elderly woman, with a briefcase at her feet and blue chiffon scarf protecting her hair from the sea spray, stepped away from the rail and came over to Matt. "Ne'er mind him, son," she said kindly. "Some folks are born rude. Al Swanson's one of them. He's a miserable fella."

A few other locals seated in the foredeck nodded in agreement. Matt shifted from his mom's side to an empty bench.

Em, who was looking over the side at the churning water, squealed in delight. "Mom, look—jellyfish! Hundreds and hundreds of them. They're following the boat!"

Sandie looked. The water was thick with translucent pink bell-like creatures of varying sizes, some as big as footballs, others as small as a baby's fist, trailing the wake of the ferry.

The lady in the chiffon scarf peered over the rail next to Em. "We call them moon jellies, dear. When the light of a full moon hits them, it's like the stars have fallen into the sea. It's quite a sight. But they're not really following the ship. The ferry's creating a current that's dragging them along."

Sandie took a quick look at Matt behind her. He was slumped over his backpack. She tried to stifle her irritation. Was he drawing? He looked like he might be. But since Em was thoroughly engaged with the jellyfish, she decided to let him be.

The ferry ride lasted about fifteen minutes. As soon as the ship docked, the pedestrians streamed off to waiting tour buses, bike rentals, or their own cars left in the parking lot.

Sandie stepped off the ferry and onto the island, immediately spotting Renard's right-hand man, Simon Butler. He was leaning against a Range Rover, reading the newspaper, looking exactly as Sandie remembered: a handsome, thirty-something ex–football player, with a bad knee and lots of attitude. As he spotted Sandie, he tossed the paper into the front seat and jogged to greet her.

With the leather satchel and her messenger bag bouncing against her hips, Sandie ran to him. They met in the middle of the parking lot in a swinging, wild embrace. When the twins caught up, their mom and Simon were laughing and crying and making complete fools of themselves.

"Matt and Em," said Sandie, pulling away at last, "this is Simon."

Em smiled and shook Simon's hand. Matt nodded, keeping his hands in his pockets.

Sandie was about to make Matt take his hands from his pockets when Simon spoke. "It's lovely to see you both. I help run your grandfather's business." He opened the car doors. "My son, Zach, lives at your grandfather's place too. He'll be thrilled to have some company his own age."

From the ferry behind them, car horns were blaring.

The twins looked over at the parking deck. The first two rows of vehicles were exiting the ferry, but the rest of the cars were caught behind Al Swanson's truck. He and a few of the ferry crew stood in front of the truck's cab, gazing in utter bewilderment at a jellyfish the size of a beach ball that was firmly attached to the windshield.

TWELVE

The sign on the impressive wrought-iron gates read THE ABBEY. Simon tapped a button on the car's dashboard, and the gates slowly swung open. As they drove through onto a narrow lane shaded by a canopy of trees, they could see the water of Largs Bay on their left, but to their right there was only a wilderness of other trees and foliage. Up ahead, the edges of a brick structure were visible behind a tall stone wall with an arched gateway. When the Range Rover drove out from the cover of the trees, even Matt gasped.

"Our grandfather owns this?" asked Em.

Simon smiled. "Welcome."

"Wow," Matt managed. "It looks more like a castle than a church."

Simon nodded. "It's built around one of the oldest fortified tower structures remaining in Scotland," he explained.

The tower on the right was about fifty feet taller than the one on the left, and had a flagpole flying the Saint Andrew's cross and another flag showing the abbey's crest—a majestic white stag with enormous wings. The central structure connecting the two towers was three stories high and topped with a series of turrets that Em decided were part of the abbey's living space. She'd spotted the shadow of a figure darting away from one of the turret windows when they'd pulled into the courtyard. In the distance, perched on the promontory of Era Mina, was another Celtic tower that Matt thought had to be at least a hundred feet tall.

"When the original parts of the abbey were built in the thirteen hundreds," explained Simon, while Matt, Em, and Sandie climbed out of the car, "the monks needed protection as much as they needed a place to worship. Auchinmurn was regularly under attack from Vikings and pirates and sometimes other Scottish nobles who wanted the island for their own, so the tower you can see was used as a lookout."

The twins couldn't stop gawking at the amazing structure before them. Matt especially was fascinated with the carved detail on the tower's cornices—gargoyles of teeth-baring, two-headed dogs.

"Now, how about a quick tour of the grounds, to give your mom a chance to catch up with your grandfather?" Simon prompted.

"Sure," said Matt, still gazing at the building.

"Yes, please," said Em.

"He's in the library," Simon told Sandie in a low voice.

Her heart fluttering, Sandie lifted the satchel and her bag out of the car, crossed the courtyard, and went inside through two massive oak doors set in an arched medieval portal.

"Now, you two," said Simon, turning back to the twins. "Let's head down to the jetty first."

He led Matt and Em through the tower's arched gate to the rear of the abbey. They walked along a path that wound its way through vegetable gardens and flower beds, bordered by the same ancient stone wall.

"Do you like to garden?"

"We live . . . lived in an apartment in London," answered Matt. "We grew some herbs once in a pot."

Simon laughed. "Our housekeeper, Jeannie, will be recruiting you both, I'm sure. These are her gardens, and she grows most of what she cooks for us."

"What if you want a burger?" asked Em, not a vegetable lover.

"That she negotiates with the local butcher."

They left the secluded garden path and walked out of the shade across a manicured lawn. On the far horizon, the islands their mom had pointed out to them loomed even larger, and in every direction on the water, there were boats of all sizes. The closer the three of them came to the water, the less perfect the lawn became, until it eventually rolled into a rocky shoreline and a pebbled beach. The jetty looked modern but well used, with two bench seats at the end. The linked boathouse was a heavy wooden structure, built to withstand the powerful winds and storms coming off the Atlantic.

"Do either of you like to fish?"

Matt and Em looked at each other. In unison, they shrugged.

"Never done it," said Matt.

"That'll change too."

Matt and Em were still a bit stunned by the sheer size of the abbey, its grounds, and its breathtaking vistas, but Matt in particular was in awe of the Celtic tower perched on the point of the smaller island across the water.

"It's pretty impressive, isn't it?" Simon said, noting Matt's interest.

The three of them walked out to the end of the jetty.

"I've read a lot of books about ruins and castles," said Matt. "But nothing compares to actually seeing it."

"He's a dork about that kind of stuff," Em cut in. Matt ignored his sister's taunt. He was far more interested in the history looming in front of him. "Why would monks have a watchtower built over there on the smaller island and not over here?"

Simon hesitated for a beat. "I think the answer has something to do with the smaller island being the first line of defense during an invasion. The tower would have had a better view of the sea to the north, which was the direction most of the invaders, especially the Vikings, would have come from. But you'll learn about all that when you start your lessons."

"Lessons? We're going to go to school here?" asked Em incredulously.

"Yes, Em," said Simon, smiling at her reaction. "Your grandfather and I will be your teachers at the abbey. Now, shall we continue our tour?"

The twins were so stunned by this information that they simply nodded.

Em and Simon walked back up the jetty to the shore, but Matt stayed behind, staring at the tower. It didn't make any sense. When these lookout towers were built, their primary function was to warn the castle's inhabitants or the surrounding town of approaching invaders. Usually a lookout would ring the bell at the top of the tower and, if necessary, fire flaming arrows or catapult pots of boiling tar at the invaders to slow their advance. And sometimes, but not very often, the towers were used to protect people from the invaders. This tower was far too narrow to protect more than a few people. Not only that, but its position and its few arrow slits were all wrong for fending off invaders.

"Matt, are you coming?" called Simon.

Matt ran along the jetty to catch up, deciding that this was a pretty cool place. The abbey was as impressive at the back as at the front, but for different reasons. The front hinted at the medieval fortress it once was, but the rear suggested a very modern mansion. Expansive windows replaced sections of the stone walls in the main part of the building; the cloisters on the western side had been renovated to create studios for students and artists in residence at the abbey. At the far edge of the studios, a grove of birch trees stretched back to the beach. About twenty steps into the first line of birches, a large mirror of colored glass hung between two of the trees in a sort of hammock of silver chains. Identical pieces hung from the next four birch rows, creating an overlapping line of glass all the way to the water.

Tearing her eyes away, Em looked back at the abbey. There was something strange about the windows that she couldn't quite work out. They walked across the lawn to the former stables and peeked inside. Two had been converted into garages, but it was the cloisters on this side that made Em smile the widest, as they housed a full-on gym and a pool. Their grandfather was clearly loaded.

"Do either of you like to swim?" asked Simon, sliding open a heavy glass door to reveal the pool and gym equipment.

"I love it!" said Em excitedly.

"So-so," said Matt, not wanting to look overly impressed.

Simon smiled to himself at the difference between the twins' levels of enthusiasm. "That's it," he said. "Tour's over."

He led them up to a flagstone terrace, furnished with two umbrella tables and groupings of chairs and loungers. French doors were open onto the terrace from a kitchen. Em stopped and stared. That's what was niggling at her about this place. All of the glass—on the windows, the doors, even the cloisters—was smoky and dark. From the outside, no one could see into any part of the abbey.

Pretty sure the monks didn't put that in, she thought.

"Ready to meet your grandfather?" asked Simon, welcoming them into the biggest kitchen they'd ever seen.

THIRTEEN

Before Matt and Em had the opportunity to enjoy any of their favorite foods—and there were lots of them spread across a massive oak table—a cheery-faced, gray-haired woman in an old-fashioned apron came dashing across the room, scooped Matt and Em into her arms, and pressed them against her ample bosom.

"Will ye look at the two of you. Oh, my. Not bairns anymore."

Eventually she released them from her squishy embrace, although to Matt it had felt like more of a stranglehold. Keeping them at arm's length, she exclaimed, "Och, yer your dad's doubles all right." She sighed, pulled a hankie from her apron pocket, and dabbed her nose and eyes. "You must be starving—and parched too, I've nae doubt." Heading across to a refrigerator that looked bigger than their entire kitchen in London, she gave Simon a flick with a tea towel. "I ken Simon didn't offer you anything to drink 'fore he gave you the grand tour, eh?"

"Matt and Em, this is Jeannie," laughed Simon, ducking a second swipe from her tea towel. "They should meet their grandfather before they eat."

"Nonsense!" Jeannie poured three glasses of juice and set them at places already arranged on the table. "Zach's ready for his lunch, and these weans have been on a train all night. If Mr. R wants to meet them, they'll be in here when he's ready."

Jeannie shifted out in front of the table and gestured in sign language to someone behind Matt and Em. Em turned to see a boy maybe a year older than her and Matt. He was about Matt's height, with cropped blond hair, was dressed in a T-shirt, baggy cargo shorts, scuffed sneakers, and no socks, and was gesturing back at Jeannie. Zach. Simon's son.

"Is he deaf?" Matt asked Jeannie curiously.

Before Jeannie could reply, Zach grabbed the back of Matt's stool and turned it so Matt was facing him. Em tensed. She wanted these people to like them both. She wanted to live here. She felt safe here. She didn't need Matt picking a fight the first hour of their stay.

Zach pointed to his lips.

"You read lips," said Matt, obviously impressed. "Cool. I'm Matt." He shoved his hand into Zach's and looked the boy directly in the eyes. "And this is my twin sister, Em."

Zach smiled and then signed something, keeping his eyes on the twins as he did. Jeannie translated.

"So who's the eldest?"

"I am," answered Matt, carefully watching Zach's gestures.

"But only by six minutes," interrupted Em. "We lived with our mom in London, but . . . some things happened there, and now we have to live here." She looked over at Jeannie. "At least, I think we do."

Jeannie smiled and nodded.

"Well, I live here with my dad," signed Zach. "My mom died when I was born. I don't remember her."

He stopped moving his hands, gulped down his juice, filled his plate with sandwiches, and, before darting out the French doors with his lunch, turned and signed again to the twins.

A voice with a deep, melodious Scottish accent spoke from the other side of the kitchen. "Zach says he'll catch up with you two later."

The twins swiveled on their stools as a tall man with thick white hair stood before them.

If asked, the twins would've said they'd expected their grandfather to look like an older version of their dad. Admittedly, they only had a vague idea of what their dad looked like, based on a few holiday pictures and a couple of snapshots taken days after they were born. But from those, he'd been tall but fairly scruffy, with shaggy dark hair and a stud earring.

The man standing before them in the kitchen was anything but scruffy. He wore lightly pressed jeans, a blue dress shirt rolled at the cuffs, and a pair of polished tan hiking boots. There was a puckered scar on his right forearm that looked like some kind of bite mark.

Renard smiled at the twins. Em thought he looked handsome and kind. Matt thought he looked intimidating. *He doesn't look anything like Dad.*

"So . . . I see you're enjoying your lunch," Renard said. "You don't remember me, do you?"

The twins shook their heads, their mouths full.

"Well, you were very young when you left. When you're finished, meet me out in the garden. I want to see what you can do."

"I'm still not sure that's such a good idea," said Sandie, coming over to Em and taking a few chips from her plate.

"If these children are going to be under my protection," said Renard, "and under my tutelage, then I want to see first-hand what they are capable of."

Matt and Em glanced at each other.

"You heard what happened at the National Gallery," continued Sandie. "You know how this will change things with the Council. In fact, you knew all about the incident before I even called you. How was that possible?"

"That would have been because of me," said a woman about the same age as their mom, stepping inside from the garden. "I was in Glasgow yesterday picking up supplies for next term. I had lunch with a friend of a Council member. It's all he could talk about."

Dressed in a short navy sundress and high wedge sandals,

with rows of chunky silver bracelets lining her arms, the woman looked regal. Despite her silky black hair held off her face with rubber safety goggles, her thin nose and wide hazel eyes reminded Em of a painting she'd seen once of a Native American princess. The woman was the opposite of softly freckled, fair-haired Sandie, who, in paint-spattered jeans, scuffed cowboy boots, and a shirt she'd slept in, looked as if she'd been mucking around on a horse ranch.

"Mara! I didn't know you were back at the abbey," said Sandie in surprise. She hesitated for a beat before awkwardly embracing the newcomer.

"Yes, I came back." Mara stepped away from Sandie's cursory hug. "When Renard opened the abbey as an art school a few years ago, I decided to join him and teach."

I don't think Mom is glad she's here, Matt.

Oh, don't be so dramatic.

Quickly, Simon made the formal introductions. "Em and Matt, this is Mara Lin. She and your mom and I—"

"And Malcolm," interjected Mara, pulling the goggles from her hair.

"And your dad," continued Simon, "were all at university together. Not only does Mara teach with your grandfather, but she's also an amazing glassmaker."

"Did you make the installation on the trees out there?" Em jumped off of her stool, rushing to the French doors. "I noticed it when we were taking our tour. It's . . . it's ridiculously gorgeous."

"I'm pleased you like it," said Mara, following Em to the doors. "It's a copy of a much larger piece I created for a hotel in the States."

Simon joined them. "What's really cool about it is when you walk through the installation toward the water, the mirrors create this weird illusion that you're walking into what you've just left behind."

"Could you teach me how to make glass, Mara?" Em asked.

"I'd love to." Mara put her hand on Em's shoulder as they walked back to the table. Em noticed her fingers were dotted with thin cuts and pinhead-sized burns from her work.

Matt was more interested in how deeply his mom was frowning at Em and Mara.

Renard went over to a large desk and took a sketch pad and packet of chalk pastels out of one of the drawers. "Matt, Em," he said, "shall we go?"

When Renard made up his mind, it was pointless arguing. Which was why, when they'd disagreed ten years ago over the twins' futures, Sandie had packed up and left. But running was no longer an option, as Sandie was no longer in a position to protect the twins on her own. She had to let Renard do as he wished.

The twins were staring at their mom, well aware that something complicated was going on among the adults in the room, including Jeannie, who was drying the same glass for the third time. Finally, their mother spoke.

"Fine. Walk with your grandfather. Do what he asks."

FOURTEEN

Em lagged behind as she and Matt followed their grandfather across the lawn, under another arch in the stone wall, and past Mara's mirrored installation swaying in the breeze, trailing him deep into the forest. They were climbing. At one point, through a break in the trees, they spotted the water far below them. Every few minutes, Em thought she caught a glimpse of someone following them, but she dismissed it as a trick of the branches shifting in the wind and her anxiety over why they were being taken so far from the abbey. Matt was working hard to keep up with his grandfather, whose strides were long. Every few steps he skipped a little, to stay at his side.

"What should we call you?" Em said, sprinting a few yards to catch up.

"What would you like to call me?"

"What's your name?" asked Matt.

"Mason Renard Calder, but everyone calls me Renard." Their grandfather smiled. "Jeannie, of course, yells 'Mr. R' far too much."

"Well, I think we'll just call you Grandpa, then," said Em breathlessly.

The older man chuckled. "That sounds good to me. Now, I have something to ask of each of you. Tell me about your special drawing abilities."

Don't tell him anything!

Matt, don't be stupid. It's why Mom brought us here.

Well, I don't trust him, so don't tell him everything.

The trees had thinned. The three of them hiked out to a rocky clearing. The road to Seaport was far below, and behind them in the distance they could see the flags flying from the abbey's tower. Beyond that lay the far edges of the jetty and the tower on Era Mina. The peak of the hill before them looked as if someone had peeled back the grassy earth to reveal a rocky underbelly.

Their grandfather sat down on a ledge of slate and regarded Em. It seemed that he had sensed she would be the spokesperson in this conversation.

"Sometimes when Matt and I concentrate and imagine things and then draw them, we can make the drawings come alive," Em blurted out. "But we have to draw the same picture, and we have to really concentrate together."

"So it's important that you're drawing together, is it?"

"Yes," lied Em. She knew she should probably tell him the whole truth, but she trusted Matt more, and her brother had insisted, for now anyway, that they should keep some of their secrets. And besides, it had been only yesterday that the twins had discovered that if they could share the image telepathically, then only one of them needed to draw to make the picture real. The jellyfish on the truck had been their second attempt; the doorless wall at the apartment their first.

"So what happened at the National Gallery?" their grandfather asked. "Have you ever crossed into a painting before?"

"Well . . . only once," Em said, telling the truth this time. "But then yesterday we were hot and mad at our mom. We were both thinking about swimming as we were drawing and then . . . splash! We were in the water."

"When we draw," Matt explained, getting tired of listening to his sister answer every question, "it's weird and kind of cool because we can see beyond the paper and our pencils. Like we see what's underneath the colors and the shapes and the lines and . . . and—"

"Light," Em jumped in. "And we always see light."

"And then," said Matt, frowning at Em's interruption, "the thing we're drawing creates itself around us." He looked directly at Renard. "It's like watching one of those films where they've speeded up the time and you see a flower grow in sixty seconds. I can sense Em drawing the picture in my head, and she can sense me in hers."

Their grandfather's stare felt like a pin pricking the edge of

Matt's brain. It was not a pleasant sensation, and he wanted it to stop.

"Are you like us?" Matt asked, turning away from Renard's gaze. "Is that why Mom brought us here? Can you make your drawings real too?"

"My dear children," said their grandfather, "hasn't your mother explained any of this to you?"

The twins shook their heads. Renard took a deep breath.

"You are both quite different from me. You see, like your mother, you are both Animare. But, like your father, you are developing a Guardian's abilities too. You are unique, my dears. Quite extraordinary, in fact. Have you heard the terms before?"

"Maybe. I don't know," said Em, racking her brains. Matt scuffed his Nikes into the dirt as if he wasn't that interested, although Em could tell he wanted to know everything—especially the part about their dad.

"An Animare," continued their grandfather, stretching his legs out in front of him and tilting his head back to catch the warm afternoon sun, "is a supernaturally gifted artist who has such a powerful imagination that they can alter reality when they paint or draw. Simply put, if they choose to do so, an Animare can animate their own art."

Em sat silently, the word "Animare" rolling around in her head. It was the strangest thing she'd ever heard, and yet she wasn't frightened or shocked. Somehow the knowledge made perfect sense.

"Now," Renard went on, "because of the damage an Animare might do in the world—"

"We'd never do anything bad," Matt interrupted indignantly.

"Let me finish," said their grandfather. "Think about what might happen to you and your sister if the TV or the newspapers learned that you had the ability to bring your drawings to life."

"They might want us to use our drawings to help people, and they would never leave us alone," said Matt, thinking.

"Or hurt people, if you got into the wrong hands. . . ." Renard let the words linger in the air. Em thought about what they'd done to the man in their apartment and the truck driver.

The man in the apartment was trying to hurt us, Em. That's different. And the truck driver?

That was a bit of fun!

"Because an Animare may be a danger to others or themselves," continued their grandfather, "and because if the world knew of an Animare's existence it could pose a threat to everyone, an ancient guild of men and women with their own set of powers exists to protect the Animare. I am one of them. We are called Guardians, and some of us are more powerful than others. The most powerful Guardians make up Councils, who keep things in order. Our sacred, sworn responsibility is twofold: to prevent the world from knowing about Animare and Guardians, and to protect the Animare and Guardians from the world." He paused, leaning forward on the rock face. "There are five Councils in the world, each monitoring and, if necessary, containing our kind."

"How?" asked Matt, digging the toe of his sneaker deeper into the dirt.

"Well, first of all," said Renard, "a Guardian has what's called 'inspiriting' powers, a range of psychic abilities that allow him to manipulate an Animare's imagination."

I don't like the sound of that! Matt kicked a cloud of dirt into the air.

Pay attention. Em gave Matt a withering look. He crossed his arms. *See? I inspirited you.*

Get out of my head, Em.

The twins turned to their grandfather, realizing he'd stopped talking, as if he knew they'd been communicating telepathically to each other.

"Sorry," said Em sheepishly.

Renard continued without comment. "Secondly, every Animare has their own Guardian, a protector assigned to him or her. This happens at a special ceremony in front of the Council."

"Do we pick our Guardian?" asked Em, taking off her sweat-shirt and tying it round her waist.

"Sometimes," said Renard, "but usually your Guardian is someone who has developed a special connection to you."

"Like you love them?" asked Em.

Matt squirmed.

"More like the way you and Matt are connected to each other because you're twins. A Guardian and their Animare have a psy-chic connection to each other's minds and imaginations. For example, Mara is an Animare, and Simon is her Guardian."

"Does that mean Zach is becoming a Guardian?" asked Em, while at exactly the same time, Matt asked, "Who is my mom's Guardian?"

Laughing, Renard put his hands in the air in surrender. "One question at a time, please. I may have a great mind, but it can get overloaded. Yes, Em—Zach is becoming a Guardian. Our powers are hereditary." He turned to Matt. "And your dad was . . . is your mom's Guardian."

Again, Em was not surprised by how natural all this strange information felt.

"So do we have Guardians yet?" she asked, finding the whole idea of a special connection to another person incredibly romantic.

"Normally the Council formally approves or assigns the Guardian when an Animare turns sixteen. So no, you don't have Guardians yet, and your Guardian needs to be at least sixteen too."

Renard paused for a second, staring out at the deep blue water of the bay, realizing once again how complicated his son and Sandie had made things by having children. The Fourth Rule was there for a reason. A mix of Animare and Guardian powers was . . . dangerous.

"The Council has never seen the likes of you two," Renard continued, "so we may have to help them decide about your Guardians when the time comes."

"So have we inherited powers from our mom *and* our dad?" Matt asked.

He was more fascinated by this information than a discussion of any future Guardian. At last an adult was treating him like a person and not a child.

His grandfather nodded.

"Are we the first Animare also to be Guardians?" continued Matt, staring into his grandfather's eyes.

"I know of no others."

Matt held his grandfather's stare for a long time. "You're not telling us everything," he said, standing up.

Matt, don't be a jerk.

Renard smiled at his grandson. "I'm not ready to tell you everything, Matt, because you're not ready to hear it yet."

Em felt frightened. She and Matt had never thought about what they could do in quite as serious a light as her grandfather was suggesting. Even though they'd always placed their abilities in the same category as being really good singers or amazing football players, they knew they were different from most children. They'd always understood they had to keep their abilities to themselves, but they'd honestly never thought that their imaginations were such a big deal. And here was their grandfather, telling them it really was a big deal; such a big deal, in fact, that an ancient guild existed to protect and watch them. Em couldn't decide if this made her feel better or even more anxious.

Now their grandfather was walking down the hill a little way, waving for them to follow him. "Your mother should never have taken you from here in the first place. But I'm grateful that she has brought you back to the abbey so you each may learn what it means to be an Animare the way she did, and, depending on how your powers evolve, so that you may learn to use whatever Guardian abilities you have the way your father—"

Renard didn't finish his sentence. Instead, he walked to the other side of the outcropping of rock at the pinnacle of the hill. "Enough talking. Let me see what you can do."

Handing each of them a chalk pastel, he passed Em the sketch pad he had picked up in the abbey kitchen, open at a clean sheet of paper. Then he pointed up to the peak, known as Lion's Rock.

"Please animate this for me."

FIFTEEN

Everything went terribly wrong as soon as the twins put chalk to paper.

First of all, no one had told Matt or Em the rock was supposed to look like a lion. They stared at the cliff formation carefully for a few beats and then decided it was something else entirely. Secondly, the twins knew a test when one was placed in front of them. Their grandfather had the authority to say whether they remained on the island or not. Matt and Em wanted to impress him.

And so the twins set the sketch pad on the flattest surface they could find and, with their grandfather hovering behind them, began to draw.

"I'll take the front," whispered Em, as her fingers whipped across the page. "I'm better at heads than you."

"Fine," said Matt. "Anyway, I've a great idea for the tail."

The twins were fast. Within seconds, a tremor rumbled up from inside the peak. As their grandfather watched, the huge rock started whipping from side to side. Mighty jaws burst from the rock face—but not lion's jaws. Reptilian jaws. The curve of what Renard had always thought was a lion's mane was suddenly and shockingly the thick slate scales of a *Tyrannosaurus rex*.

The monster thrashed its head back and forth, trying to free itself from the face of the hill. Before Renard could respond, think, yell, or even kick the sketch pad away from the twins, Matt finished the creature's tail, which blasted from the rock with a spinning saw blade at its tip. The creature was massive: part dinosaur, part Transformer.

Intuitively, the twins kept a section of their drawing attached to the hill, to prevent their creation from escaping its source. Sitting back on their heels, they grinned proudly at the power-ful beast lurching and lunging and roaring into the heavens as it attempted to tear itself from the hillside.

But the geology of the hill was no match for the power of their drawing. The saw-tail ruptured from the rocks and ripped into the ground inches from where their grandfather stood. He threw him-self down the hillside, screaming to the children, "Stop drawing!"

But it was too late. The creature was fully animated.

The twins' pride in their success quickly turned to terror as they understood what they'd created. Especially when the dino-saur thrashed its steel-bladed tail at them both.

"Tear it up!" yelled Matt, dodging out of the way.

The T. rex thrust its huge, snorting nose forward and knocked a screaming Em and the sketch pad in different directions.

Renard scrabbled back up the hill and stopped in shock. Tucked inside the tree line, digging in the soil with his back to the monster, was Zach. Yelling a warning was useless.

The dinosaur spotted Zach at the same instant as Renard. It stood up on its hind legs and let out an ungodly roar.

"Destroy the drawing!" Renard shouted. "Zach's over there— the creature's seen him!"

Em screamed. Matt tore the page frantically, but he wasn't quick enough. The dinosaur crashed into the copse of trees where Zach was digging—then blew apart in an explosion of light and shards of color.

Matt and Em sprinted over with their grandfather. Zach was gone.

Suddenly a high-pitched whistle pierced the air behind them. They turned and cheered when they saw Zach picking himself up off the ground a few feet down the hill. The boy ran into Renard's arms. Then, self-conscious at his show of emotion, he pulled away. He signed something in the air. Renard looked at Em and then back to Zach. "Why are you thanking Em?"

"She yelled at me to get out of the way."

"How on earth did she do that?"

"In here," he signed, and pointed to his forehead.

SIXTEEN

At about the time Matt and Em were animating Lion's Rock on Auchinmurn Isle, six men and four women were seated around a massive mahogany table inside a suite of private rooms at the Royal Academy, London. Two seats were empty—one at the head of the table and the other next to an elegant woman wearing a diamond-encrusted watch. Two Celtic coins were set at every place at the table, one gold and one silver, each with a spiral design on one side and the image of a winged stag on the other. The Council had been waiting for more than half an hour for their leader to appear. Most were getting impatient; a few were angry.

The high walls in the room were covered with ornately framed paintings of varied styles and periods, more than half of which depicted fantastic and mythological creatures of the air and the sea. On the wall behind the woman with the diamond watch were paintings of a basilisk—a monstrous bird with the wings of a pterodactyl, the tail of a snake, and the body of a cockerel—and a kraken—a giant squid with tentacles large enough to engulf whole ships. Another wall displayed sirens, selkies, and sea serpents. The most impressive piece of art was a floor-to-ceiling tapestry hanging next to the double wooden doors.

Stitched in the early Middle Ages, the tapestry's colors had remained unnaturally vibrant and chillingly bold. It depicted the grendel, a giant, apelike monster, rising out of a dark swamp. Behind him there followed an army of skeletons led by a hooded monk on a black stallion. Ribbons of fire flowed out behind the monk.

The blond woman who had chased the twins from the Kitten house was pacing in front of the windows. She was agitated and kept flipping open her phone to check her messages. "Given the mess Arthur has left in his wake," she said, "I need to return to the National within the hour."

A man with iron-gray hair and impeccably white shirt cuffs glared. "Blake, if you hadn't been outwitted at the Kitten mansion, the twins would be here now. Instead they're back with Renard where we can't touch them."

Blake looked resentful. "There was nothing we could do."

"This is hardly the first time Renard has put himself above the Council," said an athletic man with jade-green eyes, turning a signet ring on his little finger as he stood by the double doors.

"You know as well as the rest of us, Tanan, that Renard's feud with Sir Charles over the leadership of this Council is only getting worse," said Sir Giles.

Tanan Olivier ran his fingers through his short dark hair, his handsome face furrowed with concern. "So you think Renard is provoking the split?"

"Who else could have convinced so many to question our authority? Renard wants us to reform rules that have been sacred for centuries, ancient tenets that go back to the beginning of our time. What gives him the right?" snapped Sir Giles. "Sir Charles has been more than patient with Renard."

"We must make our decision about the Calder children, irrespective of where they might currently be," said the elegant woman, checking her sparkling watch for the fourth time. She lifted a pencil and began to doodle on the pad in front of her. "And what about the reports that the Hollow Earth Society has re-formed? This split in our ranks is diverting our attention from what is potentially a serious situation."

The other members of the Council shifted uncomfortably.

"The Society was wiped out years ago, Henrietta," said a mousy younger woman named Frida Adler, sitting across the table.

"The Hollow Earth Society is *not* re-forming, and is not the subject of this meeting," replied Sir Giles firmly. "Renard's grandchildren are. We gave them a reprieve at their birth. It's time we reconsidered that decision."

"If the Hollow Earth Society is indeed active once again," said

Luigi Silvestri, a portly Guardian who had traveled from Italy for the meeting, "then that makes the twins all the more dangerous. Either way, they should be bound immediately."

"But Luigi," said Tanan, now spinning a pencil between slim fingers, "if you allow the rumors about the Society to affect today's decision, you will be violating the most sacred of your ancient rules—that a child's imagination cannot and should not be bound—for something that may not even be true. The Calder twins are only twelve, remember. Binding them would be repugnant—"

"Given what they did at the National Gallery yesterday, Tanan," Blake interjected, "the twins are already more powerful than any Animare we've ever known. Age cannot come into it. The Council allowed them to remain with Sandie until now because she assured us she could control their development."

"A decision, I might add," said Henrietta de Court, smiling at Sir Giles, "that Sir Charles fully supported."

"Yes, well, I've always thought they were dangerous," said Luigi angrily. "The Calder twins are living examples of why we must hold steadfast to our traditions and rules. Those children . . . they're . . . they're *scherzi di natura*. Freaks of nature!"

There were murmurs of agreement around the table.

"I haven't heard anything about the Hollow Earth Society since university," said Frida absently.

"Hollow Earth is a *myth*," said Sir Giles, thumping his fist on the table and rattling the tea service at its center. Frida shrank back against her chair. "We all know that an Animare's drawings have a limited existence beyond the Animare's imagination. To believe that somehow there's a place where these"—he waved his hand in front of the tapestry of the grendel—"these beasts and other creatures have been trapped is beyond absurd."

Tanan strode across the room and placed his hand on Sir Giles's shoulder, trying to calm him, but to no avail.

"Despite the rumors of the Society's resurgence every few decades," Sir Giles ranted, "this Council has never found any proof that Hollow Earth is anything more than a tale told round campfires. As Luigi stated, what we should be discussing is that the Calder twins are an abomination of our kind. A dangerous hybrid of Animare and Guardian. And that's why they should be bound!"

The room erupted in a cacophony of shouts and accusations as the members of the Council weighed in on whether or not the Calder twins were indeed an abomination. Putting her fingers to her lips, Blake let loose an ear-piercing whistle to restore order.

"Ladies and gentlemen, please," said Tanan. Tall and immaculately dressed in a gray tailored suit, he cut a commanding presence. "You are Councilors. You are above petty squabbles. The fate of the imaginations of two young Animare is in your hands. This should be a solemn undertaking."

"Where is Sir Charles, anyway?" asked Henrietta restlessly. She gazed at the empty chair at the head of the table.

The double doors opened and Vaughn Grant entered the

room, carrying an ivory box inlaid with the images on the Celtic coins still lying untouched in front of the Council members. He handed the box to Henrietta. Taken aback by the gesture, Henrietta quickly adapted and shifted to the empty seat at the head of the table. Vaughn placed a phone in the middle of the table and set it to speaker.

"Sir Charles, everyone is present," said Vaughn, taking Henrietta's former seat.

"Good, good." Sir Charles Wren's voice sounded reedy and cold. "My friends, I am unable to join you for this important vote because of a matter beyond my control. I have, however, let Vaughn know my vote, and with your permission he will act as my proxy. As has been the case since the twins were born and he took his stance on our rules, Renard's chair at the Council table will remain empty. He will not have a vote in the matter before us."

The gathering murmured its consent.

"Before the vote proceeds, let me say I am as saddened as all of you at Arthur's sudden death . . . and in such a brutal manner. I know that you'll trust my associates Tanan and Blake to remain on top of this and to keep us all informed."

Again, the gathering murmured its consent.

"Now, to the Calder twins. We must make a decision today about their future."

"Sir Charles," said Frida, leaning forward to be heard. "We have never taken such a vote without the Animare in question being present. It's a violation of our ancient protocols."

"Unfortunately, the twins are already in Scotland," replied Sir Charles dismissively. "We will take our vote without them present." Through the speaker, the Council could hear muffled voices and what sounded like an ambulance siren. "As you know, twelve years ago Sandie and Malcolm Calder violated our Fourth Rule. By all means, love and marry, but an Animare and a Guardian must never have children together. The mix of abilities can result in a fusion too dangerous to control."

"Hear, hear!" acknowledged more than a few around the table.

"There is not one example in our history of a child's imagination being bound. But I would posit that in all our history, there have never been two Animare so powerful at such a young age."

"Sir Charles," interrupted Tanan, "we could learn a great deal from the Calder twins by studying them instead of binding them. A vote to bind them will only widen the growing split among us surrounding this issue. I suggest a compromise. Do nothing about the Calder children until they face the full Council on their sixteenth birthday."

"I appreciate your position, Tanan," barked Sir Giles, "but you don't have a vote."

"The gold coin will be a vote for waiting until the children are sixteen," stated Vaughn. "The silver for binding immediately."

Tanan and Blake retired to the window and began to talk in low voices. Henrietta de Court slid the box to Sir Giles, who immediately picked the silver coin and dropped it into the box. He passed the box to Luigi Silvestri, who also picked the silver coin. Frida was next, dropping her gold coin into the box. This went on around the table until every member of the Council had chosen a coin and cast their vote.

Vaughn slipped Sir Charles's silver coin into the box and returned it to Henrietta de Court. She unlocked the brass latch and emptied the coins in front of her. She counted.

"The vote is five silver coins," she said, "and five gold."

She stared at the two coins in front of her. She picked up the gold one.

PART TWO

SEVENTEEN

THE MONASTERY OF ERA MINA
MIDDLE AGES

If Solon had not been in such a hurry when he dashed along the wooded path from the monastery's stables to the abbey, he might have observed the eerie quiet of the forest around him. No morning birds were singing. No animals were scavenging for their breakfast underfoot. No wind was rustling the treetops. It was as if the forest was holding its breath, waiting to exhale when the coming danger had passed.

If Solon had not been in such a rush when he sprinted up the narrow stone steps of the abbey's north tower, he might also have taken a moment to glance out through the arrow slits in the thick wall, spotting the outline of a longship beached at the island's cove, its short masts and square sail cloaked in the dim light of the coming dawn.

But Solon was excited, missing both of these occurrences, because this morning the old monk would begin inking the final image in *The Book of Beasts*, exactly four years to the day after he had first started this momentous task. Today was also Solon's thirteenth birthday, and to honor the day the old monk had promised that Solon could assist in the inking. Solon could hardly contain himself.

At the top of the abbey's fortified north tower, Solon stopped in front of a wooden door. Carved in relief at the center of the door was the image of a winged white stag: a peryton. On either side, equidistant from the carving, were two brass handles. Solon pulled a key etched with the monastery crest from the pouch he had hooked to his leather belt, maneuvering it into an opening hidden under the peryton's wing. Solon turned the key counterclockwise and pressed his ear against the carving, listening for the complicated series of weights and pulleys shifting inside the thick wood. When he heard the final weight drop into place with a sharp *click*, Solon flattened himself against the door. With the carving digging into his back, he stretched his arms and grasped each of the handles.

When he was sure of his grip, Solon took a deep breath and pulled the handles inward. Immediately the door flipped backward, tilting Solon upside down and placing him on the other side of the wall. Without a moment's hesitation, Solon released the handles, expertly somersaulting off the door seconds before the handles locked down against the wood, trapping anyone still holding them. The door flipped another forty-five degrees, crushing against the stone floor anyone who remained trapped in the handles.

Solon released the breath he'd been holding and let his stomach settle. He was in a small antechamber, no bigger than a monk's cell. It was pitch dark. Solon edged forward, his arms outstretched, until he reached a second door. This one opened without any tricks, leading Solon into the turret room, filled floor to ceiling with manuscripts and scrolls. This was the monastery's scriptorium, the place where the monks kept all their written work. The only light filtered in through an arched stained-glass window set into the peak of the roof, turning the room into the inside of a kaleidoscope every time the clouds moved across the sky.

The monks had built the scriptorium at the top of the north tower decades earlier, to protect the illuminated manuscripts from the ravages of fire and the destruction of robbers. When the old monk had first shown the room to Solon, the boy had been unable to stay for more than a few minutes at a time, his senses so overwhelmed by the power of the images captured in the scrolls and manuscripts. Solon had felt as if his head was going to burst. It was on that day four years ago that the old monk knew conclusively that Solon was a very special apprentice with imaginative powers of his own, and someone the old monk could trust with the monastery's secrets. And so he had.

The most important secret Solon had learned was that a few of the monks could make their art come alive: a magical power that they mostly kept to themselves, using it to make their manuscripts more beautiful than those of any other scribes in Europe. Many of the kings and queens and scholars who owned a manuscript illuminated by the monks of Era Mina felt as if they were transported to another world when they read. The monks called themselves Animare, which Solon knew meant "gives life to" from the Latin he was learning.

Solon was always a little stunned when he first opened the scriptorium's door. Although the old monk had taught Solon how to concentrate, how to use his mind to quiet the explosion of sounds and images in his head, Solon couldn't help letting his imagination loose whenever he was near the books. When fetching a scroll, sometimes Solon would stand in the middle of the room, allowing the drumming inside his mind to rise to such a crescendo that when he closed his eyes he could see the images from the manuscripts as if they were all flashing in front of him like the flip-books he and the old monk made to entertain the village children.

He loosened the straps on a leather portfolio that he'd left leaning against the wall the night before. He placed the final two pages for *The Book of Beasts* into the portfolio, separating the sheets of vellum with squares of silk.

Solon looked down at the rough image of the final beast, the last one to be illuminated and the most horrible of all. He shivered and clamped his mind shut. Even the old monk had been resisting this page. The beast was a nightmarish one, perhaps the most feared of all the beasts in this part of the world: the grendel.

The grendel was known in songs and poems all over the kingdom as the "corpse-demon" or the "death-prowler," the "mud monster" or the "serf of hell"—a monster damned for eternity to crawl in the netherworld, the hollow in the earth between heaven and hell, feasting on the dead. The grendel was the reason most villages in the kingdom would place freshly butchered animals around the site of a recent grave, hoping the grendel would take the animal corpses, leaving their loved one's body safe in the earth and thus their soul free to rise to the heavens.

The old monk admitted to Solon that he feared if his power to control his imagination failed while illuminating the grendel, there would be no stopping the monster from slipping away from the pages and digging itself deep into the island. Even the abbot, the old monk's Guardian, had tried to convince him to leave the page blank.

Solon slung the portfolio over his shoulder and was about to leave the scriptorium when the monastery's warning bell rang out from the roof of the south tower.

"Invaders! Invaders!"

Solon froze, listening in horror as the monk sounding the alarm suddenly fell silent. For a second there was nothing, and then the monastery erupted in screams and flames.

EIGHTEEN

Inside a private suite at the Royal Academy, Sir Charles Wren was studying an ancient map of Scotland. A tapestry rustled on the wall behind him as the door opened, and Tanan and Blake entered the room. Gesturing at them to sit, Sir Charles pushed the map aside with his bandaged hand.

"I know you're anxious to get on with your task for me," said Sir Charles, "but I felt it important that we meet before you leave for Scotland."

"We know what must be done, Sir Charles," said Blake.

Dressed in skinny jeans and a cropped jacket, Blake Williams looked more prepared to take on the paparazzi than a powerful Guardian. But Sir Charles knew better. He trusted Blake implicitly. She had worked for him for a long time, coming under the protection of the Guardians as a young teenager when her father, a brilliant graphic artist in New York and an old friend of Wren's, had found it increasingly difficult to control his powers and had been bound by the American Council of Guardians. Since Blake had not inherited her father's powers, she had been given the choice of remaining in America with a distant aunt or committing herself to Wren's care and authority. She'd chosen the latter.

Tanan, on the other hand, was a recent discovery, whose talents Sir Charles had quickly found useful. The man was photogenic and personable: important traits when dealing with the media. Since Arthur's murder, Tanan had skillfully controlled the press, helping create and perpetuate the story that the painting *Witch with Changeling Child* had been stolen and that Arthur's death was a tragic consequence of the art theft.

"Sit, Tanan. Please."

"I'm fine, Sir Charles," replied Tanan, twisting the ring on his little finger. "I'll be sitting on the plane for long enough."

"Very well. Let's get started." Wren used his uninjured hand to operate a remote. The lights dimmed, and a flat screen emerged from the center of the table.

A recent image of Matt, Em, and Zach fishing off the jetty at the abbey appeared on the screen. They had been with Renard for a month now, and seemed oblivious to the camera focused on them from a boat across the bay. They appeared comfortable in their surroundings, looking like typical soon-to-be teenagers passing time on a late summer afternoon. Even in the short time since

JOHN BARROWMAN & CAROLE E. BARROWMAN

they had left London, Matt had grown. He and Zach were easily a few inches taller than Em, whose hair in the photograph was cut in a chunky chin-length style that made Sir Charles think of a Japanese cartoon character's hair. Matt's hair was still shaggy and unkempt, his love of scruffy old T-shirts still intact.

"We know now, unequivocally," said Sir Charles, zooming in on Matt and Em's faces, "that each twin is developing the imaginative powers of both an Animare and a Guardian. According to one of my Guardian contacts in Glasgow, the girl currently seems to be the stronger at sensing emotions, and her abilities to read people's feelings are emerging faster than her brother's. The boy, I hear, still has a temper."

Sir Charles's wrapped fingers twitched, the recent memory of what the twins had done to him the day they fled their apartment and trapped his arm in the wall still fresh in his mind.

"We may have lost the vote to bind the children, but I will not lose what Sandie Calder stole from me. That said, it is imperative that the twins are not hurt when you capture them and persuade Sandie to release the contents of the satchel in exchange for their lives."

With another click of the remote, Sir Charles changed the image on the screen. This time the photograph showed the twins on their bikes, waiting at the island's ferry dock. In quick succession, Sir Charles flashed up three photos of the twins and Zach leading a group of tourists into an island cave on the beach.

"It seems the twins and Simon's son have found a way to . . . 'entertain' the tourists in order to supplement their pocket money."

Tanan shifted, clearly impatient to leave. Ignoring him, Sir Charles continued to speak.

"The twins have learned well from Renard these past weeks. They know something about who they are and what they are becoming. Do not let your guard down, and do not fail to bring me back what I've waited for so patiently."

Sir Charles walked across the room and stood in front of the tapestry. He spoke with his back to the table.

"Tanan, you've served me well these past months, but don't mistake my trust for weakness. I need the contents of that satchel. And the Council must hear about none of this. Do you understand?"

"Perfectly."

Vaughn entered the room, carrying a small first-aid pack.

"Are you sure you want them to use this, Sir Charles?" he asked, opening the lid to display two vials of clear liquid and two syringes.

Sir Charles took the kit and passed it to Tanan. "We can't have those twins doing something clever again," he said, dismissing Vaughn, Tanan, and Blake with a wave of his damaged hand.

NINETEEN

E m was dreaming. It was the kind of dream where she was aware she was dreaming, but she couldn't scramble her mind out of it. Her dreams were always so much more powerful now than they had been when she was younger.

She was clinging to the face of a high cliff during a storm, an angry sea pummeling the jagged rocks beneath her. Soaking wet and shivering with fear, Em looked up to the dry tip of the mountain. Beneath her, furious waves were swallowing up men and women and animals, tossing their bodies against the rocks. Em tried again to wake herself up, but her thoughts felt heavy in her head. She tried to climb up the mountain, away from the vengeful water, but her arms and legs were numb.

Em knew the story of Noah's Ark, about how God had sent a

flood to cleanse the earth of all its wickedness, and she knew that for centuries artists had been using the Bible as inspiration. She had somehow dreamed herself into a painting called *The Deluge*, which she'd seen with her mom on one of their trips to the National Gallery.

Averting her gaze from the bodies thrashing in the water beneath her, Em made herself focus on what she thought had to be the edge of the painting, where a young girl had been dashed against a flat rock. A shimmering white angel floated above the girl, weeping.

Em felt so sad for the drowned girl that she too began to sob. Losing her grip on the rocks, she tumbled into the darkness.

And then Em *was* the girl on the rock, looking up at the shimmering angel.

The angel leaned close to Em's cheek and whispered, "You are a freak of nature." Then the angel morphed into a demon, and Em realized she wasn't dreaming anymore.

She could feel something pressing against her chest, trying to suffocate her. Gasping for breath, Em forced her eyes open, only to face a deformed dwarflike creature with small, beady, yellow eyes sitting on her chest, slobbering and snapping its needlelike teeth close to her cheek. She thumped the side of the demon's head with her fist, but the dwarf grinned even wider. Its tiny hand reached over and covered her mouth. In her head, Em screamed as loud as she knew how.

Seconds later, Matt burst into her bedroom. Em appeared

to be in a violent wrestling match with a creature that Matt could barely make out in the dark. It shimmered above her like a demonic puppet. Em, eyes wide in terror, was scratching and pummeling the creature's face and head. He grabbed a tennis racket from behind the door. But before he could swing at the creature's head, Em sat bolt upright, gasping for breath, and the creature was gone.

Matt sat on the edge of the bed and held Em's shoulders. "It's okay. You're okay. Just breathe. Big air. Big air."

When Em's breathing had steadied, Matt went into the bathroom that separated their rooms and poured a glass of water. He handed her the drink.

Em could feel her pulse slowing. She took a sip of the water and lay back against her pillows.

"Was it the same dream?"

"Uh-huh."

"We should tell Mom."

"She's got enough going on right now, getting ready for her exhibition in Glasgow. I don't want her to worry. I can handle it." Em put her hand on her chest. Her ribs ached. Maybe she *should* tell an adult. Maybe she wasn't handling "it" as well as she thought.

"We should at least tell Simon or Grandpa. They warned us our imaginations might get a bit out of control when we approach our thirteenth birthday."

Em nodded and gulped down the rest of the water. When she

turned to put the empty glass on her nightstand, the creature was perched there, grinning at her.

Frantic, Em scrambled out of her tangled duvet, pushing Matt onto the floor as she struggled to stand up. She looked again, and the creature was gone.

"What the—?" Matt looked up at Em's bed. The horror was now sitting on top of Em's pillows, grinning at *him*.

"Em!"

With an audible scream this time, Em threw herself across the bed, pounding the place where the creature sat. This time it exploded into sharp fragments of white light that went flying across the room, hitting the walls like tiny bolts of lightning and then fizzling to flashes of nothing.

Lying on the bed, Em began to sob from exhaustion, frustration, but most of all from fear.

"Come on, Em . . . Em!" Matt soothed helplessly. "You've imagined worse things. You've experienced night terrors since we arrived on the island. Grandpa said they'd stop when you got older and could control your imagination better—"

"Don't you think I know that?" Em cut him off. "I'm not upset because of that, you idiot."

"I don't get it, then. What's wrong?"

"I'm not imagining this night terror, Matt. It isn't mine. Someone else is animating it."

TWENTY

The next morning, at the far end of the kitchen, Matt and Zach were working on a massive scale model of the abbey as it had once been. They had already created the exterior of the structure. Now they were working on the medieval village, which had been rebuilt inside the monastery's stone walls after a Viking raid had laid waste to the original.

When their grandfather had assigned the project, Matt hadn't been very pleased. He had loved making models when he was younger, but had since lost patience with them, finding it difficult to remain so focused for long periods of time without feeling the need to snap, strike, or unintentionally animate something.

A couple of weeks into Renard's project, Matt had figured out how to concentrate to the point where he felt, for the first time in his life, that he could let his mind unwind a little. Eventually, he realized that had been his grandfather's reason for the project in the first place: to use the detailed precision work of the model to train Matt's patience and help him control his imagination.

Matt was poring over old drawings describing the layout of the abbey, while Zach was measuring, cutting, and gluing balsa wood for the roofs of the village. While they worked, the boys stopped every few minutes for Matt to sign a word or two to Zach about their plans for the day. Like his sister, Matt had grasped the basics of sign language in a short time, and after only a few weeks, he and Zach were already good friends.

Renard had business to attend to in Glasgow, so the children's lessons had been canceled. He and Jeannie sat at the kitchen table, finishing their coffee prior to Renard taking the ferry to the mainland. Renard was reading the newspaper. Jeannie was adding notes to a recipe.

"Hasn't Em come down for breakfast yet?" Renard asked, glancing at his watch.

"She didn't sleep too great last night," said Matt.

"Another nightmare?" Zach signed.

Matt shrugged, not wanting to say any more when Em had asked him not to.

His grandfather put the newspaper down. "I thought her nightmares weren't happening as much."

Zach knew immediately that Matt wasn't sharing everything.

But Zach was no more inclined to betray Em's confidences than Matt was.

"I think this was the first one she'd had in a long time," said Matt.

Simon came into the kitchen, dressed in faded jeans and a paint-spattered T-shirt, wielding a hammer. Out in the garden, Mara pushed a tarp-covered painting on a handcart across the lawn, toward her studio in the renovated cloisters of the abbey.

"How's Sandie's art show coming along, Simon?" asked Renard. "Is Mara helping?"

Simon accepted a cup of coffee from Jeannie. "I doubt it. Sandie doesn't want anyone to see anything yet. The only reason she's letting me near her studio is because she needs her frames built quickly, and"—he twirled his hammer like a baton—"I'm the man with the tools."

Simon was pouring milk into his coffee when Em wandered down the stairs and into the kitchen. "You're still half-asleep, Em," he observed.

Em was rubbing her eyes, completely unaware that a shimmering apparition from her imagination was following her into the kitchen.

"That's so gross," signed Zach to Matt.

Matt was relieved to see that the illusion close at his sister's heels was not the horrible creature from last night. Instead, the apparition looked a lot like the actor who played a vampire in Em's favorite film.

"Eww," said Matt.

Jeannie, who was rolling out dough at the corner of the kitchen island, rushed to Em, waking her completely with an embrace. The apparition disappeared. Embarrassed, Em slouched over to the table, ignoring the boys.

"Listen, hen," said Jeannie, pouring Em a bowl of cereal, "not to worry, they've all done the same. When your dad was a wee boy, he brought Robert the Bruce downstairs with him once, his horse too . . . so no fretting." She tousled Em's hair, returning to her baking.

"So what's on the agenda today, since you have no lessons with me?" asked Renard. "It's the first sunny day of the holidays. I expect the island will be packed."

We're counting on it!

Em glared at her brother. "We're going round to the hill above Seaport," she explained. "Zach thinks he's found another Celtic burial mound that absolutely no one in the entire history of the island has ever discovered before. It's just been sitting there, waiting for us to come along."

Zach looked up from gluing a roof on the miniature village, aware that Em had spoken about him but having missed the full gist. Matt signed what she'd said. Zach made a face at her, and she smiled back.

Simon laughed. "Well, heed your grandpa's warning. The roads will be packed with tourists. Be careful on your bikes. Which reminds me," he added, pulling three packages from the desk next to the pantry. "These are a bit early, as they were meant to be Matt and Em's birthday presents, but they may come in handy today."

The children tore open their gifts simultaneously.

"A sports watch! Thank you, Simon," said Em, hugging him across the table.

"Ah, they may look like watches, but they are so much more." Simon took Zach's watch, tapping his fingers across its face a few times. Instantly, Em and Matt's watches beeped, a text message from Simon appearing on their screens.

"I'm tired of replacing Zach's lost phones, and Renard and I thought that since Em and Zach's telepathic connection is getting stronger than ever, with these units Matt can communicate with Zach more directly too. I've created each watch with phone and Internet capabilities. Plus, each one connects to my unit here at the house." He held up his wrist.

"Simon, these are brilliant," said Matt, immediately texting Zach, who was already fastening his to his wrist. "Thank you."

TIME 2 GO

Quickly the boys tidied up their project, while Em finished her cereal.

"Can I expect the three of ye for lunch?" asked Jeannie, loading the dishwasher. The three children hesitated for just a beat too long.

"We'll let you know, Jeannie," answered Em, hoping to cover the awkward pause, "but we'll probably pick something up in town."

"If yer lucky ye will. There'll be queues everywhere. I figured ye'd rather hae these." She opened the fridge, pulling out three lunch bags. "Here's a sandwich, an apple, and some chocolate cookies for each of ye."

Em accepted hers, hugging Jeannie tightly around her ample waist. "You're the best."

They said their good-byes, rushing out through the French doors. Simon and Renard watched them sprint toward the nearest stable, where their bikes were kept. From across the lawn, Sandie stepped out of the doors of her studio.

"Remember the rules. No drawing in public," she yelled after them.

"We won't!" yelled the twins in unison.

Technically, we're not going to draw in public.

TWENTY-ONE

Y ou know the three of them are up to something, don't you?" said Simon to Renard as he waved across the lawn to Sandie, who waved back and returned to her studio.

"Indeed," said the twins' grandfather. "But they deserve a little freedom to play as well. They've been cooped up in this place for too long. I'm sure Auchinmurn will survive whatever they have planned."

"It's not Auchinmurn I'm worried about," said Simon. "There's something going on in London. Since Sandie fled with the twins, I hear the split among the Guardians is growing. The twins' continued freedom is fueling Sir Charles's anger that he lost the vote to bind them. He's been having a lot of meetings at the Royal Academy recently."

"Wren will always monitor the twins' abilities; you know that," said Renard. "Fortunately, the majority on the Council are intelligent enough to see the value of education over Sir Charles's medieval approach."

Simon nodded, checking that his watch was indeed tracking the children. Three tiny blue dots illuminated a map on the watch face.

"Still, it pays to be watchful," continued Renard, retrieving his newspaper from the kitchen table and heading for the terrace. "I don't trust Wren to leave them alone, despite the Council's vote. I don't think he'll do anything while they are on the island with me, but still I'm pleased that you have activated a GPS program in the children's watches. You can monitor them from your unit when they're out of my psychic reach."

"I've heard more, Renard," said Simon, following. "The rumors about Malcolm and the Hollow Earth Society have surfaced again."

Renard set his paper down on a wrought-iron table outside, running his fingers through his thick hair. For a second, Simon had a sense that the older man had made a decision and was about to say something to him—but then Mara headed out of her studio toward the kitchen, interrupting the moment.

"Renard, there's a reason you trust me with your intelligence gathering," Simon said, as Mara approached. "I'm good at it. The rumors have resurfaced because of the twins' exceptional powers. If they can animate themselves in and out of a piece of art, then

Duncan Fox and his original Hollow Earth Society were onto something after all. Hollow Earth may well be "real and eternal," as Fox prophesied. You must admit the twins are transforming at a rate that's truly unprecedented. Soon they might be able to do things that even *we've* only imagined possible."

"Keep listening and keep me informed," said Renard. "I know you're the best. But also know this. As long as I'm around, Malcolm is not a threat to the twins. You need to trust me on that."

Simon shook his head, not happy with Renard's response.

"Okay. How about this?" Renard placed his hand gently on Simon's shoulder. "After the twins turn thirteen, I'll tell them as much as I know about what might be in their future, including the rumors about their father and Hollow Earth. Deal?"

"Deal," said Simon reluctantly.

Renard was keeping something back. But there was nothing Simon could do about it.

Matt led the way out of the abbey grounds, with Zach in the middle and Em bringing up the rear. When they reached the wrought-iron gates, Matt dodged his bike into the cover of trees.

"Are you ready?" he signed to Zach.

"Sure," Zach signed in reply. "My dad's clever, but he's not good at keeping secrets."

Zach pulled his laptop from his backpack. His fingers flew across the keyboard. Over the last few years, Zach's technological abilities had been evolving just as fast as the twins' imaginative powers. He could design a code for anything, his mind intuitively wired to the infinite possibilities of programming code. Matt and Em watched in awe as lines of code scrolled across his screen.

Do you need us to do anything, Zach?

Not yet, Em.

After a few minutes, Zach signed that he was ready to upload the software patch he had created. Balancing the laptop on his bike saddle, he double-tapped the face of his watch.

On the count of three.

Em nodded, counting out loud, "One, two, three."

In unison, they each tapped an icon on the screen on their watches, and simultaneously Zach hit return on his laptop. The download bar on Zach's computer screen filled, and their watches beeped when the patch was uploaded. Zach closed his laptop, sliding it back into his pack.

"My dad's GPS will now follow a route I've created around the island," he signed with a grin. "As for us, we're off-line and on our own."

TWENTY-TWO

As the kids biked across the island's hiking trails, they avoided the majority of the tourist traffic on the main road. When they reached the ferry port to Largs, they realized how right their grandfather had been. It was still early, but already long lines were snaking out from the information center. The island tours were filling up at every run, and the rental shop was running low on bicycles.

"What do you think?" asked Matt, scouring the crowd.

"How about that American family over there renting the tandems?" signed Zach.

"How do you know they're American?" asked Em, as they watched two adults and four children fastening their helmets and sorting their gear.

Zach tapped his mouth. "Good eye."

"He read their lips," said Matt, pulling a handful of flyers from the front pocket of his backpack. "Zach and I will head to the cove and get things set up. Let us know when you're close."

The boys pedaled back in the direction they'd come, while Em kept her eyes on the American family. When they'd pulled out onto Beach Road, she followed them.

Beach Road was really more of a paved lane. Whenever two oncoming cars needed to pass each other at one of the island's sharp bends, one of the vehicles had to swerve onto the verge of the hill or pull onto the stony beach. As the American family reached the first bend in the road, the traffic was at a standstill. A car pulling a caravan had taken the curve without checking the mirror on the side of the road, sideswiping a tour bus coming the other direction. Both were locked together.

For most of the traffic stuck behind the obstruction, the late summer weather, the calm sea, and the peaks visible on the nearby isles were far too beautiful to make it an incident worth complaining about. A few people walked out onto the pebble beach to get around the blocked road, some settled onto the hillside to wait, while the rest turned and went back the other way.

Em was now directly behind the American family, who were debating whether to risk wading through the low tide to get around the bend, turn back, or wait until the obstruction was removed.

"Sometimes it can take the tow truck hours to get here," Em

offered, "and that's if Mr. Ralston is even at the garage when the call comes in. He's probably off fishing on a day like this."

"Are you a local?" asked the mother. The youngest son, who looked about five, was sharing her tandem.

Em wheeled her bike closer. "It's bound to happen again—it always does. You don't want to spend your entire day waiting around." She dropped her voice to a whisper. "I know a really fun thing for your family to do that's not too far from here."

Em felt a surge of warmth emanating from the woman. She glanced at the husband, balancing a girl of about seven on the back of his tandem, and the warmth deepened. Em could tell they were good parents, that they were genuinely thrilled to be on holiday, and that they wanted their children to really enjoy themselves too.

Renard had been teaching Em to pay attention to the way people made her feel. Someday, he said, it might save her life. She knew this particular situation was not what her grandfather had had in mind, but she also knew, like Matt and Zach, that she was really tired of being told what she could and couldn't do with her own mind. Plus, what was the real harm in practicing some of what they'd been learning?

Em concentrated on the younger children next. The boy seemed focused and distracted at the same time. She couldn't figure out what she was sensing from him until he climbed off the back of his mom's tandem and stood feet crossed, bouncing on his toes.

Em laughed to herself. He needed to go to the bathroom.

The girl was willing to do whatever her parents suggested, but Em was feeling something else, another desire that was overwhelming the first. The girl was getting hungry.

The older children, two boys aged about ten and eleven hanging at an appropriate distance from their parents, were far easier for her to assess. Both were clearly bored with everything they had done so far on this trip. In their opinions, Em was the first interesting thing that had happened since the vacation began.

"My family used to work in television in London," said Em, telling the tale she had rehearsed with Matt and Zach, concentrating on the mother. "Now we live on the island with my grandfather. He owns a lot of the land along the far coast of the island. Every summer for a limited time, my family presents a reenactment of one of the most famous moments in the island's history. There's a performance beginning in an hour if you're interested."

Em handed the mom one of the flyers she and Matt had drawn, advertising *The Battle of Auchinmurn*. Her fingers glanced across the mom's hand. The woman was already convinced, enthusiasm flowing from her.

"Oh, Tom, let's go," she said excitedly. "We'll be supporting some local enterprise and I'm sure the boys will learn something unusual about Scotland."

"I'm hungry," whined the little girl. Em remembered Jeannie's packed lunches. "We have sandwiches."

The eldest of the two boys spoke up. "C'mon, Dad, everything we've done so far on this stupid vacation has been so lame."

"Yeah," said his brother. "You're always telling us we need to try new things. Let's do it!"

"I don't know," said the dad, looking at his family and then down at the flyer. The picture the twins had drawn on the front was of an angry Viking standing next to his longship. Suddenly the Viking on the flyer thrust his sword out of the page toward the dad, who yelped, instinctively ducking.

"Jeez Louise! Lori, did you see that?"

"Hologram," lied Em.

"Well, young lady," he said, laughing, "I guess you've got yourself some customers."

TWENTY-THREE

Em led the Nelsons from Nebraska—Tom, Lori, and their four children—back round the island to Viking Cove, a rocky inlet on the southeast point of Auchinmurn. From the air, the cove looked as if something had taken a bite out of the rock, leaving an empty slice tucked from the view of passing boats. Because the beach was layered with uneven slabs of limestone—unlike the sandier beaches on the rest of the island—the cove was no more than a passing highlight on the island's tour.

I'm ten minutes away.

We're ready.

The Nelsons followed Em along Beach Road, then onto a forest path, heading toward the sea. About five minutes along the trail, they reached a dilapidated fisherman's shack, where they parked their bikes, continuing on foot across a rocky plateau that eventually stepped down to the cove.

The view was so stunning from this promontory that Em had to wait for Mr. Nelson to snap a number of photos of his family with the Celtic tower as a backdrop. When they eventually climbed down to the cove, haunting Gaelic whistle music rose up to greet them from wireless speakers Zach had installed under the rocks.

"Oh, listen, kids," said Mrs. Nelson, helping her youngest children down off the ledge. "Maybe there's a leprechaun hidden in that cave."

Puhleeze, thought Em, but let the statement pass. "Welcome to the site of one of the most famous events in Auchinmurn's history. If you'll please take a seat." She pointed to a long wooden bench inside the mouth of a cave hidden under the overhang of rocks. "I'll see about sandwiches, and getting your tickets." Em smiled up at Mr. Nelson. "They're five pounds each. Children under five are free."

"Oh, of course," laughed Mr. Nelson. "You're quite the entrepreneur. Good for you."

He counted twenty-five pounds into Em's palm. She thanked him and ducked inside the cave, returning quickly with Jeannie's lunches, which she handed over for another four quid.

Once the Nelsons had settled, the children having eaten all Jeannie's chocolate cookies and the cheese sandwiches, Em dropped a curtain over the cave's entrance. Pulling a rope divider in front of the bench where the Nelsons sat, she darted behind a black screen that Matt and Zach had built from old painting canvases. A row of lights strung along the roof illuminated the space.

The Gaelic music came on again, the tune echoing eerily off the rocks. A silver light appeared in the center of the black canvas, spreading out to the edges as if the film projector was too hot, melting the film. The lights went out.

"Woot! Woot!" exclaimed the older Nelson boys.

The two younger children shifted closer to their parents. The lights came up, gradually revealing a stunning sight on the screen—a painting of a bustling village square, obviously from a very long time ago. The fortified monastery tower loomed in the background, thatched cottages surrounded the square in the forefront, and, beyond that, a square-sailed ship floated on a sliver of sea.

But what brought a gasp from Mrs. Nelson and an "awesome" from the older boys was that everything in the painting was in motion: shoeless children chasing each other while dodging slop thrown from an open cottage window, fat men drinking and brawling outside a tavern, two rosy-cheeked women gesturing and joking with a laughing monk, a farmer feeding his horse, a band of musicians leading a wedding party through the square, chickens foraging in the dirt, dogs fighting under a tree, and a pig spinning on a spit.

"Looks like a Brueghel painting, doesn't it?" said Mr. Nelson to his wife. "Very clever how they're doing that."

"Shhh!" Mrs. Nelson said.

I told you to copy something else.

Shhh! Get out of my head, Em.

The lights dimmed. This time when they came on again, one of the rosy-cheeked peasant women from the painting, her shoulders wrapped in a woolen shawl, stepped out of the lively scene and appeared to stand before them in the cave.

Mr. Nelson clapped his hands.

The peasant curtsied, and the whole family applauded enthusiastically.

"Good morrow, strangers. Welcome to the Middle Ages!"

The voice had a pleasant highland lilt. Em had recorded Jeannie's voice last week, saying she needed it for a project she was working on with Simon. Jeannie had been thrilled to oblige.

Good morrow? Really, Em?

It sounds historical.

Hysterical, maybe.

"Focus!" signed Zach to them both.

They were all hidden in the darkness behind the canvas screen. With his computer, Zach was controlling the lighting, the prerecorded sounds, and dialogue, while the twins were animating drawings they'd planned out beforehand from Renard's stories about the island. They were drawing on a storyboard that they had rigged behind the screen. Each square of the storyboard, and there were many, contained an outline sketch. As Matt and Em used their imaginations to fill in the image, their animations appeared to burst through the black canvas in trails of color and light like holograms. The screen created an illusion for their audience that the images were somehow being projected from behind the canvas.

"My name is Morag," said the peasant woman. "Many centuries ago, I lived in the village near the Monastery of Era Mina. I'd like to tell you the story of how my son, a thirteen-year-old boy, saved the children of the village from slavery during a bloody Viking raid."

"Is she real?" asked the Nelson girl.

"Of course not, sweetie," whispered her mom. "It's special effects."

"It's called CGI," said one of the older boys. "Computer-generated images. It's brilliant! Can't she just be quiet and watch?"

Morag stepped to the side of the screen. The boisterous village behind her was now quiet as dawn approached.

"It was the day after market day, when under the cover of dawn a band of Norsemen invaded the island. Without warning, they torched the village, forcing us all inside the protection of the abbey's fortified walls."

As the twins started filling in the next outline sketch, another painting of the village square filled the screen, one with terrified villagers fleeing from a swarm of encroaching Norsemen. The invaders' torches engulfed the thatched houses, and flames flickered out of the screen so realistically that, for a second, Mrs. Nelson thought she could feel the heat of the blaze.

Careful, Matt! You'll singe her eyebrows.

Zach hit the sound effects, and the tolling of the monastery's warning bell made the Nelson children jump. Zach hit another key, and the screams of terrified villagers filled the cave.

Nice, Zach.

"I'm scared," said the Nelsons' little girl.

"Oh, it's just pretend, sweetheart," said her mother, pulling her closer. "Those bad men can't hurt you."

Morag looked directly into Mrs. Nelson's eyes. "After they torched our homes, the Norsemen shepherded us all into the square. Then they began to round up our children. All except Solon, my son, an apprentice to the monastery and a very brave boy."

A painting of the monastery courtyard came alive on the screen. The Vikings, their longswords dripping with blood, began rounding up the village children.

"But the villagers were not going to let that happen without a fight," added Morag.

"Why do they want the children?" the Nelson girl whispered.

The cave filled with villagers—pitchforks, spades, and knives in hand—charging the Norsemen, while the children pelted them with horse manure.

I think we're scaring the little girl, Matt. Maybe we should stop.

Aw, no! We're almost at the best part with Solon and the beast.

Mr. Nelson and the boys were loving every minute of the battle that was unfolding in front of them. A Viking came flying out of the screen, rolling into the corner of the cave, where he disappeared in a flash of light and color. The youngest boy was so excited, he stood up and cheered, the apple he'd been saving for later falling from his lap and rolling against the screen.

Darting under the rope, the boy crouched and grabbed his apple, as two villagers brandishing pitchforks leaped off the screen, one after the other, in pursuit of the Viking. The second villager stabbed the Nelson boy before tumbling into the darkness.

The boy let out a terrified, pain-stricken howl. His mother, seeing blood gushing from her youngest son's leg, screamed in panic, and because her mother was screaming in panic the little girl began to scream too.

Lights, Zach! Quickly. Lights!

TWENTY-FOUR

Largs was bustling with tourists enjoying the last gasp of a glorious, sunny August day when Renard stepped onto the pavement outside the train station. He'd left the island that morning for the Kelvingrove Art Gallery in Glasgow, not long after Matt, Em, and Zach had biked from the compound. Now he was on his way back.

He removed his suit jacket, folded it over his arm, and, dodging the heavy traffic cruising along the promenade, walked smartly to the ferry dock.

Once on the ship, he settled himself on the upper passenger deck. He was about to unfold his newspaper when he felt a weight, a distinct pressure, pushing on his chest. Gripping the ship's railing, he closed his eyes, allowing the vision he knew was coming to take form.

When he opened his eyes, a boy of about four or five years old stood on the deck in front of him, an apple in his hands. The boy was wearing a University of Nebraska T-shirt and had a bandage around his thigh. On closer inspection, Renard could see the boy had horse manure smeared across his arms.

"Mr. Renard, are you all right?" asked one of the ship's crew, walking through the apparition as it dissolved around him. "You look awful pale."

"I'm fine, Jimmy. Thank you. The heat plus a tiring day, is all."

Renard fished his mobile phone out of his briefcase, speed-dialing Simon. No answer. He scrolled down and dialed Sandie. Nothing. Mara—no answer. The children's new phones. Nothing. Dead silence.

Where was everyone? Why weren't they answering their phones?

Renard was angry rather than panicked. He knew that he would have sensed if something tragic or terrible had happened on the island. He was also angry because the vision of the little boy with the apple had come from Em. She was not yet fully aware of the deep connection Renard had with her as her Guardian powers strengthened, but the boy with the apple was obviously something she had witnessed or, worse still, created sometime that afternoon. It had affected her significantly.

Renard pushed his way off the ferry, cutting to the front of the waiting line, running to his car in the parking lot. Normally a patient man, Renard used his horn more times on the journey to the abbey than he had ever done before, forcing drivers and pedestrians out of his way.

The gates to his home were wide open when he turned into the grounds, his tires spraying gravel in all directions as he raced along the lane and skidded to a stop in the abbey's front courtyard. Before he had climbed from the car, Mara was already outside the front doors.

"Calm down, Renard," she said. "Somehow our communication network was infected with a virus. That's why the gates are open. Simon is convinced that it wasn't an outside hacker. He's working on correcting it. We should be back online soon."

"I'm not bothered about that. It's the twins and Zach. Where are they?"

"They're fine," Mara soothed. "At least, we think they're fine."

"What do you mean, 'we think'?"

"Simon received a text from Zach around lunchtime."

"Lunchtime?" said Renard, appalled. "That was three hours ago! I've been picking up a vision from Em. An unsettling vision."

Mara lifted Renard's briefcase from the backseat and followed him inside while filling him in. "Directly before the system crashed, Simon checked the GPS he'd installed. The three of them were on the hiking trails north of the old church in Seaport. Probably looking for the burial mound they thought they'd found."

Renard exhaled slowly before marching into the library to a cabinet near a grouping of leather chairs, where he lifted out a decanter of whisky, pouring himself and Mara a drink. Renard had only taken a sip when Simon stormed into the room, slamming his laptop onto Renard's desk, which sat facing the arched window with a view of Era Mina and the bay.

"Zach was the one who crashed our system."

"What!" said Renard.

Simon was as white as chalk. "He wrote a piece of code that simulated my GPS program so that we couldn't track the three of them when they left the compound. Somehow he's patched it into our network. But the little monster isn't as smart as he thinks. His program hit a glitch. And when it tried to repair itself, it corrupted our entire system."

Renard sat down on a leather sofa, rubbing his hands across his face. "What was he thinking?"

"You've got to give the kid credit for ingenuity," said Mara, trying to repress a smile as she finished her drink.

"Not funny, Mara," said Renard. "Who knows what damage he might have done?"

"Well, you know one thing. Zach wouldn't have done this without the twins' approval, if not their help," said Simon.

"Oh, I'm well aware of that, Simon," said Renard. "I don't know what they were thinking either. They may still be learning, but they know the rules."

Simon worked on his laptop for a few more seconds before closing it. "Good news is, the damage wasn't too bad. We should be fine now."

"Good," said Renard, finishing his drink. "That leaves me to deal with the boy with the apple and the manure on his arm."

Renard was describing his vision on the ferry when Sandie came through the open library door to join them.

"Hey, did I miss the invitation for cocktails?" she asked. She caught the anger in Renard's eyes immediately. "What's wrong? Where are the children?"

"That, my dear," said Renard, "is the question."

TWENTY-FIVE

The children were exactly where most children love to be on a sunny summer's day: perched on the beach wall, eating ice-cream sundaes. Behind them, the Seaport Café was packed, its outdoor deck spilling customers onto the sand to enjoy their frozen treats.

Zach, Matt, and Em were watching a game of volleyball, oblivious to the man and woman sitting at one of the umbrella tables. The blond woman was dressed in a white halter-neck dress, and the man was impatiently tapping the ring on his little finger against his coffee cup.

"At least Mr. Nelson didn't ask for a refund," said Em.

Matt licked up the last of his sundae, lobbing his plastic bowl into a nearby garbage container. "That family got way too excited about a tiny scratch and a little cow dung. Their boy was fine."

"Thanks to Zach's quick thinking," said Em. "If he hadn't told Mr. Nelson that he'd fallen against the screen and accidentally stepped on the boy with his cleats . . . well, who knows what would have happened?"

"You could have tried to make them forget what they saw," said Matt. "You know, that inspiriting thing Grandpa told us about."

"I've never done that before," said Em. "I'm just glad that you did what you did, Zach," she signed. "You saved the day!"

Zach's face reddened. Quickly gathering up Em's bowl and his own, he walked over to the bin to mask his blushing.

"We should've known the whole story would be too scary for young children," said Matt, oblivious to Zach's embarrassment. "The children with that last family from Edinburgh, though—they were the perfect age. How old do you think they were, Em? 'Cos that's who we should stick to next time."

"They were our age," laughed Em. "Still, it was pretty easy to convince their mom and dad to follow me, especially when the dad figured he could have a pint on the beach while we entertained his children."

"How much did we make?" signed Zach.

Em pulled a pencil case from her backpack, surreptitiously counting the bills stuffed inside. "Sixty quid. Not bad." They high-fived each other.

"Celebrating something?" asked a woman, appearing next to Matt on the steps.

Em jumped with fright.

"Oh, I'm sorry! Didn't mean to startle you." She pointed at a man sitting at one of the umbrella tables, who lifted his cup in acknowledgment. "We heard from a fellow tourist that you children conduct a reenactment to anyone interested in learning more about the history of the island. We'd like to take your tour, and, of course, we're happy to pay you double since it's so close to the end of the day."

The woman took a thick pile of bills from her bag. Em was feeling uncomfortable. There was something vaguely familiar about the woman. Had they met before? She took a closer look at the man at the table. He looked fairly harmless, but there was something about him. He waved. It didn't help Em's unease. Maybe she was just getting tired.

I don't like this woman, Matt, and there's something weird about her husband.

Matt ignored her. "I think we could do one more show before it gets dark," he said, standing and brushing sand from his cargo shorts.

"I think we should get home," signed Zach, sensing Em's discomfort.

Em was under no illusion that they'd spent most of the day breaking the First Rule of being an Animare—never to animate in public. But she had convinced herself that they had done their reenactment in such a way that no one in their audience would ever know that what they were seeing was real. Technically, she felt, they'd got round that one.

But giving one more performance when they were both tired and not as focused as they should be would violate the Second Rule of an Animare—always be in full control of your imagination.

Let's get Matt out of here.

Em and Zach each grabbed an arm and forcefully yanked Matt across the street to where they'd left their bikes.

"Maybe another day," the woman called after them. Then, more quietly to herself, "Most definitely another day."

TWENTY-SIX

S o how much trouble are we in, Jeannie?" asked Em.

Sandie had cornered them in the back of the stable when they were putting their bikes away. She'd been livid when they'd admitted what they'd been doing.

"It's hard to say, lass," Jeannie answered. "They've been in the library since you returned, and not one of them has come in here since. I made a treacle pudding as well. Usually Mara and Simon have their spoons out before I've even served it, but not this afternoon." Ladling thick pea soup into their bowls, Jeannie smiled sympathetically at the three of them.

"We said we were sorry," snapped Matt, tearing into a crusty roll. "What more do they want?"

"Son, that bread never did a thing to you," said Jeannie,

staring at the pile of crumbs covering his place mat.

"Sorry." Matt dropped the remains of the roll onto his plate. "So how did they find out in the first place?"

"One of the things ye two should heed—and quickly—is that when it comes to this island and his kin, nothing gets past your grandpa. Nothing."

"Mom said that he had got a projection of the Nelson boy from me," Em said.

She had decided that she was prepared for whatever punishment their grandfather set for them. She'd also already made a decision that they wouldn't run their performance at Viking Cove again. When the little Nelson boy had screamed in such abject terror, she had felt as if someone had stabbed her. She did not want to feel that way again. Ever. Today would most definitely not be repeated.

"I've lost computer privileges for a month," signed Zach.

"As well you should," said Jeannie. "I couldn't get any of my programs on the telly this afternoon. The whole screen was a big box o' nothin' because of yer fiddling."

Zach drooped. "Sorry."

For the rest of their tea, Matt, Em, and Zach concentrated on eating, hoping that looking penitent enough would mean that any punishment coming their way might be muted by their obvious remorse.

When they finished their sticky treacle pudding and excused themselves from the table, they each tackled a section of the monastery model in silence, continuing to look as contrite as possible.

Mara came into the kitchen, stopping first to scoop a taste of pudding out of the dish with her finger.

"Wow, you're really doing a great job with this." She crouched down, peering into the village square, where Matt was painting a hay cart. "Is this how you got the idea for your performance thingy?"

Matt nodded awkwardly. "Em was studying the artist Brueghel with Simon, and Zach was making a comic about the Battle of Auchinmurn with my mom, so we just put the two things together when we were . . . um . . . animating."

"Plus Grandpa has told us about Solon and the monks so many times," added Em.

"Certainly can't fault your source material." Mara smiled. "Well, come on now. Renard wants to see both of you in his study." She turned to Zach. "Your dad is waiting for you in the stables, Zach. Something about scrubbing the boathouse?"

TWENTY-SEVEN

Renard's study was at the front of the abbey, on the second floor of the north tower. Matt and Em took their time getting there, neither of them in any hurry for the impending telling-off. As they paused outside the door, tears welled up in Em's eyes, and Matt nervously clenched and unclenched his fists.

"I know you're both out there. Come on in," boomed Renard's voice.

Their grandfather was standing at the window, looking out at the Celtic tower on the promontory of Era Mina.

"Matt, do you remember that first afternoon when you and Em arrived on the island?" he asked, turning to face them.

Matt was wrong-footed. He'd been sure they were just here for a telling-off.

Why is he asking us about that?

"Humor me, Matt," responded Renard.

Matt's and Em's eyes widened in surprise.

"Don't panic. I can't hear the words you're actually tele-pathing," he said. "I just know when you are, so I simply made a reasonable assumption, given the circumstances." He looked from Matt to Em. "So, Matt. *Do* you remember that first afternoon?"

Matt nodded.

"And do you remember what you asked Simon, when he gave you a tour of the gardens?"

Frowning, Matt joined his grandfather at the window. "Yes! The Celtic tower. I couldn't understand why it had been built as a watchtower when it was so narrow and all the arrow slits were in the wrong side."

Renard shifted over so Matt and Em could stand next to him at the window. "The tower faces the island and not out to sea because the tower was not built as a watchtower as Simon told you. It was built as a prison."

Matt and Em gasped.

"It was built for an Animare," Renard continued, "a mad old monk who one day, so the story goes, became so deranged that he became a threat to himself and all around him. His Guardian, the abbot of the monastery of Era Mina, knew something had to be done. Even then we had rules that Animare and Guardians lived by."

Em stepped in. "Some of the monks who lived here were Animare?"

"They were indeed. The monastery of Era Mina was the first full community we know of that was organized to protect Animare and to support their artistic abilities away from the scrutiny of the wider world."

"So what happened to the old monk?" prodded Matt.

"The historical records are sketchy, but legend states the monk was illuminating a manuscript and lost control of his imagination, animating a terrible monster that wreaked havoc on the island. So his fellow monks, who loved him dearly and couldn't bear to hurt him, built the tower, situating it in such a way that the monk could sit at the window and see the comings and goings from his beloved abbey, but if he animated anything it would be contained within the tower."

Matt slumped into the nearby armchair.

"That's very sad," said Em. "Was he able to keep his manuscripts?"

"I don't know, Em. The monks had to protect themselves and the village from his imagination somehow. If they did let him continue working with manuscripts, I think they hoped that the height of the tower and the thickness of its walls would have made it very difficult for him to sustain his imaginings for very long. He'd have been too old to project them very far."

"But this is the twenty-first century," Matt blurted out. "You're not going to lock us up for what we did today like we're deranged or something, are you?"

Renard let out a little chuckle. "I wasn't going to suggest that,

Matt. I just wanted to illustrate how dangerous an Animare was considered back then. Because, sadly, there are a growing number of Guardians who wouldn't hesitate to lock you both up. Your mixed birthright is seen as dangerous for our kind and the world. Notwithstanding the fact that the Council voted not to bind you, you are still seen by many as a threat."

"What happens when someone is bound?" Em asked nervously.

Renard retrieved a key, some sunglasses, and a pair of earplugs from his desk and slipped them into his pockets. "I want to show you both something. It will help you understand."

The side wall of the mantel in Renard's office was embellished with a shield displaying the abbey's coat of arms. Tilting back the shield, Renard revealed an electronic keypad. He punched in a series of numbers, and the paneled wall next to the stone fireplace slid open to reveal an elevator, not much bigger than an old telephone box.

Matt had always suspected that the abbey would have secret passageways, but this wasn't what he'd expected. The elevator looked more like the kind of high-speed elevator you'd find in a modern London office building or a fancy hotel. Its interior was steel and chrome—no fixtures, no panels of any kind.

"Shall we?"

The elevator doors closed with a hiss behind them. Before Matt could complain about his ears popping and his stomach somersaulting, the doors opened onto a dimly lit passageway with a row of lights pulsing along each side of the stone floor, diminishing to a small, dark rectangle in the distance.

"That was cool," said Matt, about to step out. "How far down did we come?"

"Wait!" said Renard, grabbing Matt's arm and holding him back. "I need to disengage the security."

Renard pressed his palm against the elevator wall next to the doors. A heat outline of his hand morphed red, then green. When it turned blue, the pulsing lights in the hallway quickened. Matt pressed himself back against the rear wall because it looked as if it was suddenly moving forward, traveling at some speed along the passageway.

"Grandpa, I feel sick," said Em.

"Close your eyes, Em. It's an optical illusion," said Renard. "We're not really moving at all."

"Brilliant!" exclaimed Matt.

Renard pulled Em next to him. "It's a little disconcerting when you first experience it, but it's part of a sophisticated protocol that uses the pulse and the illumination to control access. Simon designed it."

"What would happen if you didn't disengage it correctly?" asked Matt.

"The elevator seals shut."

"And then what?"

"That's simply it."

"Oh."

When the pulsing lights slowed to a steady heartbeat, the elevator appeared to stop. Now there was a door directly in front of them.

"I told you about the old monk locked in the tower not to teach you a lesson and certainly not to terrify you." Renard tousled Matt's hair. "I told you about your Animare ancestor to help you understand what you're about to see in this room, and so that you appreciate the significance of who you are becoming."

Renard pulled the key, the sunglasses, and the earplugs from his pockets. "Em, you should wear these."

"Why?"

"Your Guardian abilities are emerging more strongly right now than Matt's. That's why you can sense emotions more easily and why you and Zach can read each other's minds. This room may affect you more intensely."

Em slipped on the shades and tucked the earplugs into her ears. Renard unlocked the door. Matt stepped into the room first.

"Wow!" he said, gawking at maelstroms of yellow, black, and green exploding across a canvas directly in front of him.

Em followed her brother into the cavernous space. Immediately she felt herself pulled to a small painting in a gilded frame, protected under a thick Plexiglas case.

She crumpled to the floor and lost consciousness.

TWENTY-EIGHT

I told you they weren't ready to be down there!"

"I'm sorry, Sandie—I thought they were. They need to know more about who they are."

"I don't care how well-meaning your motives, Renard. You put my daughter's mind in jeopardy and—"

Matt was sitting at the foot of Em's bed. He was tired of the squabbling, especially since it reinforced his disappointment at having to leave that amazing room and return to the surface when Em had collapsed.

He knew what had happened wasn't Em's fault. As soon as she stepped across the threshold, she had looked as if someone had slapped her hard across the face. Her eyes had rolled up into her head, then she had crumpled to the floor.

Em stirred on her bed.

"I think she's waking," said Matt. When Em opened her eyes, she felt as if she had fallen into the final scene of *The Wizard of Oz*, with Zeke, Hunk, Auntie Em, and Uncle Henry peering down at Dorothy. Only Em's Kansas was a spacious bedroom in an ancient abbey, with her grandfather, her mom, Matt, and Zach gawking at her.

"Where's Toto?" she croaked, smiling weakly.

"Hey, sweetie. How are you feeling?" asked Sandie, kissing her daughter's forehead.

"Okay, I think."

Zach passed her a glass of water, and she took a sip before asking, "What happened?"

"Go downstairs and tell everyone Em's awake and talking," Sandie ordered Zach.

"Were you ever worried that she wouldn't be?" Zach signed.

An almost imperceptible glance, a silent admonition, flashed from Sandie to Renard. Zach caught it, and decided to let the question go. He would ask his dad what Sandie had meant later. He waved at Em, then hurried from her room.

Sandie looked at her children. "The place your grandfather wanted to show you . . . It's a place where . . ." Her words trailed off, tears welling up in her eyes. "Where they store artwork by former Animare."

What are they talking about, Matt?

I don't know, but I want to.

Sandie turned to Renard. "Seeing those works of art changes everything, Renard—the way you see the world. You know that. When you know what's down there, it can breed suspicion, mistrust, even madness."

"Not to most Animare, Sandie." Renard reached across the bed and squeezed her hand. "It didn't to you or to Mara."

"But it did to their dad," Sandie said, snatching her hand from his. "He was never the same after he had seen all those paintings. I want to . . . I have to protect them from that path."

"Keeping them in the dark is no way to help them live in the light," said Renard gently.

"Hello?" interrupted Matt. "We're in the room, you know. We can hear you."

"Mom, we can handle it," said Em. "They were just paintings."

Sandie closed her eyes. "Oh, Em. They are so much more than that."

Renard took Em's hand. "That room is one of five vaults hidden all over the world, containing art created by Animare who, at the height of their imaginative powers, either refused to contain their imaginations or lost control of their power. After the Council voted on their binding, their imaginations were . . . de-animated by their Guardian and another powerful Animare, reduced to radiant energy and bound in a work of their own art."

Em pulled herself up against her pillows. "I don't understand. These Animare died?"

"In some cases the binding of their imagination resulted in

the artist's death," said Renard in a low voice. "To be bound, to lose their imaginative powers, reduced other artists to madness or worse. Sometimes it simply left them empty, a shell of a human being."

"Oh man, I saw van Gogh's painting *Starry Night* down there," Matt gasped.

"So was van Gogh an Animare then?" Em asked, thrilled by the connection to such a famous artist.

Renard sighed, resigned to all he would have to tell them. The time had come, and he didn't like what lay ahead one bit.

TWENTY-NINE

When Matt had walked into the vault, the room had astonished him but not overwhelmed him the way it had overwhelmed his sister.

"The room was filled with paintings," he explained to Em enthusiastically. "Each one was glowing, like it had a halo of light coming from it." He jumped off the bed again, as if pacing would help him find the words more easily. "Em, when I looked into that picture—*Starry Night*—I felt like . . . well, I don't even know what it was I felt."

Sandie stepped in. "You felt bliss, Matt. Euphoria. Joy. Van Gogh's painting transported you beyond reality for a fleeting moment."

Confused, Em looked at her mom. "But how come it's down there? We've seen *Starry Night* in a museum."

"It's down in the vault because van Gogh's imagination is bound within it," Renard explained. "But it's a copy. You see, when the binding decision is made, the Council of Guardians can either bind the artist's imagination or the artist's entire being, depending on the circumstances. If an artist is bound, he or she can choose which painting to be bound in. The *Starry Night* in the vault is not identical to the original, but it's close, and Vincent himself painted it." He paused for a beat. "Poor Vincent was an unusually sad case. He went mad before his imagination was bound. His own mind was never able to come to terms with his Animare powers. Sadly, Europe in the nineteenth century didn't appreciate him much, either."

"Is that what happened to the old monk in the tower?" asked Em.

Renard tilted his head. "Perhaps, but I'm inclined to think that the old monk was, quite simply, old. His mind had lost its sharpness, and even his Guardian could do nothing to help."

"You said before that some Guardians on the Council want to lock us away like that," said Matt. "Didn't you?"

"Your mom and I will not let that happen," said Renard firmly. "One of the wonderful things about being an Animare is that when you create a work of art normally, without animating it, your art can move anyone who views it to the same heights of joy and pleasure that Matt experienced in the vault. For most Animare that is enough, and they live happy, productive lives, creating great art."

Sandie snuggled closer to her daughter. "Your grandfather and I just want you both to be happy, to be able to live your lives without any fear, no matter what you choose to do," she said. "Unfortunately, when you were born, some Guardians wanted to bind your powers right away because your dad is a Guardian like your grandfather."

Matt was about to interrupt, bursting with questions about the vault and about his dad. His grandfather lifted his hand. "Let your mom finish."

"A Guardian—like your dad—and an Animare like myself are forbidden to have children. But we did. I came to the abbey as a young woman to learn under your grandfather's guidance and to have a place where I could work on my art—" Sandie's voice broke.

"And you fell in love with our dad," Em jumped in, squeezing her mom's hand.

Sandie nodded. "But a few years later, when you two were born . . ." She stopped, looking to Renard for help.

"Some on the Council suggested separating you instead of binding you," said Renard, leaning back in his chair, "because they feared how strong your imaginations could become if you grew up together."

"Kind of like in *Star Wars*," said Matt.

Em rolled her eyes, deliberately this time.

"Was our dad one of those Guardians who wanted to hurt us?" asked Em.

Renard looked frozen in his chair. Sandie answered quickly, "Of course not!"

For most of their early years, the twins had held on to the belief that their dad was caught up in some grand scheme for good that kept him away from home. But as more birthdays had come and gone, they'd started to entertain the idea that their dad was not in their lives for some other reason. Sandie's story that he had simply abandoned them hadn't sat well with Matt when he was small. It wasn't resting any easier at almost thirteen.

"One afternoon," Sandie continued, "not long after we'd arrived in London, your dad left the apartment and never returned. No one has heard from him since."

She's lying, Matt.

How do you know?

I can feel it . . . like a clicking in my head.

"So will this happen to me again?" Em asked, letting her mom's lie stand for now. She was feeling sleepy.

"For a Guardian, the intensity of the emotion, the rapture, that emanates from a bound painting can be hard to absorb," explained Renard. "Where Matt felt only the positive that came from the painting, you absorbed everything van Gogh felt when he was painting, Em—his sorrow and his joy. You were overwhelmed. Your brain crashed, like one of Zach's computers."

"But why me and not Matt?" said Em.

"You seem to be developing your Guardian side—your empathy—more strongly at the moment," said Sandie.

"Your imaginative powers are evolving differently in each of you," explained their grandfather.

"So can we go back down to the vault some other time?" asked Matt.

"Of course, when Em's stronger," said Renard. "But looking at the art of an Animare in full control of his or her imaginative power can be just as exquisite. So, for a while, we'll stick with the works on public display in art galleries and museums." Renard lifted Em's hand to his cheek. "I'm so sorry for your pain. Now get some sleep. In the morning, Simon's going to take the three of you shopping in Glasgow."

"But aren't we going to be punished for what we did today?" asked Em, snuggling under her duvet.

Sandie went over to Em's desk, picking up the pencil case stuffed with their ill-gotten gains. "Not if we give this money to Seaport Primary School for art supplies," she said. "Then I think we can call it even."

"Okay," said Em, just relieved to be able to put the injured little boy out of her mind.

THIRTY

Dinner was a quiet affair that evening. Matt said very little, digesting what Renard had told them. He was also snubbing Zach, believing he had poured out the full details of what they'd done in the caves under minimal pressure from the adults.

At the other end of the table, Zach was sulking because of the dressing-down he'd received from his dad for crashing the abbey's network. He was also anxious about Em. She'd looked so pale when Renard carried her upstairs to her room.

It was a relief when finally they all went to bed. En route to her own room later, Sandie stopped to check on the twins, easing open the door to Matt's room first. He was wrapped in his duvet, mumbling in his sleep. Sandie untangled his cover as best she could without disturbing him, then stepped down the hall to her daughter's room.

She laughed aloud at what confronted her. Stepping into Em's bedroom after she'd fallen asleep was like falling into a wonderful 3-D movie. Favorite characters from Em's imagination were shooting back and forth above her bed like colorful comets—a young Victorian girl chasing a street urchin, two teenage boys with wands, a Gothic-looking witch on a broom, a superhero in a green cape, a beautiful mermaid riding a kelpie.

Sandie perched on the edge of the bed, resting her hand on Em's forehead. One by one, the characters exploded in vivid bursts of light, leaving tails of silver stardust in their wake. Sandie waited until the room was free of all Em's imaginings before getting up and leaving, gently closing the door behind her.

Crouching in the corner, the changeling grinned, licking its thin, cracked lips, its yellow eyes piercing the darkness.

The next morning, a heavy atmosphere covered the whole abbey. Matt was the last one to come downstairs for breakfast. Grunting to Jeannie, he poured himself a bowl of cereal, splashing milk all over the counter. Picking up the *Times* crossword and pen that Renard had left on the table earlier, Matt began to scribble across the page, lightly at first. He was remembering how embarrassed he had felt when Em and Zach had ganged up on him at the beach, when that weird couple had asked to see their performance. Zach and Em had been doing that a lot recently. He didn't like it.

His doodling became more aggressive. Suddenly, one of the characters from the Rice Krispies box jumped off, sprinted across the kitchen counter, and leaped onto the sink in front of Jeannie, who screamed, picking up the pan she was washing and splatting the little figure in an explosion of color.

Matt grabbed his head, howling in pain when the character exploded. He rubbed his temples, shocked that he'd felt the character's demise in his head. That had never happened before.

Renard, Simon, and Sandie rushed into the kitchen. Zach and Em came running too.

"What on earth is wrong wi' everyone this morning?" Jeannie yelled at no one in particular, waving the pan back and forth in the air as if she was batting away imaginary missiles. She glared at Matt. "What if I hadn't caught that wee man and he'd headed outside? The gardeners are here!"

"Matt, for pity's sake!" snapped Sandie, as Renard gently eased the pan from Jeannie's grip. "After everything we talked about yesterday, you're still not getting how serious this kind of messing around is, are you?"

For Matt, this was the last straw. "I'm tired of you telling me what to do, what to think, what to eat!" He swept his cereal bowl from the table, sending it crashing against the wall.

"Stop yelling at Mom!" screamed Em. "It's all you ever do."

"Something bad is coming, Simon," said Renard, guiding Sandie away from the enraged and shaking Matt. "I can feel it. It's affecting all of us."

Sandie looked appalled that she'd lost her temper. "I'm so sorry, Mattie. I've been feeling weird all morning."

Renard gathered everyone in the living room. He left Mara alone in her studio, merely sending Jeannie to check on her.

"What's happening, Grandpa?" asked Em, feeling the tension in the air like something dark pressing down on her.

"Someone or something is psychically affecting us all, you and Matt more than the rest of us," Renard told her. He turned to Simon. "Take the children to Glasgow as we'd planned. I'll see what I can discover from here. It may be nothing. We may all just need a break from each other, that's all."

"No surprise there, then," said Matt, stomping out of the room.

Matt, Em, Zach, and Simon waited for the ferry from the mainland in a jagged silence, afraid to say anything that might disturb the precarious balance of civility. As the ferry disgorged its isle-bound passengers, Matt spotted the woman who had confronted them by the café at the beach yesterday. She was driving onto the island in a blue van, with her husband at the wheel. Matt was about to say something, but as he glanced at Em, she glared back at him.

Stuff it, he thought, and kept his silence.

THIRTY-ONE

The trip to Glasgow was just what they all needed. When the train from Largs pulled into Glasgow Central, Matt was singing along to his iPod. Even better, his singing wasn't bothering Em and Zach in the slightest.

Simon had a number of stops to make, buying supplies for the children's art camps that he and Sandie sometimes taught at the abbey. Matt, Em, and Zach promised to be on their best behavior, swearing to wander the shops and nothing more. Simon relented, agreeing they could meet up in a couple of hours.

Everyone was as good as their word. As a treat, Simon took them to his favorite restaurant in the city center for a dinner of fish and chips before catching the train back.

"Did you know our dad really well, then?" asked Em, sipping a milk shake while they waited for their orders.

Simon nodded. "Mara, your mom, a couple of others, and I began our studies under your grandfather at the abbey when we were a bit older than each of you. I came to develop my powers as a Guardian, and your mom had come to learn about her abilities as an Animare. Your dad, of course, was already there. We went to university and then returned to the abbey afterward."

"Are there other places in the country where Animare and Guardians can learn?" asked Em.

"Of course, Em. And not just here, in other parts of the world, too."

For the rest of their meal, Simon managed to find enough entertaining stories about the old days at the abbey to keep them all in good spirits.

"So did you and Mara ever double-date with my mom and dad?" asked Em.

Simon laughed, while the boys grunted their shared displeasure at this turn in the conversation. "Not really. Although, if I remember right, Mara and your dad were close. They went out a few times before he started seeing your mom. In fact—"

Simon suddenly clutched his hand to his throat, gasping for air. Then he slumped forward onto the table.

"He's choking on his food," screamed Em.

Zach looked confused, signing madly that his dad had finished eating way before they had. Something else was wrong.

A man from one of the other tables came rushing across the room, pulling Simon upright to perform the Heimlich maneuver.

Simon recovered enough to push him away. "Not choking. I'm okay."

"Are you sure? You don't look too good, mate."

"Need some fresh air."

With considerable effort, Simon stood and signed to Zach to pay the bill from his wallet. Putting his arms around Matt and Em, he let himself be guided outside.

"Flag down a taxi, Em," he gasped, his entire body twitching. "Something's wrong at the abbey. I can feel it."

In the taxi, Simon drifted in and out of consciousness. Em tried to phone home, but she kept getting Jeannie's voice mail. When she called her mom, there was no answer either, and Renard's phone kept going to the answering machine in his study. If Mara was in her studio, she wouldn't have her phone with her—she hated the distraction.

"I thought your dad had fixed the network, Zach."

"He had!"

Simon was barely lucid, and appeared to be in terrible pain.

"How are we going to get Dad on the train without calling attention to ourselves?" Zach's hands were a blur. "We can't have someone phoning the police or an ambulance."

We need to do something, Em.

Zach did his best to make his dad comfortable, humming softly to him and stroking his head, while Matt and Em tried to think of all the ways they might "do something" without violating any of the Animare rules they'd agreed to last night.

This is a special circumstance.

I agree.

Em pulled her sketch pad from her bag, flipping to a clean page.

Wait until we get closer to the station.

"Are you kids sure you don't want me to take you to the emergency room?" said the taxi driver when they turned into the station entrance. "It's not far."

"He'll be fine once his medicine takes effect," lied Matt. "Really. Thanks, though."

Ready?

Em nodded, concentrating while Matt sketched quickly. Using a silver marker from the set in her bag, she shaded the edges of the drawing when he'd finished.

"Stop over there," said Matt to the driver.

Zach paid for the taxi using money from his dad's wallet, while Matt and Em hauled Simon into the wheelchair that had appeared at the curb. The twins jogged alongside the wheelchair as Zach pushed it, doing their best to keep focused, the drawing clutched in Matt's hand. They darted through the crowded station to the platform, making the 7:05 p.m. train to Largs with only moments to spare.

When they had Simon settled, Matt wheeled the chair to the

end of the carriage, checked no one was watching, and tore up the drawing. The chair evaporated in a puff, leaving an imprint, like a burn mark, on the floor where it had stood.

As the train passed through the many stations on the way to Largs, Simon revived enough to accept a bottle of water. Soon, he was sitting up and coherent, although momentarily confused to note that they were already on the train. When they arrived in Largs, he was himself again. Without asking how they had managed to get him onto the train, Simon hugged each one of them.

"You told us that something bad was happening at the abbey," said Em, her panic building the closer they got to home.

"It was. So let's not dawdle."

The four of them sprinted from the train station across the crowded main street to the ferry, the Range Rover in the parking lot on the other side.

Simon tried not to think about what he knew to be true.

Something bad had *already* happened.

THIRTY-TWO

Tendrils of fog unfurled over the island like long fingers, poking into its coves and crannies, its slopes and crags. When the ferry docked, steaming mussels and roasting chestnuts for a beach party tinged the sea air, slowing traffic in both directions as everyone gawked at the huge, smoking, oil-drum barbecues dotted across the sand.

By the time Simon had driven the Range Rover through the gates of the abbey, darkness had dispelled the fog and everyone inside the vehicle had a headache. Simon tried to play down his growing anxiety, but Em and Matt both felt a dull throbbing in their minds as soon as they turned into the grounds.

Simon turned off the headlights and cruised slowly along the lane toward the towers in near total blackness. When the abbey loomed in front of them, it too was in darkness. Simon pulled off the road and into the edge of the forest, branches scraping against the car as if they were scratching to get inside.

"I'm scared, Matt," said Em.

So am I.

"Squeeze down between the seats," said Simon. "Stay inside until I let you know it's safe."

Simon had only taken two steps when he heard the car doors ease open, the children's footsteps shuffling behind him. He ducked into the forest, letting Matt, Em, and Zach follow. He was far too worried to fight with them.

As the four of them walked into the darkness, it took shape in front of them. A shadow rose above the tree line, a hulking, black, apelike beast with torn slits for eyes and a gaping fleshy mouth. Matt gasped. Em screamed. Zach grabbed Em's arm, pulling her away.

Someone inside the house is animating the forest, thought Simon in horror, pushing the children into a copse of trees.

The beast charged at them. They were helpless, easy prey.

But then the beast exploded into bright yellows, reds, and blues in the darkness above their heads, harming no one. *We should have been killed*, thought Simon in astonishment. When an Animare brought a drawing to life, it was no illusion.

But before Simon could process what had happened, a strix swooped along the treetops, its demonic owl eyes glowing red. Diving at the tree directly above their heads, the bird split apart, shooting spears of blackness that morphed into flying monkeys scampering up the nearby trees.

Simon grabbed Em in realization. "You and Matt are doing this. These creatures are your fears! You're creating them with your imaginations."

"I'm sorry. I'm scared. I can't help it," Em sobbed.

"Yes, you can." Zach took Em's hand, looked into her eyes, and smiled. He turned to Matt. "You can control them, too."

"I'll try."

"Do your best, both of you," added Simon grimly. "Otherwise we'll be slowed down even more."

They reached the abbey's front door. The twins' fears were muted but still palpable in the carved relief of the monastery crest—the peryton was bursting from the wood.

A trail of color flashed across the courtyard behind them. Matt turned in time to see Em's dwarfish night creature dart under the stone arch and into the garden. But then Simon pushed open the abbey doors, and the awful scene in the hallway drove the creature from his mind.

It looked as if a hurricane had struck. Paintings lay slashed on the ground; side tables were overturned; vases were smashed. A trail of torn pages and ripped books lined the floor from the library to the bottom of the stairs, where Renard's broken body lay. Jeannie was cradling his head in her lap, weeping. Mara was kneeling next to them, bleeding from a gash on her forehead.

Em felt as if she was back in the vault again, only this time, her heart, not her head, was about to burst. She threw herself onto her grandfather.

"Mara, draw something. Make Grandpa wake up, please!"

"It doesn't work that way, Em. We can't animate people." Mara pulled Em into an embrace. "We've called for an ambulance. It'll be here soon."

"What happened?" Simon demanded.

"It was right after dinner," said Jeannie, red-eyed. "Mr. R felt the anger in the abbey getting heavier. He sent me to fetch Mara. I found her, poor thing, out cold on the floor of her studio."

"Someone attacked me," said Mara. "I didn't see who. I'm so sorry. I could have done something if I'd been with him. I could have drawn . . ." She stifled a sob.

Simon used the bottom of his shirt to wipe the blood gently from Mara's eye. "This is not your fault." He scanned the room. "Where's Sandie?"

"We couldn't find her," said Mara, choking back more tears. "She's gone!"

THIRTY-THREE

Within ten minutes, the grounds of the abbey were packed with emergency vehicles. An RAF helicopter had landed on the back lawn, before airlifting Renard to the hospital. Jeannie had gone with him. And now a paramedic was helping Mara into an ambulance.

Wrapped in blankets, the twins and Zach sat in the front courtyard on a bench. Behind them, the woods were full of shifting shadows. Every few seconds, something would fly out from the darkness—a screaming banshee, a rotting corpse, a shrouded phantom—dissolving to nothingness as it flew into the bright lights of the courtyard. The hellhound gargoyles twitched on the abbey's turrets, trying to wrench free of their stone moorings.

Simon came outside, observing the chaos that the twins'

fears were creating. It would only be a matter of minutes before a policeman or an emergency worker noticed too. Sitting next to Matt, he put his arm around his shoulders. Zach had taken Em's hand. The darkness behind them gradually quieted, the shadows slowly faded.

The chief constable for Ayrshire and Western Scotland was a tall, elegant, middle-aged woman named Clarissa Bond. She'd arrived at the abbey within thirty minutes of her deputy informing her who was involved in the attack. Renard was well-known in Scotland for his philanthropy, so any attack on his property, never mind his person, was immediately considered a high-profile crime. Chief Constable Bond was also one of a handful of people in public positions of power and influence who knew of the Animare and the Guardians.

She walked over to the bench, crouching in front of Matt and Em. "I'm sorry about what has happened to your grandfather, but he's a very strong man, and I'm sure he'll pull through."

"What about our mom?" asked Matt, shifting out from under Simon's embrace. "She's not here."

"She wouldn't go anywhere without us," cried Em.

"Whoever did this to our grandfather must have taken her!"

"It's likely, I'm afraid," said the chief constable. "In case she's hurt and still on the island, we're doing a thorough search. Try not to worry." She patted Em's leg sympathetically. "I've notified the authorities on the mainland. We have alerts at all the airports and at every train station up and down the coast. I've sent two men to check the ferry to see if anyone remembers seeing anything out of the ordinary this evening. Unfortunately, tonight's beach party means the entire island is swarming with strangers."

She could be hurt somewhere, Matt, or else when the abbey was being attacked, she would've drawn something to stop it. Why didn't she help Grandpa?

But if she was hurt, wouldn't Simon be in pain or something?

He's Mara's Guardian, remember, not Mom's. Dad was Mom's Guardian.

The chief constable stood up, motioning to Simon. "May I speak with you privately?"

"Zach," signed Matt, shifting over on the bench as Clarissa Bond and Simon walked together to the far side of the courtyard.

"Read their lips. Telepath Em what they're saying, so your dad doesn't see you're eavesdropping."

Zach leaned forward.

Are you listening, Em? The policewoman is telling my dad that whoever did this was looking for something. She wants my dad to walk through the abbey with one of her officers and . . . and, uh, see if he can tell if anything is missing.

Em relayed the conversation to Matt, trying to concentrate on the rest of what Zach was telling her. It was strange, having two voices in her head at the same time. *She wants to know if Simon can tell if your mom did anything to stop whoever it was. I think she means did she draw anything?*

I know what she means, Zach!

You don't have to yell.

Sorry. Sorry. What else?

Zach turned his gaze across the courtyard again.

Dad wants to know why she's asking. . . . She says, uh, because if Sandie had drawn something to defend everyone, then she'd be here. And if she didn't, it might mean she was involved. There's no evidence she's been kidnapped. My dad says that's rubbish.

"Well, it is," snarled Em.

"What is?" asked Matt.

Em filled him in. Matt felt his anger building again. He sat on his clenched fists, breathing deeply—in and out, in and out—trying to use the breathing techniques Renard had taught him to help control his temper. The gargoyle above the door flexed a claw.

Zach was still concentrating on the conversation on the far side of the courtyard. *Dad says if Sandie had been drugged or knocked unconscious like Mara, then she wouldn't have been able to draw anything.*

They watched the chief constable call for one of her forensic officers, who climbed from the back of a police van carrying a plastic evidence bag. She showed the sealed plastic bag to Simon.

She's asking Dad if he recognizes this. She says her crime-scene people found it in Mara's studio.

"What's inside the bag?" asked Matt. "I can't see from here."

What's in the bag, Zach?

Dad's looking at it, but I can't see either. Whatever it is, Dad is saying he's never seen it before.

The children watched as Simon returned the evidence bag to the crime-scene officer. The chief constable shook Simon's hand, then they walked back toward Zach, Em, and Matt.

Did you see what it was that time, Zach?

It looked like a plastic first-aid kit.

It was the early hours of the morning before the abbey finally settled for the night. There was still no sign of Sandie. Jeannie had called from the hospital around midnight with the news that Renard's wounds, although numerous, would heal easily, but the head injury was more serious. Until the swelling went down in his brain, the doctors had put him in a medically induced coma. Simon sent everyone off to their beds with big mugs of hot chocolate. Zach was climbing into his bed when his watch flashed a text from Matt.

MEET ME IN THE KITCHEN AND DON'T WAKE EM.

WHY? typed Zach.

COS SHE WON'T LIKE THAT I'M GOING TO BREAK MORE RULES.

THIRTY-FOUR

Sneaking down the servants' stairs was the best way for Matt and Zach to avoid disturbing Em or Simon. Jeannie had remained at the hospital with Renard, and Mara was still being treated in the emergency room. Navigating the kitchen in the dark was easy because of the floodlights spilling in from the gardens.

Matt opened the refrigerator, pouring each of them a glass of juice. Zach fished a handful of chocolate cookies from the jar on the counter.

"If we can figure out what the intruders were looking for, it might give us a clue as to why they took your mom," signed Zach, before dunking a cookie in the juice. The chief constable's idea that Sandie might be involved in some way was completely ludicrous. Sandie would never do anything to hurt Renard.

"We need to get into Mom's studio." Matt ate his cookie in two quick bites, washing it down with one gulp of juice. Wiping his mouth with the back of his hand, he said, "I think Grandpa keeps a spare key in his desk in the library. Let's go."

The dark foyer was more difficult to navigate than the kitchen. Almost immediately, the boys stumbled over two broken chairs that the police had shoved against the wall, their clumsiness echoing in the cavernous hallway. They froze, Matt listening for any movement from upstairs to suggest they'd been discovered. Nothing. After a few seconds, Zach began to step over the chairs, but Matt grabbed his T-shirt, pulling him back.

"I can hear something in the library."

"The intruders might've returned." Zach looked worried as he signed. "We should go get my dad."

"Wait. I want to check it out first."

Trying not to think about Renard as they passed the bloodstains at the bottom of the stairs, the boys darted to the library.

"Still hear something?" signed Zach.

Matt nodded. "It's weird. Sounds like a cat scratching."

"Seriously, we should wake my dad."

The library doors were locked.

"These doors are never shut up like this." Zach shifted closer to the door, trying the handles for himself.

"I need to know what's going on in there," said Matt.

He pressed his ear against the door. The distant scratching persisted.

Without warning, a hand shot out from the darkness behind them, thumping Matt on the shoulder. Both boys jumped with fright.

Draw something, genius.

It was Em. She punched Zach in the arm next.

Hey, why'd you hit me?

For not waking me up.

Pulling a small sketch pad and a stubby pencil from her dressing-gown pocket, Em began to draw. While she outlined the library's doors, Matt concentrated, imagining his hand on top of hers, tracing every stroke. When she was almost finished, he began shading in the drawing. As he did so, the wood at the center of one of the double doors began to shimmer. Within seconds, Matt was able to put his eye against a perfectly placed peephole that had materialized in the wood.

What do you see?

Hard to say. . . . It's a person, for sure.

Hey, it looks like a monk!

"A monk?" said Em, forgetting to keep silent as she pushed her brother out of the way and looked for herself.

She saw a tall figure in a dark, hooded robe rummaging in Renard's desk. Instinctively, she sent the thought to Zach.

Maybe it's a ghost. Zach frowned.

There's no such thing.

Says you.

As if their thoughts had charged into the room, the hooded

figure cocked its head, staring directly at the peephole. Em fell away from the door with a gasp, feeling as if someone had poked her in the eye.

"It does look like a monk. But I think it's an animation," she said, trying to stop her voice from shaking.

"How can you tell?" signed Zach.

"When Matt and I animate a drawing, we can always see a shimmering kind of glow around it. Either it's that monk or something else in that room has been animated."

Zach took Em's place and peered inside the room. Instead of seeing a monk as Em had suggested, he found himself staring at a grotesque, dwarfish creature scuttling toward the library doors.

"It's some kind of gnome or goblin." Zach backed away. "Now I'm definitely getting my dad."

Matt and Em glanced at each other as Zach raced upstairs. Panicked, Matt took another look. The creature was grinning up at the peephole from the other side of the door.

It's your night terror, Em.

Em looked. Her complexion shifted from pale to ashen. *Will you stop saying that? I keep telling everyone, I didn't imagine that thing!*

Looking into the peephole again, Matt listened as the creature slowly clawed its way up the other side of the door, tearing at the peephole.

Grabbing the sketch pad from his sister, Matt tore up the drawing. A wave of light rippled across the wood, and the creature shrieked, the door instantly healing over. The twins fled under the stairs. The scratching and screeching from the other side of the library door was getting louder.

Simon came bounding down the stairs with Zach at his heels. At the same time, Mara, her arm in a sling, walked in through the front door.

"What's going on?" she said at once. "Why's everyone down here in the middle of the night?"

"The twins think there's an animation in the library."

Mara stared at the twins, noting their sketchbook. "Whose?"

"Why won't anyone believe me?" raged Em. "It's not mine!"

"What's not yours?" asked Simon and Mara in unison.

"The thing in the library," said Em, close to tears. "It's been coming into my room late at night, getting into my dreams, but it's definitely not come from my imagination. It's nothing to do with me."

"We can talk about that later," said Simon. "For now, let's deal with what's behind the door." He looked curiously at Mara. "How did you get back? Ferries don't run at this time."

"A friendly fisherman gave me a lift," Mara answered. She set her handbag on the ground. Pulling out her sketchbook, she rested it on a table in the hall, ready to draw with her good hand. She nodded at Simon, who unlocked the library, pushing the double doors open wide. The room was empty.

"Are you sure about what you all saw?" Mara said.

The three children nodded.

"Look," said Em, pointing to the back of the door. They all shivered. Pencil-thin claw marks had been gouged deep into the wood.

THIRTY-FIVE

Exhausted but far too wired to sleep, Simon, Mara, and the kids decided to investigate the library, giving it more than the cursory walk-through Simon had completed with the chief constable earlier. Hoping to find something that might suggest a reason for Sandie's disappearance, they all moved around the room, eyes peeled for anything that seemed out of place. Possible sources of the animation the children had seen were not discussed, as the twins and Zach restacked books onto the shelves, and Simon and Mara poked around in Renard's desk.

It's not fair, Zach. Simon and Mara think my fears animated the creature.

That's not true, Em. My dad's worried . . . but not about you. I can tell.

"Renard never kept anything of value in this room," said Mara in frustration, settling into one of the leather couches, as the children and Simon continued to scour the room.

Em dropped into the leather couch beside Mara. "Were you able to see Grandpa before the hospital released you?"

"I went up to intensive care and spoke to the doctors for a few minutes. There's no change, Em, and there may not be for a long time."

"Do you remember anything about what happened? I'm so worried about my mom." Em snuggled next to Mara.

"I remember working in my studio, seeing the grounds' and the abbey's emergency lights flashing, then nothing. That is, until Jeannie was leaning over me, telling me Renard was hurt."

"There's a lot of mess," Simon said with a sigh. "I don't know what they were looking for, and I can't find anything missing. The doors to the gardens were unlocked, but I think that was my doing. I left them like that earlier for the police."

We need to get into Mom's studio.

"Has anyone checked my mom's studio?" asked Em, ignoring the scowl from Matt, who wanted to continue investigating without the adults.

"The police checked it before they left," said Simon. "It didn't look as if anything had been damaged or moved. In fact, it looked more like . . ." His words trailed off.

"You might as well tell them, Simon," said Mara.

"Tell us what?" asked Matt.

Simon signed to Zach to stop sorting the books and join them.

"When the police searched Sandie's studio, they found a vial and a partially empty syringe that they think had recently dispensed a fairly strong anesthetic—"

"To Mom?" asked Em.

Simon shrugged, perching on the arm of a chair. "They can't tell with any certainty, Em, but the chief constable and her team did think the mess in your mom's studio looked as if it had been caused by a brief struggle, not a search."

"You mean they could have come to kidnap Mom? But why?"

Matt ran his hands through his hair in frustration. "It's not like we have any money."

"Kidnapping isn't always about money, Matt," Mara said. "Your mom is a powerful Animare. We can't rule out that she was taken because of that."

"So we're looking for another Animare or a Guardian?" suggested Em, her voice cracking from exhaustion and a growing sense of unease. "They're the only ones who know we exist."

Simon nodded. "When it's light, I'll set an internal investigation in motion."

"What does that mean?" Matt asked.

"Chief Constable Bond will handle the investigation of your mom's disappearance from the civilian side of things, but your grandfather has his own network of Guardians. They'll begin a search on our behalf."

Mara sighed. "Finding Sandie would be so much easier if their dad were here."

Simon glared at her. This sudden suggestion from Mara was as surprising as the flash of anger from Zach's dad. The twins looked from one adult to the other, hoping Mara would elaborate. Their mom and their grandfather had kept promising more details later, but with one missing and the other in a coma, the twins wondered if they'd ever find out more about their dad.

"Well it's true," Mara went on stubbornly. "As Sandie's Guardian, Malcolm would at least be able to sense if she were alive or not."

"Mara!"

"Do you know where Dad is, Mara?" Em asked, taking no notice of Simon. "Couldn't we contact him and ask him to help us?"

"I'm sure if our dad knew Mom was in trouble, he'd want to get involved," added Matt, sitting up straight in his chair.

Simon gently squeezed Matt's and Em's shoulders. "We'll find your mom. I promise. We don't need your dad's help. Mara? Enough," he added, letting his fingers graze the back of Mara's hand.

"The thing is," said Mara, her voice softening the longer Simon focused his attention on her, "we've not received any kind of ransom demand, which suggests that whoever has taken your mom isn't looking to trade for her. But Simon is right, we'll find her."

Simon is a good Guardian. He's settled Mara's frustration.

Maybe. Or maybe she's just not willing to challenge him in front of us.

"Whoever took Sandie must have a game plan for her," continued Mara, wandering over in front of the shelves they'd just sorted. "You know as well as I do, Simon, that that's not only puzzling, it's virtually unprecedented."

"What do you mean?" signed Zach, leaning over the chair behind Matt.

"In all the history of our kind, there are only a few instances of Animare breaking the rules for their own gain or being manipulated or coerced for their powers," Mara explained.

"Were they successful?" asked Matt. He moved toward the library doors to get a closer look at the scratch marks.

Mara ran her finger along the leather spines of the books above Renard's desk, stopping midway as she slid a slim volume from its place and carried it back over to the couch.

"Centuries ago, a wealthy patron of the arts and a Guardian, Grace Fortescue, admitted in her private memoirs to having coerced her Animare for years." Mara held up the book, flipping through the yellowed pages. "As a result, she built a fortune in priceless artifacts that she made her Animare create for her."

"That's terrible," said Em.

"Quite," said Mara, passing the book to Em. "But who's to say that such a relationship didn't also benefit her Animare? It makes for fascinating bedtime reading, however you look at it."

"There are perhaps two or three other examples," Simon went on, "but Mara's correct—the instances are rare." He glanced at his watch. "Good grief! It's almost dawn. I'll have to answer to Jeannie's wrath on her return if you three are tired tomorrow."

He locked up the library, following Mara and the kids up the stairs to their bedrooms. Mara turned to Simon and said in a low voice, "You do realize that there's another possible explanation for Sandie's disappearance, don't you?"

"What?"

"Sandie could have staged this entire episode herself."

"That's absurd!" Simon said in shock. "Sandie'd never abandon Matt and Em, and she'd never do anything to hurt Renard."

"She had no problem hurting Malcolm," snapped Mara. Simon watched Zach, Matt, and Em disappearing down the hallway to their own wing of the abbey before answering.

"This again, Mara? Your spite toward Sandie has always been misplaced, and I'll not dignify it with any more of my time."

Simon took the stairs two at a time, leaving Mara standing alone at the bottom.

THIRTY-SIX

The next morning, a storm from the Atlantic had anchored off the coast, with heavy winds and pelting rain making travel treacherous. Jeannie had made it back to the island on the dawn ferry before the storm broke, but the gray skies and a late bedtime were making it difficult for her to rouse the boys for breakfast. While she pounded on their bedroom doors, a lone figure on a motorcycle was carefully cresting the hill into Largs.

Flash flooding at low stretches of the main road from Glasgow had twice sent the tail of his Harley spinning; it took every skill he possessed to avoid wiping out. When he reached the ferry, he was drenched and disappointed to learn that it wouldn't leave until the storm shifted inland. Parking his motorcycle in a narrow lane behind a tearoom on Main Street, he went inside. He'd already waited years to return here. A few more hours wouldn't matter.

The boys came slouching down the stairs to the kitchen, snatching toast from Jeannie before she cleaned up breakfast.

"You seriously don't remember Grandpa telling us who Zeuxis was?" Matt asked Zach, folding a slice of toast on itself and swallowing most of it in one bite.

"The head of the Greek gods?" Zach gulped a glass of juice.

"Not Zeus—*Zeuxis*." Matt slowed his signing to spell out the letters *XIS*.

"Zeus's sister?"

Matt snorted, headed to the utility room at the back of the kitchen, and grabbed his raincoat and boots.

Em was already sitting at the hearth, struggling to pull on her wellies, trying not to dwell on what might have happened to her mom. "Actually, Hera was Zeus's sister," she said. "Oh . . . but I think she was also his wife."

"Ew!" said Zach and Matt in unison, as they wrestled with their raincoats.

"Grandpa told us that this Greek guy—Zeuxis—might have been the first Animare," continued Matt. "Apparently he laughed himself to death after painting a very funny picture of a woman."

"Och, that poor dear," sobbed Jeannie, lifting up her apron and dabbing her eyes. "I can't bear thinking about him."

Matt and Zach looked quizzically at each other. "You two are idiots," said Em, marching past the boys and slapping each one playfully across the head. "She's upset about Grandpa, not Zeuxis! Can I get you a cup of tea, Jeannie?"

"Aye, hen, that'd be grand." Jeannie dabbed her eyes. "I just keep thinking if I'd not gone upstairs so early, I could've helped."

Em brought Jeannie her tea. "Simon said that we can maybe go and visit Grandpa tonight. I'm sure they'll bring him out of his coma soon. He'll know what's happened to Mom."

Pushing open the French doors a crack, Matt and Zach squeezed out into the storm without letting too much of it gust into the kitchen.

"Where are you off to in this weather? Ye'll catch yer deaths!"

Em dashed to the door before Jeannie could stop her. "Need some fresh air, Jeannie. We'll be fine. Promise."

Outside, the rain was coming off the sea in sheets, forcing the three of them to fold into the wind as they struggled across the lawn. Between the blinding rain and the crashing waves, talking and signing was impossible. Linking arms with the boys, Em marched them toward Sandie's studio, telepathing with Matt.

Why exactly were you two arguing about Zeuxis?

I think I've figured out how that creature got into the library. It's something to do with Zeuxis.

How?

When Grandpa was telling us about the secret vault, he said that some of those paintings are especially powerful because their Animare are bound in them. What if your terror—I mean the dwarf thing, somehow came from a bound painting?

When they reached Sandie's studio, they dashed up the steps, huddling under the thick stone eaves for shelter.

Matt tried the door first. "I knew it!" he said. "Locked."

Em cupped her hands, peering through the dark privacy glass. "It's impossible to see anything. We need to get inside."

"Draw a key," signed Zach. Matt pulled his sketch pad from his raincoat's inside pocket. With Zach acting as a barrier to the driving rain, he began drawing a key.

Imagine the lock.

Em nodded, closing her eyes.

Matt's hand scribbled across the paper as if his pen were automated. When he'd finished, Em took the sketch, adding teeth to the key. Then she outlined the lock, and Matt finished it. A flash of blue light surged from under the door handle, the old lock appeared to dissolve, and, in an instant, a silver key appeared in a shiny new lock.

Zach opened the door.

"Wait!" said Em. "Mom will be okay with us doing this, won't she?"

"If we want to help get her back," said Matt, "we have to."

The twins hesitated for a second, then followed Zach inside.

THIRTY-SEVEN

L ook out!" yelled Matt, pulling Zach to the ground as a colossal wave crashed through the window of Sandie's studio.

Behind them, Em exploded in laughter.

Dazed, the boys looked up from the floor, realizing they'd ducked an angry wave painted on a wall-size mural. The image had looked so realistic that Matt had thought water was surging through the glass. Sandie had painted the wall to look as if a storming sea was directly outside, matching a similar view she had on blustery days from the real window of her studio. The fact that a storm *was* actually battering the building had made the illusion even more powerful.

Matt remained on the floor for a few minutes, getting his bearings, adjusting to the sheer number of startling images around the walls.

"Every drawing looks three-dimensional," he said, as Zach gazed around in amazement. "How did she do that?"

"It's called trompe l'oeil," Em said. "French. Means 'trick the eye,' I think. With Mom's abilities as an Animare, it makes the paintings and murals even more amazing . . . and almost real."

Matt felt like clapping. The entire studio was one trick painting after another. So many images were drawn on the walls and up across the ceiling that it was difficult to distinguish between the real objects in the room and Sandie's imagined creations.

"It's going to be impossible to search this place before Simon and Mara get back from Largs," he said at last. "They mustn't find out we're trying to figure out what happened to Mom on our own."

"Why don't we divide the room into sections?" said Em. "That way each of us can look carefully at a smaller area, and the room won't be so overwhelming."

Zach began walking the perimeter of his section. Without thinking, he reached into a glass bowl for a sweet—only to have his fingers hit against the wall, the bowl an optical illusion.

Em was briefly transfixed by one corner of the studio, which burst with exotic flowers so lush and beautiful she could almost smell jasmine, lilac, and the faint scent of her mother. Choking back tears, she shifted to the area around a long trestle table covered with paint pots and brush jars. On the wall above the table, she ran her fingers along painted images of brass hooks with antique keys hanging from them. There was a pyramid of pigeon-holes with ribboned scrolls and poster canisters inside them, and a painting made to look like a framed photograph of a Victorian woman wearing a velvet hat. The woman's hat looked to Em like a hairy black spider perched on her head. But Em's favorite was a row of fake windows painted at eye level above her mom's worktable, with views of places Em remembered from London: the steps outside the National Gallery, the Henry Moore sculpture at Westminster, the cobbled square at Covent Garden, the pond in Kensington Park.

"Hey, take a look at this. It's incredible!" Matt called from his corner of the room. Em nudged Zach. They both looked. A tower of luggage, consisting of an old-fashioned shipping trunk, a boxy black suitcase, a bulging red tote, and a brown leather doctor's satchel, which Em thought looked vaguely familiar, were painted on top of each other to look as if they were balancing precariously on a luggage cart that was collapsing from the weight. The image was as tall as the studio's door, much taller than any of the kids.

They spent the next ten minutes examining the other images in the room. Matt and Em began to feel more and more overwhelmed by the sheer volume of their mom's art and the aching sadness of their loss.

I miss her.

Me too.

Do you think she's okay, Em? Can you sense if she's okay?

I can't. I really can't.

And as much as Em hated to admit it, the fact that she couldn't sense her mother worried her most of all.

* * *

After about twenty minutes in Sandie's studio, Em lost hope. A dark shadow seemed to cover her mind. She sensed Matt's thoughts as clearly as her own, spiraling into despair beside her. They'd never find their mom this way. She was gone—maybe forever.

A spider the size of a cat suddenly pounced out of the painting of the woman with the funky hat. Leaping over two pots of paint and scampering down the table leg, the hairy black spider scuttled across the floor toward the twins.

Em screamed.

Grabbing a stool from under the table, Matt flipped it over and slammed it on top of the creature. The spider exploded in a burst of black charcoal dust. Em screamed again, as a swarm of spiders spewed from the woman's hat as if it was an egg sack. With bulbous middles and bulging eyes, they streamed across the table, washing onto the floor in thick waves.

Next, a thick, ropey vine from one of the exotic plant pictures untangled itself from its roots, slithered across the floor, and wrapped itself around Em's ankles. It tightened its grip, pulling Em to her knees.

Three bigger spiders leaped from the table edge. Landing on Matt's shoulder, they dug their legs into his neck, their hair scratching his skin like wire brushes. Matt batted them off with his hands, filling the room with more clouds of black charcoal.

Zach ran to help Em, as still more spiders cascaded from the painting. By this time, Em had curled herself into a ball, covering her head with her arms, howling as one spider after another landed on her, tangling their legs in her thick hair and nipping at her skin.

"You both hate spiders," signed Zach urgently. "*You're* doing this! You're upset about your mom. . . . All these images . . . You're losing control!"

Em was now blanketed in angry spiders, but they kept on coming.

I can't stop them!

"Help me get her outside," Matt gasped at Zach.

Ignoring the spiders scampering up their own arms, the two boys tried to pull Em toward the door. They didn't get very far. The vine was still holding her tight, squeezing the circulation from her legs.

Zach darted to the spot where they'd dumped their wet raincoats, rifling in Matt's pockets until he found the sketch pad and pencil. Matt was cloaked in the spiders too, but he was valiantly keeping as many from his sister as he could, booting them across the room when they landed near her. The air was choked with charcoal dust.

I can't . . . breathe. . . .

"Draw something!" Zach shoved the sketch pad into Matt's hands. "She's going to suffocate!"

Ignoring the hundreds of spiders thickening across his shoulders, Matt drew as fast as he knew how. He had to save his sister.

THIRTY-EIGHT

Matt drew the first thing that came into his imagination. A wooden ax with a bright red blade thudded onto the floor next to Em. With one swift swing, Matt picked it up and hacked through the vine. Suddenly free, Em was able to drag herself outside, with Matt and Zach close behind. As soon as Matt slammed the door to the studio, the spiders covering their bodies began popping like black, chalky firecrackers.

"Thinking about Jack and his mighty beanstalk, were you?" said Em a few minutes later, wiping her filthy face with her sleeve.

"If I had drawn a chain saw, I wasn't sure that it would work without electricity," said Matt.

Em laughed shakily. "I'm sure your imagination would have been a strong enough power source."

"Matt!" Zach suddenly looked electrified. "Do you realize what you just did?"

"Cracked a whopping big hole in my mom's floor?"

Em's eyes widened. "You drew the ax without me! I didn't help in any way. I wasn't imagining an ax at all. All I was thinking about was missing Mom, and getting those disgusting spiders out of my hair."

Matt shrugged, as if this development was no big deal. Inside he was punching the air with excitement. "I guess I did animate that ax on my own, but Grandpa did say that might happen eventually . . . to both of us."

"Yeah, eventually," signed Zach, tossing each of them their raincoats, "but most Animare are adults when their powers are fully evolved. You're not even thirteen yet. Think about what you might be able to do when you're older!"

The three children walked across the wet lawn to the jetty, trailing clouds of soot behind them like exhaust fumes. The rain had stopped, and the storm was passing. Zach and Em sat down on the bench at the end of the dock, while Matt skipped stones into the sea, trying to mask his excitement and nervousness at the development in his abilities.

"Well, no matter what we figured out about my powers," Matt said between skips, "that was a fairly useless hour. We didn't discover anything that could help us find Mom."

"Maybe not," answered Em, "but we learned that Mom is an amazing artist . . . and . . . and—" Something suddenly came to her. "The brown satchel!" she gasped. "Why didn't I think of it before?"

She jumped from the bench, heading toward Sandie's studio again.

"Wait!" Matt yelled, running back along the shore. Zach joined him. "You can't go in there again. You might get something worse than spiders this time!"

"What satchel, Em?" Zach signed as they caught up.

"The brown satchel on top of the funny mural with all the suitcases. Like the kind doctors in old movies carry. It looks exactly like the one Mom brought from London when Matt and I first came to the island!"

"Oh, yeah . . . I remember!" said Matt in excitement.

"I need to go back inside and take a closer look at it," Em said.

"Okay," signed Zach. "But we can't risk the walls coming to life again. This time I'm going inside on my own."

THIRTY-NINE

Zach left the twins standing outside the studio's closed door. They were supposed to be watching for Simon and Mara to return, but spent most of the time peering through the dark glass, trying to track his progress.

With the storm's passing, sunlight filled the studio with light, making every image look even more alive than before. Waving his way through the charcoal haze that still permeated the studio air, Zach went directly to the luggage mural.

Got it yet?

You'll be the first to know, Em. Now be quiet. Watch for my dad and Mara. I don't want to lose any more computer privileges because of this.

Zach was too short to reach the top of the painting where

the satchel lay. Grabbing the stool Matt had used to smash the spiders, he climbed on it and stretched his arms up the painting, trying to reach the satchel.

Your dad and Mara are pulling into the garage. You've got maybe two minutes before they see us out here. Hurry up!

Zach was aware of something tingling beneath his fingers as he touched the mural. It almost felt like . . . electricity.

Thirty seconds.

Before he could process Em's warning, his fingers hit something hard directly underneath the image of the satchel. It was a clear shelf, camouflaged in the mural with a real satchel, not an imaginary one, perched on top of it.

Got it, Em! It's real all right. And there's something underneath the mural too—some weird kind of power current.

Matt says leave the satchel where it is for now or we'll get caught with it. It'll be safer where it is. We can't let your dad or Mara know about it until we see what's inside first.

Locking the door, Zach sprinted back outside to join the twins. With only seconds to spare, the three of them plonked themselves on the end of the jetty, as Mara and Simon walked out of the garage. Matt quickly tore up their drawing of the lock and key.

Mara headed inside, while Simon came down to join them.

"What have you three been up to this morning?" He looked more closely at the state they were in. "You look like you've been cleaning chimneys. What's with the soot?"

"The flue backed up in Em's bedroom," said Matt. He gathered more stones to skip on the water. "We helped her with the mess."

"We're thinking we might walk along the shore to Seaport now," said Em, brushing excess charcoal from her jeans. "See if the storm washed up anything interesting."

"Good idea."

"Will we be able to see Grandpa this evening?" Em asked.

"I think so," Simon said. "We can go after dinner if you'd like. I heard from the chief constable this morning," he went on. "They've accounted for everyone on and off the ferry yesterday—except for one couple who came onto the island earlier in the afternoon. The curious thing is there's no evidence of the couple returning to Largs on any later ferry runs."

"So they might still be on the island?" asked Matt, alert. "And they might have Mom?"

"The police have canvassed all the B and Bs. There's no record of them staying overnight anywhere," Simon told them. "Of course, they may have found another way onto the mainland that kept them clear of closed-circuit TV cameras, but I doubt it—particularly in light of this morning's storm. I think they're still here." He stood up. "The police have every dock and boat charter under surveillance, and, as of this morning, your mom has officially become a missing person. That'll put her on every alert in every constabulary in the country."

"I guess that's good news," said Matt uncertainly.

"It is." Simon looked like he was about to say something else to the children, but his cell phone rang. He walked a little way up the beach to take the call.

Em nudged Zach. Zach peered to read his dad's lips and sent his thoughts directly to Em to avoid detection.

He's talking to someone at the hospital.

Simon closed his phone and marched across the lawn to the kitchen. Zach's mind went dark as he shut Em out of his thoughts and processed what he thought he'd read. This was something he had been working on with his dad, who had told him that there might be times in his life when he might have to keep things from Em. Zach had protested that he couldn't imagine such a time, but his dad had been right.

"What's wrong, Zach?" Em said urgently. "Who was that?"

Zach thought carefully about his response. "I think it was the chief constable. She must have told my dad something about some marks they've discovered on your grandfather's legs and ankles." He paused.

"Tell us!" demanded Matt angrily.

"Remember all I got was my dad's side of the conversation," signed Zach at last. "I may have read him wrong. But I think he said, 'Good God, bite marks. You know what that means.' Then he hung up."

"And what *does* it mean?" said Em.

"I think it means that the dwarf creature you saw in the library attacked Grandpa," Matt guessed. "The scratches on the library door looked like claw marks."

Em felt sick. "You know something?" she said. "If that creature did hurt Grandpa . . . it means there's an Animare on this island giving it orders to do a lot more than just haunt my dreams or visit the library."

FORTY

Realizing they'd have to wait until later to retrieve the satchel, and not sure what to make of all that they'd learned, Matt, Em, and Zach decided to take advantage of the low tide, and for once do exactly what they had told Simon they would do.

The wind remained strong, the sea choppy, as they trudged out onto the hard sand. The sun was out, but the afternoon felt more like a blustery autumn day than a mild summer afternoon. Plodding along the shore in a companionable silence, they occasionally picked up something shiny in case it was treasure worthy. If it wasn't, they set it on the rocks where they could later retrieve it for the trash.

"If there *was* an unknown Animare on the island," Em said thoughtfully, as they headed back to the dock for lunch, "wouldn't

Grandpa have sensed them? That creature was in my room days before it attacked him."

"You'd have thought so," Matt agreed.

Zach nudged Em, pointing to a skiff cutting across the waves. "Who's that?"

The figure operating the outboard motor was hooded and wearing dark rain gear. They couldn't see his face.

"He must have come round from the public launch at Seaport," said Em. "Where's he going in such a hurry, though?"

"Fishing off Era Mina?" said Matt. "Grandpa always says the few hours before and after a storm are the best."

"Well, he's moving pretty fast for a fisherman," signed Zach, running ahead of them toward the boathouse. *C'mon, Em.*

Em took off after Zach.

"Wait up!" Matt sprinted after them both. Inside the boathouse, Zach grabbed the binoculars from a hook near the door. The man in the fishing boat had slowed, clearly scouting the island. Zach passed the binoculars to Em.

"Did you recognize him?" she asked.

"I could hardly tell if it was a he or a she, let alone recognize them."

"Definitely a he," said Em after a minute, passing the binoculars back to Zach. "I think he's docking his boat."

Staying within the cover of the boathouse, they watched the man run his boat into shallow water on the southern end of Era Mina before climbing out and dragging the skiff up onto the beach. Then he rounded the point of Era Mina, where they lost sight of him.

"He's heading to the caves," Matt said. "What if he finds our stuff?"

Em thought about everything that she, Zach, and Matt had used to create their illusions for the tourists—their refurbished computers, art supplies, and sound equipment—all stashed in one of the Era Mina caves. The adults knew they had been exploring Monk's Cove on Era Mina, but had no idea how much of the network of caves they had staked out for themselves. "Don't be silly," she answered, with a bit more confidence than she felt. "He'd have to pick the right cave, go all the way inside, then work out which wall to climb before he'd even spot the next level of caves. If he did that, well, yes, then he'd find our stuff. But the tide's coming in. Can't see him risking getting trapped and drowning."

"You're probably right," agreed Matt, relaxing. "But who is this guy? He looks like he knows his way round the island."

Taking turns with the binoculars, they kept their eyes on Era Mina until the stranger wandered back into view, walking across the beach to the ancient Celtic tower. Wandering the tower's circumference, he suddenly stopped and crouched.

"He looks like he's examining the sand," said Matt, his eyes pressed to the binoculars. "And he's way too curious about that tower. We should follow him. See what he's up to."

"We should get the satchel from Mom's studio before we do anything else," Em warned.

"We don't have time," said Matt, glancing at his watch. "It's not likely this guy came all the way across the bay in that tiny boat. If he came from the mainland, he'll probably return it at the island rental and catch the next ferry. If we cut through the path in the woods, we'll make it. We can see where he goes from there."

"Plus," signed Zach, "whatever's in the satchel is still safer in your mom's studio than in our hands—at least for another couple of hours."

It was true that the satchel probably was safer where they'd left it, yet Em couldn't help feeling that it was something she and Matt should look at as soon as possible. But the boys had already retrieved their bikes from the stables and were racing into the woods. There was nothing else to do. She'd just have to follow them, and leave the satchel until later.

PART THREE

FORTY-ONE

The warning bell on the monastery's gate tower had fallen silent, but below, the courtyard had erupted in a cacophony of commands. Setting the old monk's manuscript on the floor, Solon crawled to the arrow slit in the scriptorium's wall. Peering through the narrow hole, he wept at what he saw.

Under cover of darkness, a band of Norsemen had attacked the village, stealing into the bay from the north. Raids had been a regular occurrence for centuries, but in recent years there had been fewer and fewer, especially on Auchinmurn. He watched in horror as the surviving villagers charged through the forest, desperately seeking the safety of the monastery's fortified walls. A line of monks, all of them skilled archers, had mustered on the parapets, shooting with speed and accuracy to keep the Vikings at bay. But the monks were outnumbered. They were losing the battle. Solon could see that those manning the heavy ropes of the portcullis would have to drop it soon, leaving any stragglers from the village to their fates.

He stared at the monks courageously holding the gates. He knew them all as friends and teachers. One or two of them were Animare, but not one would use their imaginations to defeat the invaders. Not when the monastery of Era Mina was the only place in the kingdom where Animare were protected, where they were not reviled as abominations or hunted like monsters as long as their imaginations were used in the service of enlightenment and truth.

Solon had come to know this as the First Rule. If an Animare were ever to break the First Rule, the penalty was severe—imprisonment or death. This had not always been the case, but the world was no longer the open, enchanted world in which the old monk had grown up. Instead, it was becoming a world where magic and miracles were in the hands of powerful men, and an unfettered imagination was becoming a blasphemous thing.

Solon spotted his mother charging through the gates. Then he gasped. His oldest sister, Margaret, carrying her daughter Mary, was trailing a few feet behind. Margaret would struggle to reach the monastery gates before the monks dropped the portcullis.

Come on, Margaret! You can do it. Run!

He knew only the old monk could hear his thoughts, but he willed them on nonetheless, holding his breath until he saw Margaret and Mary both safely inside.

Along the perimeter of the wall, a line of monks was pouring hot tar into buckets, preparing to drop them at the abbot's command.

But where was the abbot? Where was the old monk?

Solon scanned the chaos below. It was becoming more and more difficult for him to see individuals in the panicked sea of faces filling the courtyard. The monks were lowering the portcullis and closing the gates as fast as they could. Using pickaxes and pitchforks, a group of villagers assailed any Vikings that had got into the courtyard.

Quickly, Solon retrieved the pages for *The Book of Beasts* from the floor, intending to secure them on the shelves before leaving the safety of the tower. He planned to find the old monk and help prepare the monastery for the inevitable siege. They'd need to secure food and water, find safe places inside the walls for the women and children.

But something pierced his temple, and everything went black.

Minutes after Solon went down, the old monk and the abbot were herded into the courtyard by a second line of Vikings who had come at the monastery from the rear, scaling the seawalls and avoiding the village altogether. With the archers' attentions on the gates and the villagers' safety, this line had charged unhindered through the abbey itself, finding their two hostages along the way.

Their presence sent a wave of shock rippling through the villagers.

JOHN BARROWMAN & CAROLE E. BARROWMAN

A nimble young warrior broke from the line and climbed up onto a corner turret on the monastery's wall. Pulling his horn of ivory from its goatskin sheath, he blew two long blasts, silencing the rabble and halting the fighting.

The chief stepped into a clearing in the center of the courtyard. His feet and legs were laced in pigskin, his body draped in reindeer hide and silver chain mail, his helmet and nose guard a blush of gold. Shoving the bound and blindfolded old monk and abbot to the ground in front of him, the Viking raised his longsword in the air, holding it in two hands above his head as he spoke.

"My name is Rurik the Red, son of Logmar the Berserkr, grandson of Erik the Fierce. Put down your weapons or everyone will die!"

Beneath his blindfold, the abbot's face was the color of limestone. The old monk gasped, his body listing to the side. A cut on his head, where Rurik had thumped him with the hilt of his sword, continued to bleed. Every man, woman, and child holding a weapon let it fall to the ground. The archers, setting down their bows, moved away from the portcullis, letting the warriors outside charge triumphantly into the courtyard.

Solon! Solon! Can you hear me?

The old monk knew Solon was collecting the day's pages from the scriptorium high in the north tower.

Can you hear me?

The old monk and the abbot had been forced to their knees.

Longswords drawn, Rurik's men formed a wide circle around the terrified villagers. Four or five of Rurik's warriors moved through the crowd, fetching children and dragging them to the center of the courtyard. If a mother or a father objected, a sharp blade or a leather strap helped change their mind.

I hear you, master. Solon's voice was faint, groggy. *I hear you.*

When every child in the village was huddled together in front of the kneeling abbot and the old monk, Rurik stepped forward again, his booming voice drowning out the sobs of the children and the cries of their families.

"A century ago my family ruled these islands. The monks repaid us by stealing a priceless relic. On this day in the name of Odin, I've come to retrieve what's mine.

"You will give me what I seek, or I will take payment in your children."

FORTY-TWO

Breathless from pedaling at top speed through the forest to the ferry, Em, Matt, and Zach nodded their greetings to the man checking their boat passes at the dock. They were the last ones to board.

"I'll take a look around the boat for the stranger," said Matt, climbing the stairs to the upper deck. "You both keep your eyes on the bay in case he didn't get on the ferry after all."

He returned a few minutes later. "No sign of him. I even checked the men's room."

Taking turns with the binoculars, they stood at the stern, monitoring the bay. The ferry was about a hundred yards from docking at Largs when Em finally spotted the stranger, bouncing his boat through the waves at the southern tip of Auchinmurn.

"What took him so long?" asked Matt. "Even Jeannie could have made it round the island faster than that."

"He must have stopped somewhere," said Em. "It doesn't look like he's heading to any of the boat rental shops in Largs to return his boat, so where's he going?"

The three of them were the first off the ferry, running their bikes up the gangway, doing their best not to knock over any of the tourists exiting with them. Stopping next to cars lining up to board for the return trip, Matt took the binoculars from Zach. The stranger was now hugging the coastline, guiding his boat south.

They mounted their bikes quickly, cycling south along the packed promenade, doing their best to keep the stranger in their sights.

The afternoon sunshine had brought everyone back outdoors. Riding safely along the promenade was becoming an exasperating challenge.

"We can't let him get away from us," said Matt, more worried about losing the stranger than either Em or Zach. He'd let his mom down by not being at the abbey when she'd needed him—he wasn't going to let her down again.

"Look out!" screamed Em.

Matt had dodged out onto the street to avoid a family crowding the promenade, steering right into the path of an oncoming tour bus. Swerving up onto the curb, he used his momentum to jump his bike over the beach steps and bounce onto the sand, before nailing a perfect landing. Behind him, the driver honked furiously.

"Who the heck taught that guy to drive?" yelled Matt in rage, as Em and Zach set their bikes down on the sand beside him.

"I don't know why you're so upset. That was totally your fault," chastised Em. "You could have been killed!"

Matt glared at her. "You're not my mother."

"We're losing him," signed Zach, watching the stranger receding through the binoculars. Matt threw his bike onto the sand in frustration.

"Very mature!" said Em, jumping out of the way just in time.

Matt paced anxiously. "We need to draw something."

"Too many people," signed Zach.

"It has to be something that'll allow us to see where he's going without having to follow him directly," Matt muttered, ignoring Zach's warning. "And something that won't call attention to any of us."

"That rules out a jet pack or a speedboat," signed Zach, only half joking.

"What if we leave our bikes and get a taxi somewhere quieter?" suggested Em. Zach hadn't brought any money. Matt did have a fiver in his pocket, but he had plans for that and kept quiet about it. Picking up his bike, he locked it to a nearby stand. Then, pulling out a small sketch pad and three badly chewed pencils from his pack, he slouched against the beach wall to draw.

Mom needs our help, Em urged mutely. *If someone took her, they could be watching us, too.*

I don't care. I'm doing this.

Zach and Em locked their bikes next to Matt's. Climbing up on the beach wall, Zach kept the binoculars trained on the stranger, while Em sat close to her brother, worried she might be called on for damage control. Matt's hand was flying across the sketch pad. After a few seconds, Em realized what he was drawing. She didn't care whether he wanted or even needed her help; in her own imagination, she began to follow his every stroke. If nothing else, their combined efforts would make the animation even stronger.

Jumping down from the wall, Zach let the binoculars fall to his chest. "He's gone. I can't see him anywhere. He didn't come into shore at the memorial. I think he's gone farther down the coast," he signed.

He peered over Em's shoulder at Matt's drawing. A bird the size of an osprey with piercing blue eyes and a rounded, gull-like head was emerging.

"What's that?"

"A caladrius," signed Matt. "A mythical bird that can see the future. Renard told me about it." He shaded the bird's wings.

"You think a bird that sees the future is going to help us see where the man in the boat's going!" exclaimed Em.

Matt grinned.

"Show off." Zach shook his head. "Seriously, how are we going to see what the bird sees?"

Matt erased the top of the drawing, reworking the bird's

head. "You two had better be ready for this. I've never done it before."

At first Em didn't think Matt's drawing had animated, as the only thing visible in the sky was a plane banking into the airport. She was just about to reach for a pencil, when the most beautiful bird she'd ever seen soared out of the blue, as if the sky was a curtain it had been hiding behind. Its feathers looked like crushed velvet.

She smiled in admiration at Matt. The pupils of his eyes were eerily wide. Em's admiration morphed to panic.

A few tourists waiting in line for ice creams had noticed the bird, pointing and gawking up at it. An elderly Englishman cupped his hands over his eyes to get a better look. "My goodness," he said, "even the seagulls are bigger up here."

Now the caladrius hovered directly above the twins, its wingspan creating a current of air so strong that Em was knocked back on her heels a little. Before someone had the opportunity to find a camera, Matt concentrated on his image, sending the caladrius soaring farther out over the bay. And that was when Em saw exactly what was wrong.

Zach, a little help here.

Em's hand was cupped under Matt's elbow as she directed him where to walk. Grabbing the drawing, Zach saw Matt's eyes gazing out of the caladrius's head. Matt had sent his own vision soaring into the sky with the bird.

"It didn't quite work out the way I imagined," Matt admitted, feeling his way up the steps from the sand with Em's help. "But it'll have to do."

"What if this has permanent effects?" asked Em, worried for her brother.

"It's a risk I had to take," Matt said seriously. "For Mom's sake."

FORTY-THREE

Arms linked, Zach and Em guided Matt across traffic to the nearest bus stop on Main Street. Em was relieved to see there wasn't much of a line. The last thing she needed was someone recognizing them and reporting their antics to Jeannie or Simon.

"Matt, seriously, are you okay?" They'd never actually put a part of themselves into a picture before. Em didn't remember her grandfather saying such a thing was even possible.

"I feel a little strange but not bad," replied Matt. "Really."

"I can't believe you did something this stupid!" Em pinched her brother's arm angrily.

"Ow!"

Ask him what it feels like to fly.

"Zach wants to know what it feels like to fly."

"Great—but weird, too. Sometimes the sky is down and the sea is up, but what's really bizarre is that I can see the three of us walking to the bus stop." Matt stopped, losing his balance for a moment and tilting against Zach. "Sorry. My legs are a bit wobbly. My stomach feels like I'm on a roller coaster!"

The caladrius was swooping above the bay, skimming across the water's surface for a few seconds before soaring back up into the clouds.

"Now I feel dizzy," said Matt.

"Hey," said Em, taking Matt's weight against her for a second, "fair warning if you're going to throw up."

Straightening up, Matt tightened his grip on Em and Zach's arms. "I'll be okay, but we should probably get on the next bus. It doesn't matter where it's going as long as it's south. The caladrius can see the stranger's already past the putting green."

"Shouldn't we just find a bench and let the bird follow the boat?" Zach signed.

"We can't risk losing the stranger if the power of the animation suddenly doesn't reach that far," Em answered, pulling Matt upright as he tipped forward again, almost falling on his face.

"I think the caladrius is playing with my head," Matt said thickly. "It keeps swooping and zooming."

"That's just the way birds fly," Em said unsympathetically. "We need to get on the next bus."

Zach flagged the Troon bus down, and Em fished her pass out of her pocket, digging in Matt's back pocket for his. Clumsily, the three of them helped Matt up the narrow bus steps, ignoring the stare from the driver. They squeezed into a double seat toward the front of the bus, with Matt in the middle.

Em telepathed her brother. *Where's the stranger now?*

He's slowing down. . . . I think he's heading to the Pencil Monument.

The Pencil Monument had been built on the shore of Largs to commemorate an ancient Viking battle.

Suddenly Matt jumped back against the seat, startled.

The woman sitting behind them hugged her shopping bag tighter against her chest, tutting under her breath.

He's spotted the caladrius. He's staring up at me . . . at it. I'm going higher.

Is it anyone we know? Zach telepathed Em.

"Any idea yet who the guy is, Matt?"

"He's taken off his hooded jacket. We definitely need to get off at the stop for the monument. He's coming in toward the beach there. I can almost see his face. . . . He's not stopping at the yacht club. . . . He's docking on the rocks before the tower."

Getting off the bus was less of a commotion than boarding, mainly because Matt was getting used to negotiating his physical surroundings while his imagination soared above the clouds. The sensation was a lot like playing a video game while walking.

Arm in arm, they crossed the bridge to the yacht club and into the park. Keeping out of sight of the stranger, Em and Zach guided Matt to a picnic table hidden in the middle of a copse of overgrown bramble bushes. Matt glided the caladrius inland.

"It stinks in here," said Em, kicking a pile of empty cans and takeout containers out from under the table.

While Matt kept the caladrius circling, Zach and Em watched the stranger examine the ground around the monument in the same manner he had investigated the tower on Era Mina.

"What do you reckon he's looking for?" asked Em.

"No clue," said Matt.

"Try to draw his face."

"But I can't see the paper," Matt objected.

"You'll have to sort of feel your way, then."

Landing the caladrius on top of the monument, Matt peered down at the stranger while Em flipped to a clean page in the sketch pad, sliding it under Matt's fingers.

"Nothing clever, Matt," Em advised as she pressed a pencil into his hand. "We don't want him leaping off the page at us. Just sketch the man's face."

Matt concentrated on what the bird was seeing and tried to make his fingers work.

As if someone had dropped a curtain, everything went black inside Matt's mind. Then, just as quickly, the curtain lifted. But instead of watching the stranger examining the base of the monument, Matt was seeing something quite different. The stranger looked injured, and he was leaning against a wounded Zach. They were both in a cave somewhere.

Matt leaped up from the picnic table, tripping over his own feet and ending up on his knees next to the pile of garbage.

"What's the matter?" asked Em in alarm. "You look like you've seen a ghost."

"The guy . . . ," Matt managed. "Zach . . . is everyone okay?"

"He's just getting back in his boat," Em replied. "Zach's fine. Why?"

"I think I saw something that hasn't happened yet," said Matt, feeling sick. He felt Em and Zach pulling him back onto his feet. "It must have been the caladrius. . . . It was showing me the future."

Matt tried to sketch the stranger's face, feeling his way across the paper, wondering why he looked so familiar. The vision kept disturbing his concentration. Zach and the stranger had been lying injured in the tidal pool in the caves at Monk's Cove on Era Mina, and that was something he didn't want to share with anybody.

"I'm going to be sick," said Matt, putting his head between his legs, this time actually throwing up.

FORTY-FOUR

Thirty minutes later, when the stranger was returning the boat to a rental shop north of Largs pier, the twins and Zach were getting off a bus a few yards away.

"I can't go any farther," said Matt, still feeling nauseous. "Get me behind the wall on the beach. The caladrius can follow him the rest of the way on its own. I don't care anymore how far that is. I need to lie down."

Zach and Em helped Matt behind the wall, watching the hooded stranger retrieve a motorcycle from the public parking lot next to the pier. Leaning his head back, Matt kept the caladrius hovering above the buildings.

"He's heading back to Main Street," said Em. "Now what?"

"We let the caladrius keep following until I lose the connection."

Swooping the caladrius over Largs, Matt lifted it up into the clouds. Zach followed with the binoculars until the biker and the bird vanished toward the Haylie Brae.

"I guess he's going back to Glasgow. . . . Oh no . . . please . . . No . . . don't . . ."

"Matt, what's wrong?" Em asked urgently. "What are you seeing?"

Matt gripped his hands to his head and rolled into the fetal position on the sand.

"Matt! Can you hear me? Mattie!"

Em knelt in the sand next to her brother, not sure whether to take his hands or support his head, not sure what to do to stop his obvious suffering.

"Eyes burning . . . chest hurts. I can't breathe, Em, and I can't see anything."

"It's the bird. Zach, get the drawing!"

A man and a woman broke from the busy promenade and rushed down onto the beach. Quickly, the man removed his jacket, rolling it up and tucking it under Matt's neck. The ring on his little finger flashed in the sunlight, making Em blink. These two were the same couple that had tried to get them to perform one of their tourist shows.

"Has he had seizures before?" the man asked.

"Never." Em watched helplessly as Matt continued writhing in the sand.

The man pressed his hands on Matt's shoulders, restraining him, nodding pointedly at the woman.

Em noticed the odd look. "What's wrong?"

"I need to keep him from hurting himself," said the man, while the woman dug in her shoulder bag.

A small crowd was gathering, as Matt's convulsions were beginning to cause concern. Em was feeling very strange in her own head. Something disturbing was emanating from this couple attempting to help Matt.

"I'm calling nine-nine-nine," said a woman at the front of the crowd, taking a mobile from her pocket.

"I'm a doctor," said the man restraining Matt. He glanced at the woman with him. "And my wife's a nurse. We can get him across the street to the hospital more quickly than an ambulance."

Zach, this man isn't who he says he is. Something's weird about these two. I can feel it. They were hanging about the other day too—remember?

Finally reaching the drawing of the caladrius in the sketch pad, Zach tore out the page, ripping the drawing into pieces. Matt's eyes rolled up into his head, and his body became perfectly still. Terrified, Em threw herself on top of her brother, not feeling any relief until his breath brushed against her cheek.

Can you hear me?

"I'm calling an ambulance whether you like it or not," said the worried woman.

The man who'd said he was a doctor grasped Em's arm, lifting her off Matt and setting her behind him in the sand. "He'll be fine in a minute. His seizure's passed. But we'll take him across to the hospital anyway."

Zach, we need to get Matt away from here. These two are trouble.

Matt's sight was returning. He was startled to discover a strange man pinning him against the sand. "Hey! Get off me!" He began to squirm, attempting to get himself out from under the man's grip.

"Son, I'm a doctor. . . ."

Matt, he's lying.

No sooner had Em conveyed her bad feeling to Matt than Zach spotted the doctor's wife pulling a syringe from her shoulder bag and slipping it underhand to her partner, whose knees were now pressing hard on Matt's chest. Struggling frantically to get up, Matt saw the transfer of the syringe too. With as much momentum as he could muster, he kneed the man in the groin. It wasn't a very graceful or even a seriously debilitating move, but it was good enough to give Matt the few seconds he needed to roll free and to give Em a chance to toss a handful of sand into the woman's face.

Run!

FORTY-FIVE

Zach, Em, and Matt raced off down the beach. As Matt blinked in the bright sunshine, he was just grateful that he was able to see again. And by the time the first police car skidded up to the pier, the only person left who had witnessed what had happened was the concerned woman with the phone. The so-called doctor and his wife were long gone.

Zach guided the twins away from the beachfront, eventually ducking inside an empty bus shelter in the center of town.

"What happened there?" Em asked, gasping. "Who were they?"

"I've got a horrible feeling they were the people Simon told us about yesterday—the ones the police are looking for," answered Matt. His voice was hoarse, he had a pounding headache, and every time he took a breath, his chest hurt.

Hands on hips, Em stood in front of her brother. "And what about that fit you had?" she demanded. She punched Matt in the arm, and he yelped. "I thought you were having a stroke or something. What happened with the caladrius?"

"You won't believe it," said Matt, rubbing his arm.

"Try me."

"The stranger shot me—or rather, shot the caladrius." Matt's heart quickened as he thought about the incident. "After he got to the top of the Haylie Brae, he pulled his motorbike into a rest stop, and . . . and he looked up, grinned, and took a shot."

"With what?"

Matt glanced at Zach's questioning hands. "I don't know . . . some kind of gun. The kind hunters use."

"Is that why you had a fit?"

"When the caladrius was hit, all I could see was this explosion of colors and light, and then it felt as if I'd been shot too." Matt brushed his hair from his eyes, as if he could sweep away the memory. "The pain was terrible. My chest was on fire."

Em stared at her brother for a minute. His eyes were bloodshot and rimmed in red, his skin the color of chalk. She sat next to him, resting her head on his shoulder. "Why do you think he took a shot at the bird? Did he work out it was following him?"

"He'd have to be pretty clever to know that." Zach shrugged. "Unless he was an Animare or a Guardian. Look, I'm glad you're okay, but I think we may have an even bigger problem right now."

Across the road from the bus shelter, two police cars had

pulled in alongside each other, the policemen chatting through their open windows.

"Do you think they're looking for us?" asked Matt, standing too quickly and feeling light-headed again.

"Surely they'd be more likely to be looking for the couple who tried to kidnap Matt?" said Em.

"I can't see their lips clearly enough to find out," Zach told them. "But either way, I don't think we should hang around. If we hurry, we should be able to make the three thirty ferry. We can pick up our bikes on the way back to the dock."

They dodged out of the bus shelter and cut through a nearby garden, using the winding lanes behind the town center to make their way back to the beach where they had left their bikes, eventually reaching the ferry with ten minutes to spare.

On the other side of the Haylie Brae, the stranger lay sleeping. He had pulled into a rest stop and watched Matt's caladrius circling overheard. After he'd taken his shot, he'd climbed from his motorcycle, stretched out on the grass, and, with the warmth of the sun on his face, he had fallen asleep.

Now, as he woke, it was dusk, the sun an orange ball setting behind the peaks of Kintyre. Climbing onto his Harley, the stranger headed back into Largs.

FORTY-SIX

O h dear God, what happened to ye?"

Jeannie enveloped Matt in her ample bosom the moment the three of them stepped into the abbey's kitchen.

"Is it an eye infection?" she asked, tilting Matt's head, scrutinizing his bloodshot eyes. "Do ye have a fever?" She placed the back of her hand against his forehead. "Or is this something I'm better off not knowin'?"

"Probably better not knowing." Matt stepped away from her embrace. "But if it's any consolation, I'm okay and I learned a lesson."

"Yeah, right," signed Zach behind Jeannie's back. "Not to be such an easy target next time."

Discreetly, Matt gestured a response to Zach.

"Is there any news on Grandpa?" asked Em.

"He's still critical," said Jeannie. "Still in the coma. Are ye going to go and see him later?"

"Yes," said Matt. "I just need to lie down for a few minutes."

I'm wiped. Plus I need to sleep off this headache. Do not do or say anything about what happened today to anyone until we see what's inside Mom's satchel.

Em nodded in agreement.

Without Matt and Renard, dinner was a quieter affair than usual. After updating everyone on Renard's slow but steady progress, Mara said very little. Em and Jeannie blathered about a show on TV that they both liked, and Zach signed with his dad about the storm, about how high the tide had come in, about how many downed trees the three of them had spotted when they'd biked through the woods earlier, their hands an animated blur.

"I'm glad you're visiting your grandpa this evening," Simon told Em. "I think hearing your voices will help him immensely."

"Will he know we're there?" asked Em.

"I'm sure of it," Simon said, smiling.

"Do the police have anymore news about who may have hurt Renard and broken into the abbey?" asked Mara, helping Jeannie clear the dishes.

Simon relayed various details from the chief constable about the search for Sandie. According to the police, Sandie had completely disappeared. No trace of her whereabouts had been found anywhere.

"The more time that passes without a ransom note," added

Mara, "the less likely it is that she's been kidnapped, surely?"

"That doesn't mean she just up and left for no reason," Em said frantically.

"Of course not," consoled Mara, "but we can't rule out the possibility that she left for a reason we don't yet understand."

"Like what?"

Simon sent a scorching glance across the table.

"I guess it's not my place to say," said Mara, after an awkward moment.

Clearly the adults were keeping information back. Em felt awash with frustration. She was about to speak up when Zach intruded on her thoughts.

Don't forget we're holding out on them, too. Don't say anything you'll regret.

Simon topped off his and Mara's coffee. "The chief constable has traced every plane, train, car, and ferry from John O'Groats to the Isle of Wight," he said. "If Sandie's left the UK, she has not done so by any . . . ah . . . normal method."

"You mean she could have animated something to get herself out of the country?" asked Em, getting more juice from the refrigerator and pouring herself another glass. "Wouldn't the Guardians know if she'd done that?"

"Not necessarily," said Simon. "Remember, since your dad left, your mom no longer has her own Guardian. Renard had stepped into that role, but he won't be any help until he's well enough for us to talk to him."

"Maybe we should try to find our dad after all?" Em said hopefully. "If nothing else, he might be able to tell us if Mom's . . . okay." She couldn't bring herself to say out loud the words "dead or alive."

Mara nodded. "That's a great idea—"

Simon slammed his dessert bowl down on the table. "Why do you keep going on about finding Malcolm, Mara? For one thing, no one's heard from him in years. We can hardly afford to divert all our resources—to say nothing of the police resources—to start a wild-goose chase. For another, don't you think if he was anywhere close—and, of course, if he gave a damn—he'd have sensed something was wrong and shown up by now?"

"I'm sorry, Simon," Mara said calmly, "but I can't help wondering if Malcolm leaving them years ago and Sandie leaving them now—well, perhaps the two events are related."

Em almost choked on her juice. Zach thumped her back, passing her his water. Furious, Simon stood up.

"I don't think it's fair of you to put stupid notions like that into their heads, Mara." He gathered up his dishes. "I'm sorry, Em, but what Mara's suggesting is really not the case. Now if you'll excuse me, I need to check on a couple of things before we head to the hospital. Give me half an hour, then wake Matt and we'll head out."

Em cleaned up her place at the table more quickly than she'd ever cleaned up after dinner before. Mara's theory didn't seem nearly as stupid as Simon suggested. Not because it hurt her feelings that her dad might not care about her—because it did—but because she and Matt had considered the very same thing the night their mom had disappeared.

What if their mom's disappearance did indeed have something to do with why their dad had so hastily abandoned them all those years ago? Where did that leave them now?

FORTY-SEVEN

Zach and Em went to retrieve the satchel from Sandie's studio. Em was itching to see what was inside, especially if there was even a remote possibility that its contents might offer some insight into what had happened to her mom, and possibly her dad as well.

With a drawing of a lock and key she'd scribbled firmly in hand, she led the way across the abbey compound. Zach had brought a camping flashlight to use inside the studio; the floodlights on the grounds were enough until then. It was easier to telepath than sign in the dark.

How would we even begin to start looking for your dad, Em? Do you remember when he left?

I remember he and my mom had a huge fight. I don't know where we were, but I think it was in the middle of the night. That's what Matt remembers too. In the morning, he was gone. No good-byes. No notes. Nothing. Maybe Mara can help us? She knew my mom and dad back in the day, growing up here. But we have to ask her without telling your dad.

I know.

When they were halfway across the lawn, the power went out, throwing the abbey and its grounds into darkness. Now the only illumination came from the shipping beacon on top of the tower on Era Mina.

What's going on?

Maybe a power cut.

They waited, knowing that the emergency generator would kick in soon. But in the seconds before the lights came back on, Em heard glass breaking from the far corner of the cloisters.

Grabbing Zach, she bolted around to the rear of the building just as two figures ran from Sandie's studio, clutching something bulky. The light from Era Mina swung around and hit Mara's mirror installation, and for an instant it looked like a crowd of people surging through the trees. Zach's thoughts were instant. *It's the couple from the beach.*

Matt! Em sent her own message almost as fast. *They're stealing the satchel!*

Matt was awake in a flash. Grabbing his jeans and sneakers, he was dressed and downstairs, through the empty kitchen, and out onto the grounds in no time at all. He caught sight of Zach disappearing into the woods. Em slowed at the fringes of the trees, giving him time to catch up.

Growing up on the island, Zach knew every tree, every stream, every clearing in the forests and glens. By contrast, the fleeing couple was ill-prepared for the island's terrain, tripping and stumbling through its underbrush. Tiring, the woman glanced over her shoulder.

Zach, don't let them out of your sight. Matt and I will catch up in a minute.

Directly ahead of Zach, the man dodged clumsily around a fallen pine. The woman chose to hurdle it instead. Then suddenly they were both gone.

Zach inched closer to where they had fallen out of sight. He wanted to laugh at what he saw. They had sunk into the ground up to their waists, and were scrambling desperately to reach the branches of a nearby tree for leverage.

Breathless, Matt and Em stopped next to Zach.

They look like they're in—

Em finished Zach's thought with a grin. *Quicksand.*

Matt held up a pen, while Em held up her arm, a drawing of the clearing complete with quicksand dashed across her skin. Zach high-fived them, but there was no time for celebration. The couple may not have been going anywhere, but the trophy they'd taken from Sandie's studio most certainly was. He heard Em's gasp in his head, as clear as a bell.

The satchel's sinking. Get it!

The three of them bolted from behind the tree. Matt held Zach's feet as Zach stretched out to grab the satchel from the thick muck and pull it back to safety.

The couple didn't seem surprised to see them. The woman was still making vain attempts to pull herself from the quicksand, but with every move she was sinking even deeper.

Matt crouched at the edge of the pit. "We've been studying the history of this island. You're lucky we didn't drop you both in hot tar!"

"If you keep still, you'll be okay," added Em a little more kindly, kneeling next to her brother.

"Who are you?" Matt demanded.

"Let us out of here first," said the woman, holding her arms in the air as the quicksand squelched around her hips. "Then we'll be happy to share some personal details with you. . . ."

"You're not exactly in a position to barter, are you?" Matt pointed out.

The woman scowled. "But we're the only ones who know what has happened to your mom."

Em glanced at Matt, then at Zach.

She's lying. I wish she wasn't, but she is.

"You know we're not stupid," said Matt. "I'm guessing you even know we're Animare, since you don't seem to be freaking out about sinking in the kind of quicksand you'd normally find in a rainforest."

The man raised his arms in a mock surrender. "You win. I'm

Tanan Olivier. This is Blake Williams." He had a slight French accent, and his eyes were a jade green color Em had never seen before. "When your mother left London, she took something that did not belong to her. We came to take it back."

"And that's why Mom has gone?" Em was concentrating hard on the tone and the pitch of Tanan's voice, doing everything she'd learned from her grandfather.

"Not exactly," said Tanan.

What he's saying might be true, but he's doing a good job of masking his real feelings. I don't like him—

"You were trying to drug me this afternoon," Matt said, cutting through Em's thoughts. "Were you trying to kidnap me?"

"We felt your mother might need a little . . . persuasion to hand over the item we wanted." Blake eyed the satchel in Zach's arms. "But in the end, you weren't necessary."

"Charming," Em muttered.

"You still haven't answered my sister's question," Matt went on. "Is that why our mom has gone? Do you know what happened to her?"

"When we got to the studio on the night of those unfortunate attacks," Tanan said smoothly, "your mother was nowhere to be found."

Blake squished closer to the edge of the muck. "The only reason we decided to stay on the island was in case she returned when she heard what had happened to Renard. We got lucky with the satchel in her absence."

"Enough, Blake." Tanan turned back to the twins. "When we were searching the abbey, your grandfather was already injured, lying at the bottom of the stairs. We left as soon as we heard your housekeeper coming. We knew she'd call the police."

He's mostly telling the truth . . . but there's something else. It's like he's telling us just enough so that I can't get underneath to the full truth. I wish I was better at this.

"If you only searched the abbey, then how did you know about the satchel in our mom's studio?" asked Matt.

Tanan grinned. "Those clever little watches of yours. It wasn't difficult to add our own tracker the day Blake talked to you at the café in Seaport, trying to convince you to show us your private performance."

Matt removed his watch and shoved it angrily into his pocket. Em left hers on, figuring it hardly mattered now. Zach remained behind the twins, the satchel hooked over his shoulder, the flashlight focused on Blake's and Tanan's faces.

"Who do you work for?" asked Em.

Blake scowled. "You're getting nothing else until you get us out of here. My shoes are completely ruined."

Em turned to her brother. "What do you think, Matt?"

"I think we leave them squishing in this mud. Maybe start it boiling."

Tanan's and Blake's eyes widened.

"Nice . . . but we can't do that," Em said. "Still, even if everything they've said is true, then at the very least, they didn't try to help Grandpa when they found him. They just stepped over him like a pile of garbage and left him bleeding on the stairs."

"Maybe we should send my dad or Mara to figure out what to do with them," signed Zach, beckoning Matt and Em away from the quicksand. "I bet they can persuade them to talk more."

"Hey! You can't leave us like this," cried Blake.

"Oh, yes, we can." Em turned, holding up the drawing on her forearm. "For a while anyway, that's exactly what we're going to do."

FORTY-EIGHT

D espite their resolve in front of Blake and Tanan, Matt, Em,
and Zach couldn't agree on whether to tell Simon and Mara
about the couple, make an anonymous call to the local police, or
simply wash off the drawing and allow the couple to flee. At that
particular moment, the latter options seemed preferable to admit-
ting to Simon that they'd broken the First Rule again.

But as soon as the twins pushed open the French doors, Simon
and Mara were waiting to pounce. Instinctively, Zach tossed the
satchel into the woodpile outside the kitchen door, so that the
adults wouldn't notice it.

"Where have you been?" Simon demanded angrily.

"When the lights went out, we saw two people running from
Mom's studio," said Em, "so we decided to chase them. Matt heard

me in his head . . . and we didn't have time to get you or Mara. Plus we were afraid they'd get away . . . so we decided to trap them instead and now, ahem . . . we've come to get you for . . . you know, help."

Simon paced in front of the three of them. "You decided to chase and *trap* them?"

Em slowly held up her arm, the drawing still vibrant and shimmering. "Quicksand," she said. "We drew quicksand, and now they're stuck in it."

Mara snorted, gulping back her laughter.

"And now what?" said Simon in disbelief. "You've left them there?"

"We weren't sure what to do," Matt jumped in. "But they're not in any danger, really. The mud's warm."

Simon's temper exploded. "Oh, that's just brilliant! And I suppose when they get free, they'll just wander into town, telling everyone they were taking a lovely mud bath in the middle of Auchinmurn Woods. Don't you think we have enough going on right now without calling even more attention to ourselves?"

Zach stepped between his dad and the twins, his hands flying. "I don't think they'll say anything, Dad. They seemed to understand what Em and Matt had done, you know, with the drawing. They claimed they had been sent to get something that Sandie had taken."

"They must be working for Sir Charles Wren," said Mara at once.

"Who's Sir Charles Wren?" asked the twins in unison.

"Next to Renard," explained Mara, giving Simon the chance to calm down, "Wren is one of the most powerful Guardians in the world. He's the head of the European Council of Guardians. He and Renard have been at odds since your birth, with your grandfather in favor of changing the rules of binding, and Sir Charles and his followers adamant we remain true to our ancient traditions."

"He's a very dangerous man," added Simon, still seething. "One who has never taken easily to the passive role of a Guardian."

"What do you mean?" asked Matt.

"A Guardian must protect their Animare at all costs and take nothing in return. Renard and the other Guardians could never prove it, but there have always been rumors that Wren has used Animare for his own financial gain."

"Like Grace Fortescue?" asked Em.

"Exactly," Simon said. "Your grandfather thought that whatever Wren was orchestrating, it involved you and Matt. He had met recently with Guardians based in Scotland, and they were convinced Wren was plotting something."

"We must do something about those two in the quicksand, Simon," Mara said, pulling her phone from her jacket and glancing at her watch. "Plus you've already missed the start of visiting hours. We can fill the kids in about the rest of these conspiracy theories when you get back from the hospital."

"Have the chief constable meet you in the forest," Simon instructed Mara. "We'll give you both enough time to get there before Em scrubs off the drawing and frees them. The chief will know what to do next."

"Do you think this Wren guy has taken my mom?" asked Matt.

"If what you've discovered from these people is true, it sounds like Sir Charles just wanted something from her."

"Do you know what it might be?" asked Em in as innocent a voice as she could muster. She'd seen where Zach had thrown the satchel.

"I don't," said Simon. "I wish I did, but I don't."

For the first time that night, Em was certain that she was hearing a truth.

FORTY-NINE

For goodness' sake, where is she?" asked Simon fifteen minutes later. He was sitting behind the wheel of the Range Rover idling in the courtyard.

"She said she had to get something for Grandpa," replied Matt. Seconds later, Em darted out of the front doors, carrying a parcel the size of a coffee-table book wrapped in brown paper, and a bouquet of daisies from Jeannie's garden.

"We can't go to the hospital without flowers," she said, scrambling into the backseat.

The ferry ride and drive to the hospital were quiet, with Matt and Em lost in their own thoughts. Simon was worried that events surrounding Sandie's disappearance seemed to be escalating. Zach fiddled with their watches behind the twins, making sure they were clean of any tracking devices.

When they arrived at the hospital in Largs, a doctor met them outside Renard's private room.

"Your grandfather is heavily sedated, and he's connected to lots of machines monitoring his vital signs. But the good news is he's breathing on his own."

Em had never stopped long enough to process what a serious assault her family had experienced that night: her mom missing, her grandfather in a coma. Standing outside the hospital door, seeing the man she adored so pale and weak and connected to a medley of tubes, Em wasn't sure she'd be able to keep herself from turning into a sobbing mess.

"Can I hug him?" she asked, trying to hold back her tears.

"I'm sure he'd expect nothing less," said the doctor, leading them into the room.

Matt and Zach stood awkwardly next to the bed, doing their best to conceal their own feelings. Arms outstretched, Em threw herself across her grandfather, pressing her cheek to his heart, finding comfort in its quiet but steady rhythm.

After they'd offered their comments to the unmoving figure in the bed about the weather, the increase in jellyfish in the bay, and their lack of progress on their model of the monastery, the boys shifted to the other side of the room and perched on the window ledge. Simon went outside to chat with the doctor, while Em pulled a chair closer to Renard's bed.

"I brought you a present, Grandpa," she said, reaching for the package Simon had carried inside for her. Balancing it on her lap, she tore open the wrapping. Vincent van Gogh's *Poppy Fields*, one of the artist's less famous paintings, which Renard had bought as an investment years ago, glowed up at her.

Matt moved off the ledge. "Is that the painting from Grandpa's study, Em?"

Em set the picture on the hospital dresser, directly in Renard's field of vision should he open his eyes.

"You do know that's an original van Gogh?"

"I know that."

"You can't have a painting like that in a hospital room," Matt pointed out. "Someone will steal it."

"I don't care," Em cried. "Grandpa loves this painting. It makes him happy. I want him to sense that the painting is near him and . . . and maybe . . . maybe his connection to the painting will help bring him back to us."

"That's sweet," said Matt. "But did you tell Simon you were bringing it here?"

"I helped her wrap it," said Simon, coming back into the room. "And I thought it was a lovely idea." He hugged Em. "It's always been one of his favorites. Who knows what power it may hold?"

On their way across the hospital parking lot to the Range Rover, Simon stopped. "Who's up for an ice cream? It's a beautiful night. We could sit on the pier and watch the fishing boats go out."

Matt, Zach, and Em were appalled at the suggestion, since it would delay them even longer from finally seeing what was inside Sandie's satchel. In unison, they shook their heads hard.

Simon looked taken aback. "Okay. I guess that was a bad suggestion. But you did hear me say ice cream, right?"

"We're just tired," Em said, linking her arm with Simon's. "I think we'd like an early night tonight."

On the ferry, the children could hardly contain their nervous energy. Twice Simon had to make them sit down, as their pacing around the deck and boisterous bickering with each other was bothering other passengers.

When he pulled the Range Rover into the abbey garage, the three of them were out of the vehicle before Simon had even turned off the engine. Charging up the front stairs and yelling good night to Jeannie as they went, they agreed to sneak back down and retrieve the satchel when the adults had gone to bed.

It was one of the longest hours of their lives.

Reading a book from the never-ending pile on her bedside table, Em was curled on her window seat waiting for the kitchen lights to turn off. When they did, she telepathed the boys instantly.

All clear.

Matt watched and listened at the bottom of the servants' stairs, with Em at the hallway door, while Zach slipped outside to fetch the satchel.

Bring Matt and get out here.

Em looked across at Matt, the color draining from her face. "Something's wrong. Zach wants us outside."

Dashing out to the terrace, the twins found Zach digging around in the woodpile. "It's gone," he signed in desperation, tossing logs onto the grass. "The satchel's not here anymore!"

PART FOUR

FIFTY

THE MONASTERY OF ERA MINA
MIDDLE AGES

Solon! Solon, can you hear me?

"I will only say this one more time," Rurik bellowed. "I've come to retrieve what's rightfully mine. You have until the coming dawn to give me what I seek, or I will do as I say. I will take payment in your children."

Believing he would find an open wound from an arrow, Solon gently touched his fingers to his head before opening his eyes. His skin was unbroken.

Solon! Can you hear me?

Solon remembered he was in the abbey's scriptorium. It had been the overwhelming power of his master's words inside his head that had caused his blackout, not a Viking arrow after all. But his relief that he was not wounded was short-lived. Crawling over to the arrow slit in the wall, he stared down at the terrible chaos in the courtyard.

I'm here, master. What is it Rurik seeks?

He seeks that which he must not have—which no man must have ever again—but that is of no consequence. Right now, you must help prepare an attack and you must do so before dawn.

Solon turned away from the anguish of his family and friends in the courtyard below. Focusing his mind, he listened to the old monk's plan. And when the young apprentice was sure he understood exactly what had to be done, he set about doing it.

First, he retrieved *The Book of Beasts*, slipping the still unfinished manuscript pages under his tunic, holding it in place with the leather strap cinched around his waist. Second, he gathered as many of the old monk's inkwells as he could safely carry, placing them inside a goatskin pouch, then strapping it over his shoulder. Solon made sure the inks were protected under his arm when he engaged the scriptorium door, somersaulting safely to the outside hallway. He dropped the scriptorium key into the pouch.

Pressing his back against the cold stone walls so as not to be seen, Solon crept down the spiral stairs and out into the passage that led to the abbey's great hall. He could see a Viking sentry pacing before the doors leading to the monastery courtyard, but the double doors leading out to the sea on the other side of the great hall were clear. No sentries.

Slipping behind a tapestry hanging from the vaulted ceiling,

Solon took stock of his position. He had to get to the other side of the hall and out to the sea. The sentry paced up and down, one minute facing into the great hall and the next facing away. Should Solon make a dash for it, hoping to make it to the other side before the sentry saw him? Or should he slither across the floor, giving himself a chance to hide among the footstools, animal skins, chairs, and table legs should the guard turn sooner than expected?

Solon sprinted.

Without stopping to catch his breath, he used all his strength to push the sea-facing doors open and slipped out into the kitchen gardens, running until he reached the water's edge, the inkwells bouncing against his chest, the pages scratching his skin, reminding him of his mission.

Tossing oars into a small rowboat that the monks used to get across to Era Mina, Solon pushed himself off from the dock. The currents from the channel pulled the boat to Era Mina with only the slightest effort on Solon's part.

The apprentice leaped from the boat as soon as it hit the sand, darting around the point of the island to a small bay dotted with dark caves. But instead of heading for the caves, he removed the skins wrapping his feet and began to scale the rocky cliff face. As he climbed, the pages from *The Book of Beasts* began to tingle against his bare skin.

Are you close?

Yes.

The island was bathed in an eerie predawn light; wisps of fog lingered around the distant cliff peaks like the breath of God. Solon counted as he climbed, knowing exactly how many hand lengths he needed to take.

At the count of thirteen, he stopped. Tearing at the carpet of moss that covered the cliff, Solon revealed an opening, a tunnel carved into the cliff.

I'm inside the island.

Good. Do you trust me, Solon?

Yes . . . Yes, master, always and forever.

Good lad. Because you must let me have your imagination completely. Remember all that I've taught you.

Solon set out his materials: the inkwells, the pages of vellum. Then he crouched in the heart of Era Mina, waiting for the sun to rise.

When the dawn came, enough light spilled into the cave for Solon to see what surrounded him. He had known of the cave's existence from the stories the monks told, but he had never been inside. Only the old monk and the abbot were permitted to set foot in this damp and dangerous place and, given their ages, even they had not ventured the climb in many years.

With his brushes and inkwells at the ready, Solon stared up at the massive cave drawings etched deep into the slate-gray stone: beautiful, giant, monstrous things as old and as mysterious as the island itself. If the old monk knew who had created these magnificent images, he had not yet told Solon. The exquisite detail, the vibrant colors, the breathtaking beauty in each etching made Solon shiver in awe.

Letting his bare finger trace the deep lines of one of the drawings, the boy felt the tingling again. All his life he'd heard minstrels sing of mythical monsters, telling tales of times in Scotland's history when one or more of these beasts rose up from inside the island in times of need. Solon wondered: Would he, too, become a story told around a fire late at night? Would minstrels sing of his courage? The possibility made him smile.

He spread the page of vellum he'd lifted from the scriptorium across the damp moss floor, crouching at the ready.

It is time, Solon! Paint. All our lives depend on it.

Pressing his back against one particular cave drawing in the manner his master had instructed, Solon closed his eyes and began to paint. Using big, bold strokes, his brush swept across the length of the page, dipping in and out of the inkwells in a series of frenzied movements. Inside his head, Solon let the image take its shape and the old monk take his imagination.

The tingling washed over his entire body, making his legs want to jump and his fingers dance. But then it grew stronger, stinging Solon's flesh as if he had fallen into a patch of nettles. His gut burned. He felt sick. Swallowing bile, Solon continued painting, his brush never lifting from the parchment. He could feel the wall behind him move, as though whatever was bound in the cave drawing was pushing itself out of the rock and peat and reaching through Solon's body to his heart. As he convulsed uncontrollably, the brush fell from his hand.

You cannot let the image control you, Solon. If you do, you will fail. We will fail.

Squeezing tears from his eyes, Solon exhaled slowly and retrieved the brush. Pushing back against the cave wall, he tightened his grip on his imagination and his brush. The fire in his gut eased a little; the tremors stilled.

A few minutes later, Solon's nose began bleeding, but he was so lost to his imagination that he kept painting, his blood spilling across the vellum like crimson ink.

In the monastery courtyard, Rurik's eyes were thin white slits. He was tired of waiting. After ordering that his men remove the monks' blindfolds, his eyes swept the crowd.

"Bring me that child," he howled, pointing his sword at Mary, Solon's niece.

Margaret screamed, lunging at Rurik. Two of the Viking guards forcefully restrained her, while a third tossed Mary to the ground in front of Rurik as if she were a rag doll.

The sun was up.

With the tip of his sword, Rurik swept a braid from Mary's face, exposing her thin neck. Somewhere in the distance, a cock crowed. A crushing silence descended on the courtyard. Even the sounds of mothers weeping and the soft dirges of the monks were muted.

The abbot watched the old monk slump to the ground, noting the beads of perspiration bursting across his forehead, his breathing labored, his eyelids fluttering as if a wind was blowing on his face. The old monk's hands, tied behind his back, looked as if they were gripping an imaginary quill, his fingers twitching. The abbot looked directly at Mary's mother, who had dropped to her knees between her captors, her hands clenched in prayer.

Rurik had lifted his sword high above his head, preparing to swing, when a shadow fell over the little girl—the shadow of a man in chain mail and laced boots. The sun was just high enough to cast Rurik's own shadow low and long on the ground, but the more Rurik stared, the more confused he became. It was his shadow but it was somehow . . . staglike.

Above the Viking chief, a flying beast with the wings of a giant bird and the body of an enormous white stag swooped down into the courtyard, stabbing its antlers into Rurik the Red, lifting him into the early morning sky. The Viking's sword clattered to the ground next to Mary. Her mother broke free of her captors, pulling her daughter to safety.

Rurik didn't even struggle. An antler had pierced his heart. The stunned villagers stared as the beast's shadow on the courtyard cobbles morphed from the shape of Rurik the Red to that of a mighty winged stag.

"Solon's on its back!" someone cried.

The sight of Solon riding on the back of the peryton, Rurik the Red's body still impaled on its antlers, roused the villagers from their panicked stupor. They lifted their weapons and attacked Rurik's stunned men. Grabbing their pitchforks, spades, and scythes, the men and women of the village charged after the Viking invaders as they fled in terror from the monastery into the forest.

The abbot comforted the old monk as only a Guardian could.

"My dear Brother Renard, what have you done to yourself?"

They watched Solon guide the peryton back toward Era Mina.

"I had to be the one to awaken the cave paintings because I am oldest." Brother Renard sighed, resting his head on his friend's lap. He paused, his breathing shallow and weak. "And because although he is destined for greatness, Solon can't yet animate fully on his own, and I needed all the imaginary power I could muster."

"You used Solon as your quill?" said the abbot, stroking Brother Renard's trembling hands and calming his spirit. "And through him you conjured one of the beasts bound in the sacred cave paintings?"

The old monk nodded.

The abbot felt sad. "My friend, you know there will be a price to pay for that animation. You have broken the First Rule by creating an animated beast visible for all to see. And look at you. You may have broken your own mind."

You did well, Solon.

Thank you, master.

Animating the peryton through Solon's imagination had

drained the life out of Brother Renard. "A child's life was at stake," he whispered, looking across at the girl being cradled by her mother. "And that's worth more than ten of me."

"Why the peryton, old friend?"

Images were streaking past Brother Renard's eyes, as if everything he'd ever animated in his life was real once again. "The peryton is pure and noble. I couldn't risk letting the worst of them loose on the world."

"Of course," said the abbot, understanding at last as he watched Solon and the peryton soaring out over the horizon. "You had Solon draw Rurik's shadow as the creature's shadow, because a peryton kills only once in its lifetime—and only then in order to win its shadow back."

FIFTY-ONE

W e should've looked inside the satchel when we had our chance," lamented Em, pacing in front of the fire in the upstairs living room. Every few steps, she'd kick the leg of the couch in frustration. Her toes were starting to hurt.

"Would've, could've, should've . . . it doesn't change anything," said Matt, sticking a slice of bread on a toasting fork and holding it in front of the flame.

"You know we have a toaster for that," signed Zach, examining the charred piece of bread that Matt passed over the flame. "It's more efficient, and you're less likely to burn the bread." He set his toast down on the arm of the chair.

"But that's the best part," said Em, accepting a scorched slice from her brother. "We used to make toast this way with Mom all the time in the apartment in London."

Where was their mother right now? Was she safe? Would they ever see her again?

Matt, it seemed, was trying not to think about it as he stuck another piece of bread on his fork.

Zach pulled his chair closer to the fire. The storm earlier that day had left the abbey damp and chilly despite the later warmth of the afternoon. "If Dad had discovered the satchel, he would have confronted us about it."

"Maybe," Em said. "Unless he found something inside that he doesn't want us to see or know about."

Matt crunched on his burnt toast. "I'm pretty sure that if Simon had had the satchel," he said between mouthfuls, "he'd have been willing to share its contents with us."

"Then who's got it?" said Em, curling up on the couch and pulling a blanket over her legs.

"What about Mara?" signed Zach.

The twins looked skeptically at him.

"I know we don't want to think she might be hiding things from us, but—"

"Well, if you're thinking like that," said Em, resting her palm on Zach's moving hands, "Jeannie wasn't with us either. It could just as easily have been her."

Matt flopped onto the couch next to Em just as Zach got up

from his chair. "Why don't we at least go and look in Mara's room to put our minds at rest?" he signed.

"Now?"

"Why not? If she has got the satchel, it can only be in her bedroom or in her studio. She's not back yet from dealing with the police and those two in the forest."

"I'm not sure I'm up for any more covert activities tonight," said Matt.

"Me neither," said Em, snuggling deeper into the couch with Grace Fortescue's diary, the book she'd been reading.

Zach changed the subject reluctantly. He opened up his laptop, despite the loss of computer privileges, and paused just long enough to ask, "So what do you think's going to happen to Tanan and Blake?"

"Maybe they'll be shipped back to London for trespassing." In a burst of energy, Matt bounded across the room, leaping over the back of the couch and just missing Em's head. She whacked him with her book.

"This isn't the only seat in the room, you know."

"Maybe not, but it's the only one where I can easily annoy you."

Ignoring the twins, Zach lost himself in his computer until Em's book came flying across the room, hitting him on the shoulder. He looked up to find the twins standing at the living-room door.

"We've changed our minds. We're going to search Mara's room. Are you in?"

FIFTY-TWO

The boys had been in Mara's room fewer times than Em. They'd forgotten how fancy and fussy it was.

Draped in lush red velvet and layered with embroidered pillows, a four-poster bed dominated the room. Near the window there was a sitting area with two stiff chairs, a narrow high-backed couch, and a round mahogany end table. Covering an entire wall, paintings ranging from massive to miniature sat in gilded frames, a number of them shimmering with the soft light that comes from the art of an Animare. Two full-size wardrobes stood like sentries on either side of the door leading into Mara's en-suite bathroom, and a rolltop desk with hundreds of pigeonholes stood centered against the far wall.

"Em definitely got the better deal keeping watch down in the hall," said Matt. "This'll take hours to search."

The boys started with the wardrobes, figuring that if Mara had hidden the satchel, it would have to be in something deep enough to contain it. Matt took the one on the left and Zach the one on the right. They'd hardly begun to look when Zach started chuckling.

"I'm glad you find this funny," Matt growled. "I've never seen so many pairs of jeans outside a department store."

"You know, Em could never sleep in this bedroom."

"Why?"

Zach laughed at the thought. "Because she'd be animating these wardrobes into the character from *Beauty and the Beast* every time she fell asleep."

"Focus, Zach. Try to keep Em out of your head for at least five minutes, will you?"

What's going on, Matt? Have you found anything?

Nothing yet.

Resigned to the fact that neither of them were going to get five minutes without Em in their heads, Matt returned to his wardrobe. But neither wardrobe hid anything worse than Mara's clothes.

"We've been here too long," Zach gestured. "The satchel's not here. We need to go."

But, as they turned to leave, Zach noticed the bed's ornate legs and how high it sat off the floor. He pointed.

"Under the bed! She wouldn't have had much time between finding the satchel and leaving to deal with the police and

Blake and Tanan. Sliding it under the bed might have been her quickest move."

Lifting up the heavy brocade bedspread, Matt checked under the bed. The only thing he could see was a flat wooden box, too small to hide the satchel in. He reached for it nonetheless and dragged it out.

In the box was a padded envelope, displaying the name and address faceup:

Matt and Emily Calder

The Abbey

Auchinmurn Isle

Ayrshire

Matt shoved the storage box back under the bed. "Why would Mara have a package addressed to us?" he asked. He looked at the postmark and the return address. It was from the National Gallery, and had been posted to the island the day before they arrived from London.

Anything yet, Matt?

Something, Em. Definitely something. We'll meet you back in the living room. Stall Mara if you run into her. She's bound to be home soon.

While Zach checked that they had left everything as they had found it, Matt was still examining the envelope. It felt hard and heavy.

"Em'll kill us if we look inside without her," Zach signed.

Em's urgent voice penetrated Matt's head.

Where are you?

About to leave Mara's room.

Why?

Because she's back and she seems in a mood. She's heading straight for you.

Uh oh. Matt could hear Mara's heels click-clacking on the stairs. "Mara's coming," he told Zach swiftly. Taking the envelope, he shoved it under his T-shirt and tucked the bottom end into the waistband of his jeans. "We're going to have to do this old-school. Get under the bed."

Both boys darted to the far side of the monstrous bed, scrambling underneath. But as he did so, Matt accidentally jostled the storage box, pushing it back out where Mara would be able to see it. Outside the door, he could hear Mara digging her keys out of her bag.

Do something, Em! We can't get out of the room in time.

I'm coming upstairs as fast as I can. I don't want to wake Simon.

We unlocked her door with an animation. She'll know someone's been in!

From under the bed, Matt silently shifted the bedspread a few centimeters, giving himself a sliver of space to view the room. He nudged Zach. Mara had come into the room now, and was examining her lock with a puzzled look on her face.

"Mara! Can you . . . er . . . come back out here a second?"

Ignoring Em's voice, Mara scanned the bedroom. Now she was walking toward the bed. They were sure to be found. One . . . two . . . three . . . Just as it looked as if it was all over, Mara kicked the storage box underneath the bed and went back out. "What is it, Em?"

Shaking with nerves, Matt and Zach clambered out from under the bed and dashed behind the door, waiting for the all clear.

Mara's helping me with some girl stuff. Get out of there now, 'cos this is pretty awkward.

Making sure the padded envelope was still safely tucked under his shirt, Matt grabbed Zach's arm and they fled.

Ten minutes later, Mara returned to her room, well aware that the kids had been up to something. She smiled to herself. It was likely they'd found the package that she'd intercepted from the mail the day the twins arrived. She had to give Arthur Summers credit. His confession in the letter he'd written to the twins was the final confirmation she had needed about what had happened to Malcolm.

Mara heard her bedroom door open as she admired her wall of paintings. She turned to greet her guest with a wry and knowing smile.

FIFTY-THREE

Sitting in front of the fire's dying embers, after everyone else was in bed, Matt, Em, and Zach stared at the padded envelope on the coffee table.

"You discovered it, Matt. You open it."

Matt tipped the package upside down, letting the contents fall onto the table: a thin wooden box and a letter. Matt opened the box and lifted out the page nestling inside. As he turned it over in his hands, he recognized the thick, bold lines of the image.

"This looks like a sketch of a painting I saw in the vault. The swirling blacks, yellows, and greens are familiar." He handed the drawing to Em and Zach.

"There's an inscription on the back," said Em, turning it over.

To our sons and daughters,
May you never forget imagination is the real and the eternal.
This is Hollow Earth. Duncan Fox, Edinburgh, 1848

Em frowned. Where had she heard the words "Hollow Earth" before?

"What does it mean?" Matt asked curiously.

Zach opened his laptop and keyed a few strokes before turning the screen to show them a matching image of the print Em was holding. The text beneath the image said:

Hollow Earth, nineteenth century Scottish artist Duncan Fox's most famous work, said to depict the entrance to a mythical purgatory where all the beasts and demons ever imagined are trapped.

"Mom and that guy we met in Covent Garden, Matt—they were talking about Duncan Fox and Hollow Earth!" Em exclaimed, remembering. "Hollow Earth is a crazy legend, but Duncan Fox believed it was real. He founded a society to protect it."

"So where was I when this was going on?" Matt demanded.

"You'd gone off to listen to the musician with the weird instrument. I completely forgot to tell you about it," Em confessed. "That whole day was a crazy blur from start to finish."

"Duncan Fox must have been an Animare," Matt guessed. "Otherwise, why was his painting in the vault?"

Zach thumped the table to get their attention. He pointed at the letter.

"You're right, Zach," said Em apologetically. "We need to read the letter."

Holding it out in front of her so the boys could also see it, she began to read.

> Dear Matt and Em,
> Your mother and I have been friends for a long time. She's created amazing things under my guidance, but it's time she's allowed to be free. I trust when you're older, you'll understand. You'll realize that whatever crimes your mother committed, she had no choice. She committed them because of a secret about your father, a secret that I and Sir Charles Wren discovered by accident, and one that has kept her in our servitude far too long. For that I am truly sorry.
>
> Arthur Summers

"Crimes?" Matt said after a moment. "What secret about our dad?"

"He makes it sound as if your mom was forced to do something illegal," signed Zach. "Who's Arthur Summers?"

"We always just called him 'the yellow-haired man.'" Matt

could feel the anger rising in his throat. Their mom—a *criminal*? What on earth had she done to their dad? "Mom did some restoration work for him at the National Gallery when we were little."

Zach googled "Arthur Summers" and "The National Gallery." The first ten hits all featured the same incident.

"He was murdered," signed Zach, shifting onto the couch between Em and Matt so they could more easily see his screen.

"It says that he was killed during a robbery in the restoration lab at the gallery," said Em, aghast.

"Em, look at the date. The murder and the robbery were on the day we left London," breathed Matt.

Em read from a paragraph in the middle of the story. "According to sources, Summers was part of an international art forgery ring. His murder may be the break needed to topple his worldwide organization."

"Mom was an art forger?" said Matt, shocked at the revelation. "Impossible."

Em turned away from the screen, not wanting to read any more details of the murder. "Think about it. It's not like we knew very much about how she paid for things when we lived in London. And we did live in a nice apartment."

Unable to contain his anxiety or his adrenaline, Matt paced behind the couch with Arthur's letter in his hand. "Okay, so maybe she was blackmailed. I think that's what the yellow-haired man meant when he wrote, 'You'll realize that whatever crimes your mother committed, she had no choice.'"

"Looks that way to me," signed Zach.

Em struggled to formulate her thoughts. "But what could Mom have done or known about . . . What secret about Dad . . . What would be so awful that she would let herself be blackmailed like that?"

Matt banged his fist against the living-room wall. "If only we could ask Grandpa! I bet he would know."

"Matt, sit down!" Em said. "You'll wake someone for sure." She pulled the screen toward her again. "Scroll down, Zach. What else does it say about the robbery?"

"It says that only one painting was stolen. That one, there."

When the image of the painting appeared on the screen, Em couldn't help herself. She screamed, her heart pounding, goose bumps erupting across her skin. The boys stared at her.

"Em, what is it?" asked Matt sharply.

"The creature in that painting . . . it's my night terror—the one we saw in the library!"

FIFTY-FOUR

The next morning, Jeannie was banging around in the kitchen, sorting pans that didn't need to be sorted, when the twins came downstairs. Zach was finishing his breakfast alone. Em felt his warning in her head.

Watch out. Jeannie's in a wicked mood.

Jeannie scowled at the twins from across the kitchen table. "I suppose ye'll be wanting breakfast now too. D'ye see what time it is? It's after ten. It's not yer birthday until tomorrow, so no special favors." She slapped her dish towel against the counter for emphasis. Her accent was stronger when she was angry. "This is nae a restaurant, ye know. I have better things tae do than hang about in the kitchen waiting for folks who don't bother tae eat breakfast until close on lunchtime."

Whoa. What's got her so riled?

A wild guess—no one's eaten here this morning.

"We're sorry, Jeannie," said Em. "We stayed up too late last night, um, playing computer games."

"Just because Mr. R is nae here to keep this place running on a regular schedule is no excuse for everyone else tae forget mealtimes."

Em realized the abbey was unnaturally quiet. There was no music coming from Simon's study. Across the grounds, Mara's studio looked as if it was still closed up, the doors locked, shades tightly drawn.

"Where is everyone?"

Noooo. Don't ask, Em!

"I'll tell ye where everyone is. They've gone off early tae that new coffee shop that's opened in Seaport." Jeannie untied her apron, balling it up and aggressively tossing it into the laundry basket. "As if paying an arm and a leg for a cup of coffee makes it taste better than mine. Well, let me tell ye, it does NOT."

She grabbed her coat from the peg in the utility room, her shopping bags from the shelf underneath. "Ah wouldn't be a bit surprised tae hear that their scones don't have an ounce of Scottish butter in them." Pushing open the French doors, Jeannie stomped toward the garage, ranting the entire way about the state of baked goods on the island.

"Looks like we're on our own for breakfast, then," said Matt.

"So no one ate breakfast this morning at all? Not even Simon?"

asked Em, slicing a banana into a bowl of cereal. "Doesn't that seem weird to you?"

Putting his spoon down, Zach signed, "I'm guessing Dad's at the hospital, and Mara, too. The Range Rover's gone. But it is strange that they didn't wait to see us this morning. That's not like Dad at all."

Sitting next to Em at the table, Matt opened a tub of ice cream, scooping three big dollops into a bowl.

"Really? Ice cream?" Em remarked.

"It's dairy," said Matt, sliding the container to Zach, who added a scoop to his almost-finished cereal.

Em reached for the Glasgow newspaper sitting on the plate laid where Renard usually sat. It was a habit Jeannie refused to change even though it would be a while before Renard was eating or reading the newspaper with them again.

"It's probably good all the adults are gone," said Em, scanning the pages for any stories about an unidentified woman being lost or found. The boys thought it morbid and a waste of time, but Em dismissed their arguments. Looking made her feel useful, and being useful was at least doing something. "It'll make it easier for us to search the abbey and the grounds for that painting of my night terror."

"You seriously think it's here?"

"Yes, Zach—I do. It makes complete sense. The creature's been haunting my sleep off and on for weeks now, and it's not my creation."

"So who's the Animare that's manipulating it?" asked Zach.

"There are a few things we've learned for sure about being an Animare," Em said. "The First Rule: We can't—well, shouldn't—animate in public. Second: We have to stay in control of our imaginations. Third: An Animare can be bound in a work of his or her own art, making that art enchanted in some way."

"*Enchanted?*" Matt snorted. "You make it sound like sprites and wood nymphs are sprouting everywhere. If that creepy dwarf and the scary hooded figure in the library the other night are from a bound painting, and that same painting had something to do with a man's murder two months ago, then there isn't anything so enchanted about it."

"Then what would you call it?"

"Jinxed," signed Zach.

"Cursed," Matt returned.

"Hexed."

"Blighted."

"Okay, stop!" said Em. "No matter what you want to call it, if that painting is in the abbey or on Era Mina somewhere, it's dangerous."

"But what's it got to do with Mom's disappearance?" Matt demanded.

With the exception of a few animations they'd kept from their mom, the twins believed they'd had a fairly uneventful childhood. Now they were starting to wonder if they had been oblivious to a secret world going on around them.

"Maybe we should call Violet and Anthea back at Raphael Terrace?" Em suggested. "They've known Mom forever. Maybe they could tell us something about what she was up to when we lived with them."

"Not a bad idea," Matt agreed. "It's been weeks since we talked to them. I'll get the number from Simon's desk and call from the study."

"Matt, you can't just call them up out of the blue and be like, 'Oh hey, Auntie Vi, say, just a quick question, but did you know my mom was a crook?'" Em protested. "You'll terrify them."

Matt was already heading out of the kitchen. "That's not what I'll say," he said indignantly over his shoulder. "Besides, my call won't be completely out of the blue. Simon talked to both of them yesterday and told them Mom was missing. I'll just ask if she's been in touch, and if they happen to know of anyone Mom might have trusted that we could call for information."

Em went back to scanning the paper. As she turned to the last page, a photograph of a woman being helped into a police car in Glasgow caught her eye. She was folding the page over to get a closer look at the picture when Matt returned to the kitchen and distracted her.

"Violet sends her love," Matt said, settling back down at the kitchen table. "She hasn't heard from Mom in weeks, but she did say something very interesting. After she spoke to Simon yesterday, she and Anthea remembered that two days ago, when they were helping a new tenant move into our old apartment, they noticed that a pane of glass had been removed from the skylight. Aunt Violet says it must have happened when the apartment was empty."

"So someone might have broken in through the roof?" asked Em. Matt nodded. "Was anything stolen?"

"That's the odd thing," said Matt. "As far as they could tell, nothing was missing."

"Think it might have been your mom?" signed Zach, getting up to load his dishes into the dishwasher.

"That's exactly what I'm thinking," said Em.

"I did ask Aunt Violet if Mom had any friends we could contact," said Matt. "But she told me what we already knew. Mom kept herself to herself. The only friends she had were the few people she worked with at the galleries, and us. She said she had given a list of those names to Simon already."

Em sighed. "Too bad."

"I vote we stick with our original plan," Matt said. "Take advantage of the grown-ups being gone and see if we can find that horrible painting."

Zach smacked his spoon on the counter to get their attention. "If you two want to explore, I might go over to Era Mina to see if I can figure out what the man in that boat was looking for. Maybe he's looking for the painting too? Plus, it wouldn't hurt to check on our stuff in the cave, either."

The caladrius's vision of Zach floating injured in a tidal pool with the stranger beside him flashed across Matt's mind.

He shivered. "I don't think we should split up," he said quickly. "Let's pack lunch and *all* go over to the island. We could look for the painting later."

Em looked down at the photograph of the woman in Glasgow on the back page of the paper, while the boys cleared away the rest of the breakfast dishes. "Hey!" she said, peering more closely. "Check out this picture."

"Isn't that the woman we trapped in the quicksand yesterday?" Matt asked, staring over Em's shoulder.

"It says here," Em read aloud, skimming, "that she was taken to the hospital after she was found wandering around in Glasgow with no memory of who she was. The police are contacting authorities in the US because of her accent."

"She knew who she was when we were with her," signed Zach.

"So someone must have done something to her mind," said Matt. "What's it called when Guardians do that memory-wiping thing?"

"Inspiriting," Em snapped at him. Typical Matt, forgetting important facts. "But you need to be a powerful Guardian to be able to wipe a person's memory. Even Simon couldn't inspirit like that."

"Maybe that's what happened to Mom," Matt said suddenly. "Maybe somebody inspirited *her*!"

FIFTY-FIVE

The distant peaks of the islands of Kintyre and Bute looked majestic in the morning sunshine as the trio stood at the boat-house, pulling on their life jackets. But the brilliant beauty of the bay was in stark contrast to the growing disquiet the twins and Zach were feeling.

"Try texting your dad again," Em suggested to Zach, setting his backpack and their fishing gear—a useful cover—inside the row-boat. Matt looked at the abbey's speedboat. "What if—" he began.

"No way," said Em at once. "The speedboat would draw way too much attention. You know we're not allowed to drive it." Matt reluctantly lifted the rowboat's oars from their shelf, sliding them under the seats.

"Nothing from Dad yet," Zach signed. "My texts are piling

up. Even a phone call just goes through to his voice mail."

"Mara's, too," said Matt, tapping the face of his watch to disconnect his attempted call. Em climbed into the boat. Matt settled behind her. Zach untied the rope, pushing the boat clear of the dock before climbing in next to Em.

"Ready?" asked Em.

Zach nodded. "One day, we're going to get in so much trouble for doing this."

Pulling a pad of paper from Zach's backpack, Matt sketched their boat with the addition of a small outboard engine. Bursting into life in a flash of silver and blue, the motor morphed onto the wood behind Matt, who flipped up the tiller handle and steered them out into the bay.

"It's hard to believe that Simon and Mara could still be hanging out at a coffee shop," said Em.

"Of course it's not," said Matt. "Grown-ups can do strange things at the weirdest times, and whether we like it or not they keep secrets. They're all up to something and don't want us involved."

"That may be sort of true," Em admitted. "But when has Simon ever gone anywhere for longer than thirty minutes without checking in with us? That's why he gave us these watches."

The water was choppy, forcing Matt to concentrate on his steering, while Em and Zach kept their eyes peeled for the coastguard or a local who might recognize them and know they were too young to operate a motorized vehicle of any kind.

At last, Matt steered the boat around to a rocky inlet on the western shore of Era Mina and moored it in Monk's Cove.

"Do you hear that, Matt?" said Em, cocking her head. "Sounds like circus music. It's coming from the caves."

Matt's eyes widened. "Someone's discovered our hideout."

Once they'd explained the situation to Zach, the three of them waded ashore and headed for one of a series of caves that faced out to sea. A high-water mark indicated that most of the caves would be inaccessible at high tide.

Tapping the face of his watch a couple of times, Zach signed, "We've got about four hours until today's high tide. Should be enough to check it out."

He put on his helmet with its cave light attached to the front, grabbed a flashlight, and slipped the backpack over his shoulders. The twins put on their helmets and followed Zach into the cave.

They used the crevices and outcroppings to climb up inside the island. It wasn't particularly high, but when there had been a lot of rain, like yesterday's storm, it could be treacherous.

Matt and I are still hearing music, Zach.

Maybe we left music on last time we were here?

Em doubted it. They were always extra cautious when they left their hideout, turning things off and sealing things up, never knowing when they'd be able to sneak back across to the island again.

The higher they climbed, the more Em's uneasiness grew. Without warning, she stopped, causing Matt to crash into her.

I feel something . . . we should go back.

Hearing Em's apprehension, Zach stopped and turned. Losing his balance for a second, he steadied himself against the slick wall, dropping his flashlight as he did. It clattered off the walls, landing with a splash in the tidal pool below.

Now we definitely should go back. You've never dropped the light before, Zach.

"What's wrong, Em?" asked Matt, as Zach started climbing back down toward them.

"I'm not sure," said Em unhappily. "My stomach is flipping out, and the music is getting louder."

The vision of Zach in the tidal pool appeared again in Matt's mind. This time he couldn't stop it from lingering, which meant that Em saw the vision too. She almost lost her grip on the cave wall.

"Is that what the caladrius showed you? You said it was no big deal! Just that Zach got injured!"

"Yes, but hear me out—"

"The caladrius showed you an image of Zach drowning, and you still let him come to this cave? We've got to go back down and get out of here!"

"He would have come without us," Matt shouted. "You know that. At least this way, we can do something . . . animate if we have to. . . ."

"Animate? Is that your answer to everything?"

Angrily, Matt squeezed past Em on the ledge. "Well, we're not going back down. I want to know who's up there."

A man's voice called to them from the mouth of their cave several meters farther up.

"Are you planning on arguing for much longer? Because I wouldn't mind a sandwich if you have one, and I'd rather not have to climb down to get it."

FIFTY-SIX

Zach climbed over the lip of the hideout first. Reaching above his head, he pulled a cord attached to a string of lights, which blazed into life. The twins hoisted themselves into the cave directly behind Zach. The stranger they had followed with the caladrius stood in front of them, a flashlight hanging by his side.

"You shot me!" said Matt in shock.

The stranger held up his hands. "In my defense, I shot an animation. Impressive piece of work, by the way. Although I'm sure you realize how dangerous and stupid it was to animate something that distinctive in public."

"Did you know how much it was going to hurt me when you shot it?" yelled Matt.

The stranger shrugged. "Maybe you needed to know what being hurt like that felt like."

Matt lunged at the stranger, but Zach and Em held him back.

Matt, wait. He looks familiar. Can we at least find out who he is and what he wants before you try to pummel him?

"I like what you've done with the place," said the man, walking carefully across the slick, uneven floor to a couch where a rolled up sleeping bag, a bike helmet, and black saddlebags were stacked. "It wasn't too bad spending the night here, apart from the damp and the smell of rotting fish. There was certainly lots to entertain myself with."

The old couch faced two long trestle tables shoved together, the kind their mom and Mara used in their studios. But instead of art supplies, the tables held a desktop computer, an array of open circuit boards, dismantled hard drives, and at least two game systems.

"I can only imagine how you got all this gear up here," the stranger added. They smiled sheepishly.

"So who are you?" asked Matt, doing his best to control his anger.

"We met a couple of months ago, don't you remember? My name is Vaughn." The man sank back onto the couch, his long legs stretched out in front of him.

The man in front of them had not shaved in a while; his hair was longer and unkempt, and his disheveled clothes were very different from the sharp suit he'd been wearing when they saw him last. But Em remembered him now. "Vaughn!" she exclaimed. "Mom's friend from Covent Garden."

Zach looked perplexed, but Matt's face cleared. "Do you know where Mom is?" he asked at once.

Vaughn shook his head. "But I do have some theories about what could have happened to her. That's why I came up from London. I'm sorry about your grandpa. He was a close friend of my mom's, too. They trained together here at the abbey when Renard was a student."

I believe him.

Hard to imagine any girl wouldn't.

Em scowled at her brother.

"So how did you find us?" asked Matt, unfolding a deck chair before dropping into it.

Vaughn grinned. "When I was wandering around the island yesterday, I found the cable you'd rigged up to steal power from the abbey. That's what led me here. Ingenious."

"That was Zach's idea," said Em proudly. Zach acknowledged the compliment with a nod, finding a spot to sit where he could read the conversation more easily.

"Well done, Zach," Vaughn signed. "So I assume the main breaker is under the dock?"

Looking surprised at Vaughn's adept use of sign language, Zach nodded again.

"You're too young to remember me, Zach," Vaughn said, "but I was living at the abbey when your dad first brought you here. We all learned sign language together."

"So did you know my mom, too?" Zach signed eagerly. Zach's

question shocked the twins. Their friend had never said more than a few words about his mom; the most they knew was that she'd died when he was born.

"I didn't. Renard had only recently recruited your dad to join him at the abbey. You came as a package deal."

"So were you the one playing the circus music?" Zach asked.

Vaughn lifted a small, violinlike instrument from under his sleeping bag. "It's a hurdy-gurdy," he explained, letting the tinkling sound fill the cave. "Do you remember when you last heard this, Matt?"

"Covent Garden," said Matt, nodding. "You thought the hurdy-gurdy man was trying to kidnap me."

"He would have, given the chance," said Vaughn. "But I should add that he was actually a she disguised very well, and someone who'd been watching you both for a long time."

"Who?" said Matt and Em at once.

Before Vaughn could answer, the children's three watches beeped in unison.

"You can't possibly get a mobile signal inside this hillside," said Vaughn, frowning at the sound. "At least, not a real one."

The twins looked at their watches. The same text message flashed on each of them.

COME HOME IMMEDIATELY. SOMETHING'S HAPPENED TO SIMON.

Matt looked at Em. Em looked at Zach. Zach's hands sketched four letters.

"Mara!"

FIFTY-SEVEN

Zach grabbed his backpack and put on his helmet at once. Quickly, he headed to the cave opening with Matt and Em right behind him.

"Before you go rushing off back to the abbey at Mara's beck and call," said Vaughn urgently, "you need to know something. It's important!"

The twins stopped. Unable to hear Vaughn's plea, Zach had already disappeared down into the tunnel.

"Don't trust Mara. I found this hurdy-gurdy in her room. She was watching you in London that day, dressed up as a street musician. It was probably the easiest way to follow you all since your mom would have recognized her. I think she may even have been in the National Gallery earlier. Mara is not who you think she is."

Em didn't know what to make of this. "We really have to go," she said hesitantly. "If something's happened to Simon, we need to be there. He's been like a dad to us. But will you wait for us here so we can talk later?"

"I'll wait," Vaughn said. "But promise me one thing. Be wary of Mara, okay? Trust your Guardian instincts."

"Are you coming or not, Em?" Matt demanded, looking over the lip of the tunnel to where Zach was already far into his descent.

Vaughn grabbed Em's hand.

"Your grandfather was the one who sent me to work in London when you all fled Auchinmurn," he said. "My mission was to keep an eye on you, Matt, and your mom. With Sandie missing and Renard hurt, you may need me. I think Mara may have something to do with your mom's disappearance."

Em knew Matt had stopped his descent and was listening. After finding the envelope in Mara's room last night, their suspicions about her had grown.

"Mara was once very close to your dad," Vaughn explained. "She may even still be in love with him. I don't think she's ever forgiven your mom for his disappearance."

"But even if that's true," said Em, "why would she want to hurt Grandpa or us?"

"I don't know," Vaughn confessed. "It's one of the reasons that I had to return to Scotland when I heard your mom was missing. While I was in London spying on the Council of Guardians for Renard—yes, that was part of my job description too—I learned that Mara was doing the same here on Auchinmurn for someone else. I thought it was Sir Charles Wren, but now I'm not sure. You know I'm telling you the truth." His piercing green eyes held Em's transfixed gaze. "Don't you?"

The twins said nothing all the way down the rocky ledges. Although it was a climb they'd made often, they had never had to make it with quite so much adrenaline raging through their bodies. Silence was preferable to slipping.

Zach was waiting for them at the bottom.

"What took you so long?"

Quickly, Em brought him up to speed.

"Let's not jump to conclusions," signed Zach. His own anxiety about his dad was mounting, and he could sense Em's deepening dread.

"And how do we know we can trust this guy anyway?" Matt demanded. "He did shoot me, you know."

"Well, he was right about one thing," signed Zach. "No true signal or text message could have got to us in the cave. It must have been—"

"An animation," said the twins together, realizing at once that it was the only answer.

"But who animated it?" Em said. "Mara, or someone else?"

The three of them splashed through the rising water and out onto the beach, where they had to shield their eyes from the blinding daylight for a few minutes before getting into their boat.

Zach sat in front, the spray soaking his face and hair as Matt gunned the small engine. Every few seconds, Zach checked his watch for messages and sent more texts to his dad's mobile. Clutching Matt's drawing of the outboard motor tightly in her hand, Em tried to smile reassuringly at Zach.

Your dad will be okay.

But she knew he sensed that she was far from reassured.

Cutting across the wake of a fishing vessel heading out to the Atlantic, Matt bounced them back around the point of Era Mina and across the bay in half the usual time. When they got close to the dock, Em tore up Matt's drawing. The motor vibrated noisily, then disappeared in a shower of silver sparks, leaving the twins to row the boat up to the jetty.

In their haste and heightened emotional state, neither the twins nor Zach spotted the hooded figure climbing from a skiff near the tower on Era Mina. Robes sweeping the packed sand, the figure glided into the cave, stopping at the bottom ledge where the steps up to the children's hideout began. Cocking its head, listening to the sounds above, the figure slipped an ornately covered sketch pad from the cowl of its sleeve and began to draw.

As its hand flew across the page, the wall of the cave shook and shifted. A fissure of light flashed up the rock face, cleaving the rock in two as a fracture rose high into the darkness above.

*   *   *

Vaughn had no intention of letting the twins out of his sight. Grabbing his saddlebags from the couch, he slung them over his shoulder before following the children's path down the rock face. Halfway down, his hands began to tingle as the wall of the mountain trembled underneath him.

He tried to speed his descent, but he couldn't. The cave wall was too slick, his footing too precarious. One minute he had crevices in which to place his hands and feet—the next, the entire rock face shifted, smoothing itself over, leaving nothing for him to grasp or hold on to except air. Vaughn fell backward into the rising water of the tidal pool, bouncing off the rocks as he landed.

Outside the cave's entrance, the hooded figure tore up its drawing and walked back to the skiff.

FIFTY-EIGHT

The first person the trio saw when they entered the abbey kitchen was Mara. The twins faltered, but Zach dashed forward.

"What's happened to Dad?" he signed frantically.

"Come with me to my studio." When Mara looked at the twins, her eyes were dark. "What I have to show you will explain what's happened to Simon."

"Isn't Jeannie back from Largs yet?" asked Em, listening for sounds of Jeannie in the house. Nothing.

"Oh, I'm guessing she won't be back for a while," said Mara, flipping on the kitchen television to BBC Scotland. "Not if the news is anything to go by."

She pointed at the screen. A reporter was standing at the dock in Largs, where hundreds of people were lining the pier, staring down into the water. The camera panned the length of the ferry, which looked as if it was stuck in translucent pink jelly.

"Seems like the inevitable has finally happened," laughed Mara. "A sudden infestation of jellyfish has clogged up the ship."

Zach stared. "That's impossible. You'd need to have . . ."

He dropped his hands, feeling something twist inside his gut.

". . . animated an infestation of jellyfish to stop the ferry," Em finished for him. "Why would anyone do that?"

"Aren't you more interested in who?" asked Mara.

She's scaring me, Matt.

"Come out to my studio," Mara coaxed. "Everything will make sense when you do."

The trio didn't move. Suddenly, all they could think of was Vaughn's warning.

"You animated those jellyfish!" Em accused. "You're not going to explain anything to us. I can feel it. You're going to do something to us."

"Oh, come on now," Mara said, leaning over the kitchen counter. "If all I wanted to do was to hurt you, I could have done it years ago. This has never been about you."

"Where's Simon?" asked Matt, shifting closer to Em.

Mara opened the doors to the terrace. "You'll just have to take my word that he's okay. For now, anyway. Before we go to my studio, I'll need you to empty your pockets. Can't have you drawing anything unexpected, can I?"

Matt dumped his sketch pad and chewed pencils onto the counter. Em fished for the piece of charcoal in her pocket, snapped it in two, and brought out only half.

"And your watches, please."

The children removed their watches, setting them side by side on the counter. Before he set his down, Zach double-tapped a command when Mara wasn't looking. Then the three of them reluctantly followed Mara back outside.

FIFTY-NINE

When Mara pushed open the double wooden doors to her studio, the children felt as they often did when they entered this space—that they had stepped into a kind of medieval torture chamber. Glass-making equipment had changed very little since the Middle Ages. There was a giant kiln—high-tech and sleek, but still essentially a boiling hot oven—along with blowtorches, bench burners, rows of picks and rakes for etching designs, and three table-mounted grinding saws.

In stark contrast to her luxurious bedroom, Mara's studio was vast and gloomy. The only adornment on the dark brick walls was a high, arched stained-glass window supplying the room's only natural light. The trio knew Mara had designed and made the glass window herself. As they stood in the center of the oppressive room, Matt wondered if the Mara they had always known, the one represented by her chic bedroom, was not the real Mara after all.

Em noticed that a lot of Mara's supplies were in boxes lining the walls. "Are you going somewhere?" she asked.

Mara ignored the question, leading them across the room to a few stools and an easel covered with a drop cloth. From the corner of his eye, Zach saw one of Mara's glass figures rise a few inches into the air, then drop back onto the table. He cupped his hand under Em's elbow.

Em, try to control your fears. We'll be okay.

As Em got closer to the easel, she felt a jolt of electricity rising up from the floor, shooting into the soles of her feet. She jumped, stepping back.

Did you feel that?

They all heard the heavy doors opening and closing behind them. The hooded monk they'd seen in the library stepped into Mara's studio.

Em gasped. Matt froze. Zach stared, wide-eyed. Without thinking, Matt shoved Em and Zach away from the center of the room, trying to get as much distance as possible from the robed figure. Bumping against one of Mara's worktables, he shepherded Em and Zach across the studio until their backs were pressed against the bare brick wall. The figure had no aura.

Em, it's real. Not an animation after all.

Is that good or bad?

The monk strode across the room to the children, face hidden in the folds of his hood. Mara handed over three plastic ties.

"Sit on the floor."

Frightened at the sight of the hooded figure, the children numbly did as they were told. The first plastic tie was looped through the radiator pipe and then around Matt's wrist. The figure wrapped the second around Matt's ankle and then snapped it around Zach's ankle. Another plastic tie was curved around Zach's other ankle and tightened on Em's wrist. As he leaned close to Em, she thought the hooded figure smelled of peppermint and soap, but then the odors sharpened, and she was overwhelmed with the smell of burning wood.

Mara let out an angry yell and ran over to her worktables as one of the Bunsen burners suddenly burst into flames, shooting out balls of fire as if it was a cannon. Both boys glanced at Em.

I'm sorry. I'm trying to control my fears, but I'm really scared.

Grabbing a fire extinguisher from the wall, Mara shot foam at the burner, sending colored embers dancing into the air. They landed like bright confetti on the cloaked figure's hood.

"Control yourselves!" shouted the hooded figure. A male voice. Mara had extinguished the flames from the burner, but Em could still smell something burning. She looked down. The hem of Matt's jeans was on fire.

"Matt!"

Em yanked a cloth from a bench next to her brother, smothering the flames. Matt's ankle was raw. Matt brushed Em away.

I'm okay. Leave it. Check on Zach.

Zach was staring at the hooded figure. He looked ashen.

Zach, please snap out of it.

Em, something terrible must have happened to my dad. If he was okay, he'd be here to help us.

The realization that they were on their own was suddenly more terrifying than the robed figure looming in front of them.

"Your fears are doing this, Emily," growled the hooded figure. "I need you to calm yourself. No more fire-starting, or I may have to try burning bits of your brother myself."

Slipping the ornate sketchbook from inside his sleeve, he began to draw, his pen creating a blur of circles and lines on the page. A rocket of flame shot out of the wall directly above Matt's head, nearly taking off his ear. The three of them cowered on the floor, terrified of what might happen next.

"I need your full attention and your complete concentration." The monk slipped the sketchbook back inside his sleeve. "Can you give me that, *ma petite?*"

Now it was Em's turn to freeze. She recognized his French accent. She didn't know if she could concentrate the way he wanted her to. Zach reached over, squeezing her hand.

"Why are you doing this to us, Mara?" Em asked.

"Your doe-eyed approach isn't going to do you any good," Mara snapped. "I pledged my allegiance to another cause long before you two arrived on this island. Frankly, I'm relieved to stop pretending. After tonight, I can be free of this place."

Em let out a low breath. They should have stayed in the cave with Vaughn.

"What cause are you talking about?" signed Zach.

"Oh, you'll find out what our cause is soon enough," said the hooded figure. "But if you two want to help your mother, and your friend wants to help his father, then you will all need to help us first."

SIXTY

Tanan pushed back his hood.

"The first thing you need to do is refrain from animating anything consciously or unconsciously because you're afraid," he said. Em felt his jade-colored eyes bore into her. "I don't want to be trapped in quicksand again."

"But if you're an Animare," asked Em, "why didn't you animate a way out of that?"

Tanan ran his fingers across the cloth draped over the easel. "You were both amusing me. Letting you interrogate me with your questions, I found out a few things that have proved useful in my plans."

"And how did you get away from the police?" Em asked. "Mara called the chief constable, and . . ."

Mara raised her eyebrows. Em's voice drifted off as she realized that Mara hadn't called the police at all.

"Before I returned to the abbey with Mara," Tanan went on, "we sent Blake on her way. Thanks to a Guardian in Glasgow, another member of our Society, she'll remember very little about her adventure in Scotland."

Matt's voice shimmered in Em's head. *Keep him talking. I have a plan.*

"Why did you do that to her?" asked Em, desperately prolonging the conversation. "Guardians are only meant to inspirit people if an animation that's been created in public needs to be forgotten!"

"Blake was only with me because Sir Charles Wren didn't trust me to find what he wanted on my own," replied Tanan, waving his hand dismissively. "She had become a nuisance."

Em was aware of Matt shifting his hands behind his back so he could reach into his pocket. "What is Sir Charles Wren looking for?" she asked.

"Something your mother took from him when she left London."

"The satchel?" Em said. "What's in it that's so important?"

"What's in that satchel is of secondary importance." Tanan stepped closer to the easel. "What *I* want is something only you two gifted children can provide."

Em, tell Zach to be ready to get out of here. Get across to Era Mina. Get Vaughn.

Em sneaked a glance at Matt's free hand. He was gripping a

pointed etching tool that he must have palmed when he bumped against Mara's worktable.

What are you drawing?

A way through the wall behind us.

Em relayed Matt's words to Zach.

He'll need to animate fast. As soon as they see what's happening, they'll be all over it.

He knows.

"So what do you want from us?" asked Em aloud, trying to keep the two adults distracted. "And Mara? You were part of our family. How could you treat us this way?"

"Oh, Em. Always the sentimental one," Mara smiled maliciously. "It must be the Guardian in your DNA. I've never been part of your family. Not really."

Matt tried to focus on the etching taking shape behind him. His knuckles were bleeding, his skin rubbing raw against the hard stone with every gouge he made into the wall. Afraid Matt's exertion was becoming obvious, Zach took the conversation literally into his hands.

"Were you responsible for hurting Renard?" *Be calm, Em, no matter how they answer. We need to keep them from watching Matt too closely.*

Mara sighed wearily, as if every question they put to her was sapping her inner strength. "That night all we wanted was the satchel for Sir Charles and some assistance from your mother on another matter. But she disappeared before we had a chance to . . . ask for her help."

"It was never our intention to hurt Renard quite so permanently," Tanan added. He looked unrepentant.

Em wanted to scream. She wanted to leap from the floor and punch Mara.

Be still, Em.

"Of course, in order to maintain my cover at the abbey," added Mara, "I had to appear injured in the attack as well."

"What do you mean about Mom helping you with 'another matter'?" Em croaked.

"Blake found something important at the house in Raphael Terrace the morning that you fled London. It didn't take much for her to take it from that old woman, Violet. She didn't quite appreciate what it was at the time, and to be quite honest, nor did we," said Mara, circling the easel with a kind of nervous energy. "It wasn't until I intercepted the letter Arthur had sent to you that I knew for sure what Tanan and I had always suspected. At last, we know where Malcolm has gone."

Tanan fingered the edges of the easel. "And between your grandfather's interference and your mother's disappearing act that night," he said softly, "let's just say you two are Plan B."

Something clicked into place. The secret that her mom had been keeping for years and that Arthur Summers had discovered—the secret he had used to blackmail her . . . In that barbed moment, Em knew their mother's terrible secret had everything to do with their dad and his disappearance.

"I really am sorry about Renard," said Mara, patting Em on

the head as if she were a puppy. "Over the years I've learned a lot from him."

Easy, Em. Do not move away from the wall.

But Em couldn't take any more. She shifted onto her knees and started screaming.

"How could you have done such a thing . . . to Grandpa, of all people? He trusted you, Mara . . . loved you . . ."

"Technically, Em, Mara didn't do anything to your grandfather." Tanan pulled away the drop cloth covering the easel, exposing a painting hidden underneath. "This did most of the damage."

The cloaked crone and her evil child looked even uglier in the picture than when Matt, Em, and Zach had seen the figure of the changeling in the library. The witch appeared to shift slightly, tightening her arms around the dwarfish creature in her lap. The changeling's bulbous forehead began pulsing like a heartbeat under its skin. As the boys looked away in terror, the creature's beady yellow eyes followed their movement.

Em couldn't tear her eyes away. Her disordered mind was being pulled into the painting, the shadowy figures opening their arms to her. She could feel a terrible hunger from them, as if they wanted her warmth and her goodness. *Em, Em . . .* The wizened crone was calling, her voice melodic and comforting. Em wanted to crawl into her arms.

Em! Look away. You have to look away!

SIXTY-ONE

Zach grabbed Em's hand and squeezed. *C'mon, Em. Look at me. Look at me.*

After what seemed like the longest minute of his life, Em turned and held Zach's gaze, blinking back tears. Matt etched faster into the bricks behind him.

"So is this the painting that was stolen from the National Gallery the day we left London?" asked Em, when she was able to speak again.

Tanan seemed unable to keep his fingers away from the edge of the painting's tarnished frame. "Once the painting had served its purpose at the gallery that day by killing Arthur Summers, I gave it to Mara."

"We liked the yellow-haired man—Arthur," said Em, keeping

her eyes averted from the easel. "My mom liked him too. I'm sorry he died."

Tanan smiled. "Sweet. That day in the museum, Arthur Summers betrayed the Hollow Earth Society, despite the sacred vows he had taken to uphold our aims."

The Hollow Earth Society. Em tried to remember exactly what her mom and Vaughn had said. The artist Duncan Fox had founded it to protect Hollow Earth, assuming there was such a place—which, frankly, still sounded insane.

Tanan was still talking. "Summers told Wren about you animating into the painting, and then warned your mother what he had set in motion. Between the Council of Guardians' efforts to retrieve you and Renard's protection here in Auchinmurn, we lost you before we had a chance to use you. For his incompetence, he died."

Tell Zach to be ready, Em. And I need a major distraction.

Zach, be ready.

Zach braced himself against the wall, not sure what to expect. Without closing her eyes, Em let her worst fear churn in her stomach. The one thing she'd kept away from her imagination for days now. The terror charged into her head, a loud drumming sound, building and building until her dread freely manifested itself around her.

With a thunderous crack, the studio doors snapped open, and a raging river burst in. Torrents of icy cold water gushed in through the seams in the plastered walls, and jets shot up from the fissures in the slate floor. The deluge from every crack and crevice was so fast and so strong that the room was knee-deep in water within seconds.

Tanan was flipped against the kiln, his head slamming into its control panel. The easel wobbled on its three legs, as the ground shifted beneath it. "My painting!" he screamed.

Mara was knocked off her feet, as she tried to get across the room to the children. Without seeing exactly what he was drawing, Matt trusted his hand was following his mind's eye. Next to Matt, Zach was using his body as a barrier.

Em, what on earth did you do?

I thought . . . about how Mom might never come back. That she might be gone forever.

Tanan held the painting high above his head, as the rising water swirled around him, angrier than ever. "Get her under control, Mara!"

Mara lunged at Em, grabbing her shoulders and ducking her under the water. Em gasped and choked.

Em, it's okay. Make the water stop.

Em tried to settle her dreadful fear the best way she knew how—by imagining her mom watching a movie with her, helping her decorate her new bedroom, the soft lilt of Sandie's voice echoing in her head. And in an instant, the waters receded.

Dripping wet and unable to contain his fury, Tanan grabbed Mara's arm, shoving her to the floor next to Em. "They were supposed to be prepared for this! We need her imagination clear if she and her brother are to do what we want. Cut her loose!"

Mara reached down to cut off the plastic tie that bound Em to Zach. She stopped, turning white as she realized what had just happened.

Zach was missing.

"Where is he?" she screamed at Matt, shoving Em against the wall.

Tanan grabbed a blade from one of Mara's worktables and lunged at Matt, who instinctively covered his head with his arms. Em gasped, struggling to free herself from Mara's painful grip.

Tanan yanked Matt upright, cutting the plastic tie around his wrist to see the wall behind him more clearly. The ties that had bound Zach cracked under his foot. He stared in disbelief at the residue of two etchings carved into the stone. The first was a roughly drawn pet door—just wide enough for a tall, thin boy to crawl through. And next to it, an etching of a crude pair of scissors.

"You are going to be very sorry you did that," said Tanan, dragging Matt over to the easel where *Witch with Changeling Child* shimmered in the deepening shadows of the day.

SIXTY-TWO

Zach squeezed himself out through Matt's imagined hole in the wall, sprinted across the lawn—then suddenly stopped. Darting back to the kitchen, he grabbed his watch, his backpack, his helmet, and a set of keys from the pegboard in the utility room, before hurrying to the boathouse, where he pulled the tarp from the abbey's speedboat.

Sorry, Dad, wherever you are. You can take away as many computer privileges as you want after this day is over.

Zach slowly reversed out of the slot in the boathouse, pointed toward Era Mina, and gunned the throttle.

Tanan threw Matt to the studio floor in front of the painting. "I've not spent the last ten years of my life pretending to support

Sir Charles Wren's views on the Council so that two kids can trick me out of my destiny."

Mara dragged Em next to her brother, tore a sheet of paper from a pad on her worktable and began sketching. Iron bars shot out of the floor, inches from the twins, circling them, then morphed two feet above their heads into a massive steel lock. Huddling together for warmth, the twins felt like terrified birds.

"Em, come over to the bars," said Mara.

Do it, Em. We need to give Zach time to get to the island. Without us, he actually has to row across the bay this time.

"Hands through, please."

After snapping another plastic tie onto Em's wrists, Mara did the same to Matt. Outside, a boat engine roared to life. Tanan rushed to the door just in time to see Zach crashing through the waves toward Era Mina.

I guess Zach isn't rowing after all.

Tanan stormed back to stand in front of the painting. For a few minutes, he simply stared at it, rubbing his temples, lost in thought. Then he pulled out his notebook and began to draw. In a burst of yellow light, the changeling leaped from the crone's lap and out of the painting, scuttling across the floor to the cage, where it leaned close to Em. She struggled to pull herself away from its foul, icy breath. Close to her ear, the dwarfish creature snapped its jagged teeth up and down, up and down, then scampered out the door.

Warn Zach!

Acting on Matt's urgent advice, Em sent out a telepathic warning, repeating it in her mind over and over again every few seconds. No reply. What if something had already happened to him? Did he really know how to drive that boat?

He'll be okay, right?

When he gets to Vaughn, he'll be fine.

"What are we going to do about Zach?" Mara asked Tanan, sounding tense.

"He's no longer a concern. When he gets to the island, he'll be shocked to discover that Vaughn has had a nasty accident. Then he'll have one too."

The caladrius's vision slammed into the twins' minds at the same time. Tanan knew about Vaughn.

I'm going to be sick.

No, Em, you're not. We're going to do as they ask until we think of a way to get ourselves out of this cage. When we do, we'll get to Era Mina to help Zach and Vaughn. Now think!

Tanan flipped his hood up over his head. "Can you handle them on your own for a few minutes?"

"Of course," Mara said. "But where are you going?"

"To Sandie's studio," Tanan replied. "I left something there for safekeeping the night Blake and I broke in to get the satchel for Wren." He looked at the twins. "I believe it's time that you were formally introduced to your father."

SIXTY-THREE

Em's instincts had been right. Drops of sweat trickled down her spine. Her hands were clammy, and the drumming in her head had returned in full force.

I knew it! This all has something to do with Mom and Dad.

I know. I know . . .

Matt needed to think this through for himself. He slouched back against the bars, his fury now fusing with his fear over what the next few minutes might bring.

The strange notion that their father was somehow next door could mean only one of two things. The first was that he had come to help them find their mother, and that Tanan and Mara had taken him prisoner. The second option was much more chilling, but if Matt was being honest with himself, it seemed more likely.

Their dad was part of Tanan and Mara's plan, somehow hiding in Sandie's studio, biding his time until he could use his very own children to achieve some mysterious, shared goal.

Mara repositioned the painting near the studio doors, leaving an empty board on the easel with its clamps hanging loose. The old crone's lap was now empty, her hands clutching her ragged robes instead of wrapped around the creature. Em swore that she could hear the witch weeping through the dreadful drumming in her head.

We need to animate something before Tanan gets back, Matt. He seems to be stronger than Mara.

The twins were silent for a while, watching Mara wrap some of her glass pieces and set them into packing boxes stuffed with straw.

We need to copy something. It'll be easier to animate.

We'd still need to draw it. We're all out of paper and pencils.

Em glared at her brother across the cage. *So we're giving up?*

Mara and Tanan were very powerful together; they had put Renard in a coma and done something terrible to Simon. But Em knew that their mom would want them to try to find a way out of their predicament. She would not want them to stop trying.

Matt burst out laughing. *I love it when you think like Mom.*

"What's so funny?" asked Mara, stopping her packing. She checked the room, clearly afraid that the twins had animated something behind her back.

The scent of fish and seaweed wafted into the studio through the open doors. Matt stared out at the abbey's north tower, at the ever-present flock of seagulls perching on the balustrades, at the abbey's two flags snapping in the evening breeze. And he had an idea.

Tanan was coming back. The twins heard his footsteps on the stones outside. Em's body tensed. Matt sat up straight.

Tanan was carrying an airtight aluminum tube, the kind artists used to protect their unframed canvases from damage. The twins looked at the tube in confusion. Their mom had given it to Violet before they fled the London apartment. So why was it here?

What had Mara said? *Blake found something important at the house in Raphael Terrace the morning that you fled London. It didn't take much for her to take it from that old woman, Violet. She didn't quite appreciate what it was at the time, and to be quite honest, nor did we . . .*

Dry-mouthed, Em looked at her brother.

Be ready, Em.

SIXTY-FOUR

Matt realized the significance of the tube as soon as Tanan broke its thick wax seal and withdrew a tightly rolled canvas. His idea for escape was sidelined in an instant.

Dad's bound in that picture, Em! I bet they want us to release him somehow. Can you sense him? Do you hear anything? Feel anything?

Em shook her head very slightly at her brother, who was struggling to contain his excitement. *Nothing*.

Tanan carried the canvas over to the easel recently vacated by *Witch with Changeling Child*, placing each corner reverently under the clamps. With their backs to the children, the two adults stood in front of the painting as if it were an artifact on a religious altar. They stood there for so long that the twins thought—hoped—they'd been forgotten.

The canvas was the size of a school notebook, but the demon captured on it was truly monstrous. Its body was the size of three men, its muscles and skeletal structure visible beneath red, scaly skin. Matt thought it looked like an anatomical drawing of a body without skin. Em thought it was simply horrible.

Tanan's back was still turned to the twins. "This is a copy of Duncan Fox's *The Demon Within*, painted by your mother. Fox was a brilliant Animare in the nineteenth century. He claimed this was the first monster he saw in Hollow Earth."

Matt and Em gasped. Mara's eyes were expressionless.

"Oh yes. Fox found Hollow Earth," Tanan murmured. He was pleased with the effect he was having on the twins, and stroked the face of the monster in the picture before him. "Disturbing creature, isn't it? It's no wonder Fox went insane."

Matt glanced at Em. *I thought you said Hollow Earth was a legend!*

Em swallowed, too shocked to respond. They both thought of the strange yellow, green, and black drawing Arthur Summers had sent them; Matt remembered the painting in the vault. Zach's laptop described the picture as showing "the entrance to a mythical purgatory."

The two adults stepped away from the painting and walked over to the cage. The twins did their best to stand with as much dignity as they could muster, given that their hands were bound and their heads were hitting the top of the cage.

"When you were very young, your mother bound your father

in this painting," said Mara. "We need you to use your significant abilities to release him."

"But why would Mom do that?" said Em, her voice cracking slightly.

"Because your mother lacked your father's vision for the future," Tanan said.

Suddenly the cage began to rattle, knocking Em to her knees. Matt clenched one of the bars to steady himself. It changed into a snake, hissing and spitting venom at him, and he yanked his hand away, staring at Em.

"Are you doing this?"

"I don't know," Em cried, looking at the canvas on the easel. "Maybe. That painting scares me."

The studio floor rolled, buckled, and cracked underneath the cage, dropping the twins into a huge fissure.

"You told me you had her under control!" Tanan shouted. "Bring them here."

Grabbing the twins from the buckled and useless cage, Mara cut their ties, dragging them over to the easel. The twins instinctively took each other's hands.

"Your father, Mara, and I revived the Hollow Earth Society right after you were born," said Tanan softly, "because we believed, like Duncan Fox, that Hollow Earth was real. We understood how a very powerful Animare and Guardian together could open Hollow Earth. However, unlike Fox—who sought to protect the world from the creatures within—we have somewhat bigger plans." An expression close to rapture filled Tanan's face as he recited the lines the twins remembered from the inscription on Arthur Summers's drawing. "To our sons and daughters, may you never forget imagination is the real and the eternal. This is Hollow Earth."

Em stared at her mom's copy of *The Demon Within* stretched on the easel. The image at its center was like nothing she'd ever seen before—monstrous, skeletal, and scaly. "Mom bound Dad in this painting so he could find Hollow Earth?"

Tanan leaned close to Em. "Your mother bound him in this painting to *stop* him finding Hollow Earth!"

Help me!

For a beat, Em thought Zach must have come back to the studio. She was so sure that she turned, expecting to see him. But he wasn't there, just an echo of his voice in her head.

Zach's in trouble. We need to get out of here.

"We need you to release your father from this painting so the Society can continue its mission," said Tanan, his eyes flaring angrily. "We need your father to find Hollow Earth, and, when he does, we need you to open it."

He's insane, Matt.

Matt needed to focus on getting them out of here. He looked again at the abbey's flags.

"If you want to see Simon or your mother again," added Tanan, "you will do this for us."

"But we don't know how!" wailed Em.

"Concentrate. Feel your connection to your father—"

"We can do it," Matt said, interrupting. He squeezed his sister's hand. *Trust me and empty your imagination, Em.*

Confused, Em did as her brother suggested, sending images and emotions flying out of her head in trails of brilliant light and streams of magnificent colors. For a few seconds, they filled the studio; then, just as quickly, they exploded into a million sparkling pieces, like embers from a fire, fading to nothing. Her mother's voice popped into her mind. She forced that out into the room too.

"Good," said Tanan, relaxing. "You need a quiet mind. Now, are you ready?"

The twins turned so they stood back to back, their shoulders pressing against each other. Tanan and Mara took each other's hands, barely able to contain their excitement. On the easel, the canvas was pulsing, the monster's scaly hands twitching and flexing.

Instead of sending words to Em's mind, Matt telepathed lines, curves, dots, smudges of black, white, and silver. Instead of the rhythm of Matt's voice, Em accepted the texture and dimension of an image. Instead of sentences, Em let a picture take shape.

Suddenly it sounded as if a helicopter was hovering outside. Mara looked up, staring in confusion as all the natural light from her stained-glass window was blocked from the room. The canvas had returned to stillness as Matt had shifted his imagination to Em. There was no shimmer, no bursts of colors, no creative energy—no Malcolm.

"Something's not right," said Tanan.

"They look as if they're in a trance," said Mara, her voice displaying a twinge of anxiety. She grabbed Matt's wrist, feeling for his pulse.

The twins' eyes were closed, their heads pressed together, their hearts beating in sync, their minds creating in unison.

"This should be working," yelled Tanan, rushing forward.

But he didn't get very far. A magnificent white stag with expansive silver wings crashed through the stained-glass window, landing on top of the twins' cage, crushing it further under its hooves.

"A *peryton*!" gasped Mara.

Tanan was too stunned to move. The twins' eyes snapped open. For a couple of seconds, they stared in awe at their animation. Then Mara screamed in anger, lunging for a piece of pipe lying near one of her crates, just as Tanan reached for his sketch pad. But neither Tanan nor Mara moved fast enough.

It was as if the peryton knew their next move. It dipped its enormous white antlers, hooked them on the nearby crate, and launched it across the room. The crate landed on top of them, sending Tanan's sketch pad across the floor, colored glass showering down on them.

The twins ran to the peryton. Cupping his hands, Matt hoisted Em onto the beast, pulling himself up in front of her. The beast took one, two, three paces forward, then lifted itself back out through the smashed window.

"Nice job with the whole earthquake thing to get us out of the cage, Em," Matt shouted against the wind. "But I could have lived without the snake."

SIXTY-FIVE

Tearing pieces of crate and shards of glass from his robes, Tanan let out a feral howl, as the peryton carried the twins out through the remains of the stained-glass window. He kicked over the easel, sending Mara to the floor to retrieve the canvas of Fox's demon, then pulled his sketch pad from his sleeve, pacing like a maniac and waving it in the air like a weapon.

"Malcolm wasn't bound in that painting at all. Sandie must have made another copy . . ."

For the first time, Tanan wondered if his ambitions might have impaired his vision. Sandie had been one step ahead of him the whole way.

Mara thrust the canvas into his hands and backed away. Tanan stared down at the image. The demon's coral skin was scaly and pockmarked, its muscles and bones distinctly visible, and its bald head contained demented eyes. So if this was not the picture in which Malcolm had been bound, then where was the first copy? The satchel . . .

"I'm going after the twins," said Mara. She was about to take the canvas and return it to the tube when Tanan put his hand on her arm.

"Wait," he said softly. "I have a better idea. Let's send Fox's demon to fetch them."

The peryton landed with grace, setting Matt and Em down on an outcropping of rocks at Monk's Cove on Era Mina.

"So how long do you think our animation will last?" asked Em, stroking the beast's wings with awe.

"I don't know. I can't exactly destroy the sketch, since I used your imagination as my drawing pad." said Matt. "He feels different from our normal animations, doesn't he? Like maybe he'll last . . . forever."

The moon was full, and the water was filled with hundreds of tiny, twinkling jellyfish, like thousands of candles floating across its surface. Before they had landed, the twins had seen the abbey's speedboat beached near the tower, so they knew that Zach was here, even though none of Em's telepathic messages had been answered. Hopscotching across the rocks, the twins left the peryton preening its wings and darted inside the caves.

The darkness engulfed them immediately, forcing them to

stop and adjust their bearings. The beacon light from the tower bathed the mouth of the cave in an eerie glow, but the deeper they went, the heavier the darkness.

Behind them, tucked high on a ledge, a pair of beady yellow eyes was watching. If the twins had been concentrating, they might have been able to hear it smacking its lips, gnashing its sharp little teeth.

Matt jumped over the rocks to the ledge near the cave's entrance. His hand bumped against something heavy.

"Zach's backpack is here," he called over to Em. His fingers touched something else. "And his helmet."

A wave of fear washed over him. And then, as an arc of light from the tower swept through the cave, his worst fears were confirmed.

Two figures floated below him at the edge of the tidal pool.

"Em, over there!" he yelled, directing her with the light on Zach's helmet. Zach was sitting up against a flat rock, unconscious, his chin resting on his chest, blood dripping from a gash on his forehead. Vaughn was perched in front of Zach, as if he was sitting in his lap. Zach's arms were wrapped around Vaughn's upper body. The good news was that Zach had been able to keep Vaughn's head above the rising tide, preventing him from drowning.

The bad news was that Zach's and Vaughn's arms and necks were covered in fresh bite marks.

SIXTY-SIX

Her heart pounding, Em knelt next to Zach, gently lifting his chin. Zach groaned and smiled weakly, then dropped his head forward onto Vaughn's shoulder.

"We need to get them out of the water," said Matt, wading into the tidal pool.

With a great deal of effort, the twins pulled Vaughn up onto the rocks above the tide line. Vaughn stirred and grabbed Matt's wrist.

"You need to get out of here," he slurred.

"We will. We'll get help," Matt promised. But Vaughn had lost consciousness again.

In addition to the gash on his head, Zach had clearly twisted or broken his ankle. Em started to cry as they moved him. This

was all their fault. Tears streamed down her face as she helped
Matt lay him on the rocks next to Vaughn.

Just as they thought they were safe, it struck.

They couldn't see what hit them until it was right upon them.
A black shape, springing from the darkness, landed on Matt's
shoulders, causing him to drop the helmet light. Its teeth snapped
in Matt's ears, its foul breath chilled his skin.

Em screamed, lunging at the dwarflike creature, punching and
tearing at it, trying desperately to break its grip on her brother.
Dropping to his knees, Matt tried to shake off the grotesque creature by pummeling it against the cave wall. And all the while,
the changeling's teeth nipped and gnawed at the skin on Matt's
neck.

Em's punches were useless. The creature had somehow
attached itself to Matt's back. She scrambled back over the
rocks to Zach's backpack, barely able to see what she was doing,
her only light coming from the glow of the changeling's yellow
eyes and the pulse of light from the tower's beacon. The changeling's distorted face grinned at her every time the beacon's light
caught it.

Matt was weakening. Scuttling over Matt's shoulder, the
changeling clinched itself around his chest and began to squeeze
the life out of him.

Hunting for pen and paper inside the backpack, her fear and
frustration making her search all the more difficult, Em could feel
a drumming beginning in her head. Every time she thought she'd

grasped a pen, it fell from her fingers. If she was going to be of any use to Matt or Zach, she needed to keep control of her fears.

Where had she put that stupid pad of paper?

And then, suddenly, Em remembered the chunk of charcoal stuck in the back pocket of her jeans. Digging it out, she quickly drew a picture across the cave wall in front of her.

Roll onto your back. Now!

Matt did as he was told, and just in time. A large jellyfish dropped from the rocks onto the changeling, completely enveloping it. The changeling loosened its grip in shock. Shoving both creature and jellyfish off his body, Matt scrambled up onto the ledge next to Em.

The jellyfish had covered the changeling's entire body in a shiny pink slime. The more the creature struggled, the more the jellyfish shape-shifted to keep the changeling's flailing arms and legs wrapped in its thick membrane. When Em could see that the snapping, spitting, clawing changeling had been completely swallowed, she scooped water up from the tidal pool and dashed it against the cave wall, washing away her drawing. With an echoing *pop*, the jellyfish burst into slivers of pink and putrid green.

Em had no time to dwell on her success. No sooner had the changeling been destroyed than the alarm on Zach's watch went off. He was trying to get their attention.

The twins clambered across the rocks to Zach and knelt next to him. Zach kept straining to look over Em's shoulder at the mouth of the cave. Em heard his thoughts, weak but clear.

The beacon is flashing.

Doesn't it always?

It's Morse code.

Em frowned. *Are you sure? It could just be a fault in the light.*

Yes, I'm sure. It's a code. I know codes.

What does it say?

Hide in the caves. No time. Hide now.

Em relayed the information to Matt as quickly as she could.

"We don't have enough time to get everyone to safety," Matt said in a low voice, looking at the badly injured Vaughn and Zach. Zach attempted to sign in the darkness. "Go! Climb up and hide in the cave. If Tanan and Mara are coming, it'll be you two they want."

Em gazed at Zach. *Your dad's sending that message, isn't he?*

Zach nodded. *I hope so.*

"He's right, Em. We should start climbing." Matt's eyes were red-rimmed, and Em's chest was hurting from the effort of containing her tears.

We can't leave you, Zach.

You must.

Matt stood up and grabbed Em, dragging her toward the stepped crevices leading up to their hideout.

"Wait," she yelled, pulling away.

Digging out the piece of charcoal from her pocket again, she quickly sketched a picture of a big black blanket on a hidden stretch of wall. Without needing to be told, Matt spread the blanket over Zach and Vaughn, camouflaging them in the cave's darkness from whatever was heading their way.

The beacon on the tower flashed out the same sequence, again and again.

Hide.

Hide.

Hide. . . .

SIXTY-SEVEN

When Simon had opened his eyes, it had taken him a few minutes to organize his thoughts through the excruciating pain in his head. Something was happening to Mara. Simon could sense her heightened emotions, but he was unable to distinguish between them—fury, frustration, excitement, vengeance, pain. What was going on?

Sitting up, he realized he was barefoot and, of all things, still wearing his pajamas. His hands were bound behind his back, and he was in the rear seat of the Range Rover. Pressing his forehead against the cold glass, he peered outside. It was dark, and he was in the woods.

How had he got here? He didn't seem to be injured. He wasn't physically hurt, but he was very thirsty.

He remembered waking up quite early that morning—it may even have been the middle of the night. The voices in Mara's room weren't angry, but she hadn't mentioned she was having company. Simon recalled walking down the hall to Mara's bedroom, then nothing.

He tried to tease from his memory what had happened after he reached Mara's room, but he couldn't. Every time he thought he had an image, he'd turn it over in his mind, trying to coax it forward, but it kept scampering back into the darkness.

The best he could come up with was that whoever had hurt Renard and taken Sandie had returned to the abbey and drugged him. The couple that the twins had trapped in the quicksand?

Simon reached his bound hands between the Range Rover's front seats and opened the central compartment. Finding his Swiss Army knife, he flipped out the smallest blade and sliced through the plastic that bound his wrists. Then he climbed into the front and pressed the starter.

Nothing. The battery was dead.

Mara's emotions were getting stronger and more troubling; Simon's vision was beginning to blur from their intensity. If he didn't get back to the abbey soon in order to help her, he'd be too debilitated to move. And this time, he didn't have the twins and Zach to help him get home.

He was checking the compass on his phone to see which direction he had to walk, when he saw the long list of missed texts from Zach, ranging from early in the day to less than an hour ago.

He only had to read the last frantic message from Zach to know that the children were under threat.

Simon leaped from the car and sprinted west through the woods.

Breathless, with the soles of his feet torn and bleeding, Simon finally stopped running as he reached the abbey's security wall. A deep stab of emotion from Mara forced him to his knees. When the pain had subsided, Simon followed the wall round to the rear of the grounds, before ducking into the stables for cover.

Scanning the rear of the abbey, he could see the kitchen, brightly lit but empty. The rest of the compound was in darkness, except for Mara's studio. Her beautiful stained-glass window hung in tattered fragments from the window frame.

According to Zach's last message, the twins were being held captive by Mara and someone called Tanan—the man from the twins' quicksand, he guessed. Simon found this almost impossible to digest. How could Mara have fooled him for so long? She must have been masking her true emotions for years. He read on. Zach had escaped through one of Matt's animations and was heading over to Era Mina to get help from Vaughn. *Vaughn!* When had he returned to the island? Simon was heartsick about Mara and frightened of this Tanan, but when he reached the part about Vaughn, his panic subsided a little. Vaughn was a good man.

Simon sprinted along the tree line toward the boathouse. Climbing onto the dock, he spotted a hooded figure standing under the light of the tower on Era Mina. *Tanan*, he thought. It had to be.

Simon could sense that the hooded figure was about to animate. The twins weren't answering their phones and nor was Zach. He had to get a message to the children to warn them that something bad was coming . . . before it was too late.

SIXTY-EIGHT

The twins climbed fast, hoisting themselves over the ledge and into the cavernous space. Matt pulled the light cord. It took them a few seconds for their eyes to adjust, but when they did, they quickly noted that their hideout was just as they had left it a few hours before. Given that and the nature of Vaughn's injuries, Vaughn must have been attacked when he had already climbed down from their hideout. Matt went over to the couch, knelt down, and looked underneath.

"What are you doing?"

"Following a hunch."

The satchel was tucked behind the couch leg. Matt pulled it out.

"How did you know it was under there?" said Em in astonishment.

"I figured it had to be Vaughn who took it from the woodpile the other night. He was the only person we hadn't accounted for. Mara never had it after all," replied Matt. He stared at the brown leather bag. "And where else would he have put it? There's not exactly any cupboard space up here."

"We should have looked inside days ago," said Em.

But before they had a chance to break the lock, the lights went out, plunging the cave into complete darkness.

"Someone must have cut—"

Don't speak. Might give us away. Put the satchel back underneath the couch and let's find a place to hide.

Right. Should we split up?

Definitely.

Matt felt around the trestle table for a sketch pad and pen, tucking it under his T-shirt. Then he used the couch to climb about six feet up the wall, sliding feet first into a tunnel they had discovered months ago but had never fully explored. Em cut through the darkness to an opposite corner and shinned up onto a ledge cut into the curve of the rock.

They waited.

Do you think the peryton is still out there?

It would be pretty funny to see the faces of any fishermen nearby if it is.

Em appreciated her brother's attempts to take her mind off their situation. The last thing they needed right now was a room full of her fears.

The darkness in the cave didn't disturb Em as much as the damp. She could feel it frizzing her hair, seeping through the soles of her boots, and creeping into the muscles in her back. She shifted slightly, repositioning herself the ledge. It didn't help.

Em wasn't sure she could remain in her position for much longer. Her knees were aching and her toes were numb from the cold and damp.

Do you think he'll come soon? I'm so cold.

Soon, Em. I feel it.

The flat-screen TV on the trestle table in front of them exploded in a ball of blinding blue light. Shards of plastic and glass rained down. The light burned brilliantly for about thirty seconds and then appeared to lose energy. Soon only showers of white sparks like fireworks were shooting out from the plugs, wires, and extension cords attached to all the electronic equipment in the cave. As the sparks and the blue light dimmed, a monster's fist burst out through the computer screen at the center of the table.

Em's mental anguish almost made Matt collapse.

It's the demon from the painting!

The demon's fist uncurled slowly and stretched its fingers. The forearm was ripped, with muscles and tendons so defined it looked as if someone had sculpted it out of clay. It cracked its knuckles. One. At. A. Time.

How can that . . . thing come through a computer?

Seriously? That's what's worrying you? We have powers other people can't begin to imagine. Zach's injured because a cursed paint-

ing attacked him. And you want to know how it's possible a monster is climbing out of our computer?

Don't snap at me, Matt. I'm scared, and you're not helping!

They watched, frozen in their hiding places, as the demon's tapered talons groped and slashed across the desk with such fury that when the clawed hand swiped the computer keyboard, it went flying like a missile across the cave.

Duck!

Matt felt his scream to his sister explode in his brain, a flash of pain behind his eyes. The keyboard crashed against the rock wall inches above her head.

The monster's hand finally got a grip on the edge of the table. The muscles of its forearm vibrated against the desk as it hoisted a hulking shoulder five times the size of any man's through the sparking, hissing, blue light of the pulverized computer screen.

Can we stop him before he gets out any further?

Matt would have loved to do exactly what his twin was suggesting, to grab a shard of glass and hack and hack until that thing was sushi, but— He cut off his thoughts, remembering his sister could hear his doubts in her mind.

We should run while we still can.

A rush of fetid air assaulted them. The monster's entire shoulder was through, and its hairless head was following. Its eyes strafed the darkness. Its nostrils flared. It sniffed, cocked its head toward Em's position, and sniffed again. A black reptilian tongue flicked across its cracked lips. Its ears were like bat wings folded against the sides of its head, and the bones and cartilage of its spine were visible as it wrenched and howled and tugged and groaned until it pulled its full grotesque being out of the computer.

It crouched on its haunches on the edge of the table.

"Greetings, *mes chers*."

It was Tanan's voice.

"Get out of there, Em!" screamed Matt.

SIXTY-NINE

Em leaped from her ledge. When she hit the moss-covered slate, her legs slid out from under her, and she landed on her hip, yelping in pain. The demon whirled around to face her, rolling its head from side to side, rubbing its scaly hands together. The way out was blocked. But the monster's scales radiated a distinctive animated sheen, giving Em better visibility than she'd had a few minutes ago.

Matt looked as if he was backing down his own hidden tunnel. Lunging for what was left of the computer screen, Em threw it like a Frisbee. The demon raised its claw, catching the screen before it whizzed by and crushing it against its scaly body. It took a step toward Em, then another. Em threw herself under the trestle tables, scuttling along the floor to the opposite side of the cave.

She wasn't fast enough.

The monster took two long strides and waited for her at the other end of the cave. Em backed up against the sharp rocks of the wall. Frantically, she scanned the chamber, looking for a way to reach her brother—when she felt a tingling in her fingers. The sensation spread painfully across her palms. Within seconds, her entire hand was burning. Looking down, she watched in astonishment as a gleaming Viking longsword took shape in her hand, morphing itself securely into her grasp. Without hesitation, Em clamped her other hand over the sword's hilt, hoisted the weapon above her shoulder, and plunged the blade into the demon's thigh. The demon shrieked.

Matt tore up his sketch instantly.

It wasn't a good idea to leave the demon with a weapon. The blade ruptured down the center of its shaft, then exploded into shards of golden light, blinding the monster for an instant.

Taking full advantage of the blast, Em darted across the room and onto the couch, reaching up to the tunnel where her brother was waiting. Matt grabbed her wrists and tried to pull her up. The demon howled in rage, charging across the cave.

"Draw something to block the entrance!" yelled Em, her legs flailing.

The demon lunged at her, seizing one of her feet before slowly dragging her back out of the tunnel. She screamed.

"C'mon! C'mon! You need to get all the way inside!" yelled Matt.

Em kicked furiously at the monster's head with her free leg. Twisting around, she could see right into the demon's jade-colored eyes. *Tanan's eyes.* He had animated the demon in the same way that Matt had animated the caladrius.

The demon was tightening its grip with one skeletal fist while it batted away her kicks with the other. The more Em struggled, the more amusement she saw in its cold green eyes. She felt like a ball of wool in the paws of a very intent cat.

Behind you.

An aerosol can rolled against her back. Grabbing the container, Em sprayed mace directly into the demon's eyes. It howled, loosening its grip.

Get inside now! I'm drawing a barrier across the entrance.

Em slid her foot out of her boot, dragging herself all the way into the tunnel within a breath of a steel door slamming down over the opening like a guillotine. Instantly, the demon started clawing at the earth under the barrier, trying to dig itself another way in.

"That's not going to stop it for very long," said Matt, wriggling around to face forward. "Let's see where this tunnel goes."

Em's hand was on fire, blisters forming across the pads of her fingers where she'd gripped the animated sword. Matt glanced at her apologetically.

"Sorry about your skin. But I had to be sure the sword animated directly into your hand, or the demon might have reached it first."

{ 349 }

"It's okay. It worked."

Scuttling forward on their hands and knees, they climbed deeper into the island. The composition of the tunnel was changing as they crawled on, and Em thought the air smelled like rotting leaves.

After only a few minutes, the twins heard the monster punch its fist into the rock and yank the steel plate out like a loose tooth. There was a clang of metal as the animation dropped on the cave's slate floor. Looking back, the twins saw the demon leap up into the opening and sit there for a second, its massive girth filling the space. Then it elongated itself and entered the tunnel, slithering after them.

Draw a cave-in!

That could bring the whole tunnel down on top of us, too!

Em's hip throbbed with every movement she made. Matt's knuckles were bleeding again. With each snorting breath, the monster's black tongue flicked far out from its scaly mouth, stinging the bottom of Em's stockinged foot.

Em was terrified. What if there was venom in the demon's tongue?

One minute there was solid earth underneath them. The next minute, nothing. They were tumbling through darkness. . . .

SEVENTY

Simon had managed to reduce Mara's emotions and his own panic about the twins to a dull throb at the base of his skull. Finding Renard's emergency key for the box that controlled the shipping beacon in the abbey's utility room, he unlocked the switch box in the boathouse and stripped the wires so he could change the signal. He could only hope that Zach remembered his Morse code.

With every long and short pulse of light he had flashed, he had willed Zach to be looking at the tower. Then, after ten minutes of sending the same message—hide—Simon had looked for the speedboat to get over to the island himself.

But the boat was gone.

Mara. He had to get her to animate a way across the bay.

Simon prayed that his connection with Mara as her Guardian would be enough to bring her to her senses.

He sprinted across the lawn to Mara's studio. The closer he got, the more intense the pain in his mind and his body. By the time he reached the studio steps, he was buckled over in anguish.

"Mara," he croaked. "Are you in here?"

The studio looked empty, but Simon sensed her presence. Hobbling inside, the first thing he noticed was the mess—the smashed crates, the layers of broken glass everywhere. In the midst of the chaos stood an easel displaying a small canvas.

Simon reeled. In the days before he disappeared, Malcolm had been infatuated with Duncan Fox and this painting, his appreciation for it something that no one else understood. Simon hadn't seen the picture for years. It had lost none of its power.

A jolt of pain pushed Simon to his knees. And then he heard Mara's soft sobbing from the corner behind the kiln. Simon looked up—and froze.

"Who did this to you?"

Mara was leaning in front of *Witch with Changeling Child*, her arm fused into the painting. The evil crone grinned out at Simon as she clutched Mara's hand in hers.

"Tanan," Mara sobbed. "I thought . . . I thought we were partners. I thought we were helping each other. I was doing it all for Malcolm."

Simon was appalled. "Tanan bound you like this?"

"He's a very powerful Animare, but he's not strong enough to bind an entire person on his own."

Simon took Mara's other hand. His touch calmed her immediately. This in turn reduced a little of Simon's pain. "But what does Tanan want?"

"He wants Malcolm back. We thought he was bound in that copy of Fox's painting and that only the twins could release him."

Mara's sobs racked her body again. Simon closed his eyes, struggling to find strength to settle his Animare. It was difficult. Mara's anguish was coming from a place inside her that was full of bile, bitter, and angry.

"Why you, Mara? Why would you try to hurt Matt and Em?"

Her eyes blazed. "Because I love Malcolm. Even before Sandie came along, I loved him. I would do anything for him. He needs us to use the twins. . . ."

"Surely even Malcolm would not have hurt his own children!" Simon protested.

Mara looked coldly at him. "Those children were a means to an end for Malcolm from the day they were born. He believed when they were older and stronger, they would be the doors to Hollow Earth. That's why Sandie stopped him. We knew she had done something to him, but we never fully understood what until a few weeks ago."

There was no more time to waste on Mara's pain.

"Mara," Simon said, using the last vestiges of his Guardian

power on her. "Animate something to get me across to Era Mina. When we return, the twins can free you from this painting." Finding a scrap of paper on the floor near the kiln, he set it and a marker on Mara's lap. "Do it now!" he commanded. "It may already be too late."

SEVENTY-ONE

The twins did not fall far, but they landed hard. Em had been following so closely behind Matt that when they dropped off the end of the tunnel, she landed on top of him. He broke her fall, but the yell he gave convinced Em that she had broken his arm. He rolled onto his side, clutching his elbow and grimacing.

"That hurt."

Em pulled off her sweatshirt, knotting the sleeves behind Matt's back and fashioning a sling. Gently she eased his arm through the hoodie, taking some of the pressure off the injury.

"Where are we?" she asked in a trembling voice.

Matt was afraid that he would cry if he tried to speak.

Directly above their heads, an amber glow filled the end of the tunnel from which they had fallen. The demon was still there, its tongue flicking out into the empty air, leaving a trail of light in the darkness.

Tanan's trying to figure out where we went.

We can't give ourselves away with a light.

As quietly as they could, the twins scuttled backward until they hit the cold rock of the cave wall.

Close this end of the tunnel and we can trap him in the wall.

Like when we left London. Give me the paper and pen.

I don't have them. They must have fallen when we did.

Em started running her hands in a circle around her, stretching her body as far away from the wall as she dared in her attempts to find the pad and pen. Above them, the demon leaned out over the precipice, its head twitching and nodding as if deciding on the best moment to come in to fetch its prey.

The charcoal you used to draw the blanket. Do you still have it? We can use the wall.

In a blur of golden light, the demon jumped. It landed on its haunches in the middle of the cave. As it uncoiled itself to its full height, the sheen emanating from its scaly skin illuminated the entire chamber.

The twins gasped. The wall behind the demon was covered from top to bottom by a stunning cave drawing of a two-headed dog, a hellhound, like the gargoyles on the abbey walls.

They had found Solon's Cave.

The stories Renard had told them about the monk's young apprentice, who had saved the monastery during a Viking raid, had been the basis of their own presentation for the tourists on Auchinmurn. And now they were here.

The demon began scuffing and scratching the cave floor with its foot, like a bull about to charge.

Then it pounced.

Em gripped her brother's hand, squeezing her eyes shut. Matt threw himself in front of his sister, trying to protect her. But in midair the demon exploded, bursting into thousands of projectiles of copper light that ricocheted off the cave walls, showering the twins in a layer of thick red dust. Em wiped the residue of the animation from her face with the back of one shaking hand. "What happened?"

"Someone must have destroyed Tanan's drawing," said Matt. He was starting to feel faint; his arm was agony.

Em walked the perimeter of the cave, taking advantage of the still glowing particles of the exploded demon to inspect the walls for any tunnels or crevices that might suggest a way out. She paused in front of the relief, her fingers touching the deeply etched lines of the massive hound's two heads.

The instant she connected with the carving, the snarling heads shot out of the wall, snapping viciously. A surge of electricity soared through her arm, throwing her backward onto the floor.

Stunned, Em got to her feet. The hound was still again.

"Did you see that, Matt?"

She turned to her brother—and let out a cry. He had passed out. The jolt had not only traveled through her body, but Matt's, too. And in his weakened state, it had completely knocked him out.

Kneeling down next to him, Em took out what was left of her charcoal and sketched quickly on the cave wall. A set of stairs popped out of the rock face, leading up the precipice and back to the tunnel. If they could return the way they'd come, they'd be able to get out of the mountain via their own cave hideout.

Now all she had to do was figure out how to get her brother up the stairs too.

SEVENTY-TWO

Zach hadn't been able to telepath anything to Em for some time. But not long after the twins had disappeared up into the darkness, he had felt strong vibrations of sound shooting down the cave wall. Then, as if a thin cord connected them, he could sense Em moving deeper into the mountain.

Zach shifted Vaughn closer to him for warmth, tightening the blanket around them both. He was shivering from cold, and maybe shock, too. His ankle didn't hurt him much anymore, but it was swollen to three times its normal size.

Vaughn had been wheezing badly for the past ten minutes, but was finally regaining consciousness. Pulling himself upright, he grimaced with every breath he took. "Must have broken a rib when I fell."

"Were you hurt by the same creature that attacked me?"

Vaughn read Zach's hands, then looked closely at the bite marks on his own. "No. But it looks like it took a few bites while it was waiting here for you."

Zach explained what had happened as best he could; how he could now sense the twins moving deeper into the mountain.

"If we're going to help them," Vaughn said finally, "we need to stop Tanan. His only chance of freeing Malcolm is to hold the twins captive until he finds Sandie and the real painting. When he reaches the cave, we need to stop him."

"But how?" Zach wanted to scream with frustration. "I'm not an Animare."

Vaughn's face contorted with pain as he reached under his jacket, pulling out a sketch pad. "Maybe not. But I am. Now, my young friend, let's put an end to this right here."

Tanan had animated a boat and crossed to Era Mina. Using a brush and ink he'd taken from Sandie's studio, he'd then animated Fox's demon directly inside the children's cave, using the computer as his portal. Mara had proved useful after all with her regular stream of information about the twins. Then it had simply been a matter of chasing the twins from one cave to another. Although the demon had Tanan's vision, he had left himself enough to be able to hazily distinguish his surroundings.

He had to admit he was enjoying his little game of cat and mouse.

When he had finally trapped the twins in the second cave, he heard an engine roaring to life at the abbey's dock. It sounded like someone was mounting a rescue—too late.

With the twins trapped helplessly in the cave, and the demon pawing the cave floor ready to attack, Tanan had made it round to Monk's Cove. He would go up to the children's hideout and let the demon bring the twins to him there.

Tanan sensed something shift in the air. He looked up from his drawing. Zach was poised on the rocks in front of him, his elbow cocked, bow at the ready. There was no time to react. Zach's arrow tore through the canvas, destroying the demon in Solon's Cave, and then pierced the flesh above Tanan's black heart.

Em tried dragging the groggy Matt to the bottom of the steps she'd animated in Solon's Cave, but his arm hurt so much that she had to stop. She couldn't bear to feel his anguish inside her head anymore.

"Leave me here and get help," Matt slurred. "You'll be able to move through the tunnel much more quickly on your own."

For once, Em didn't argue. She was just helping him settle into a more comfortable position, when she heard scratching from the other side of the cave wall.

Pressing her ear against the hard earth, Em closed her eyes and listened. There was something or someone above her, on the other side. She began to yell and holler, screaming at the top of her lungs, "We're in here! In here!"

Slowly, light pierced a tiny crevice in the cave's dirt ceiling. Then it widened, and soon the entire beam from a flashlight filled the cave.

Vaughn leaned over the hole he'd torn in the hillside, his breathing even more labored than before. "Are you both okay?"

Em beamed up at him. "I'm pretty sure Matt's arm's broken, but other than that we're fine. Just really glad to see you. How did you find us?"

"That's another story altogether," Vaughn said breathlessly. "Let's get you both out, and you can see for yourself."

SEVENTY-THREE

Simon crashed the Jet Ski Mara had drawn for him up onto the hard sand at the base of the tower on Era Mina. Shoving her drawing into his pocket, he clambered over the rocky beach toward the caves, and then paused to take stock of the situation. Up ahead, he could see the abbey's speedboat. He crept forward slowly under the cover of the cliff and peered around the rocks into Monk's Cove.

The beacon light from the tower was illuminating a scene at the mouth of the cave that made his heart sing. With a blanket wrapped over his shoulders like a cape, Zach was laughing and high-fiving a man that Simon recognized as Vaughn. An archer's bow was slung over Zach's shoulder. And if that image was not amazing enough, Simon laughed out loud at the rest of the picture.

The twins were hovering above the tidal pools of jellyfish on the back of a magnificent peryton.

As soon as Simon reached the group, the extent of their injuries was obvious. Hugging Zach hard, he took out his mobile and called the chief constable, asking her to meet him on Era Mina.

The twins, Zach, and Vaughn were clustering around him. Simon put away his phone and held his hands up. "So where's this Tanan?"

Zach looked at the sand. "He's gone."

Vaughn was not going to let Zach's heroism go unacknowledged. He handed Zach the paper on which he'd animated the bow and arrow. "Zach is quite the archer. I couldn't manipulate the bow with my injuries. He had to. And he was brilliant!"

"I already knew that," said Em, making Zach blush.

Simon beamed at his son.

"By the time I got down the hillside with the twins, Tanan was gone," Vaughn apologized. "Zach's shot clearly wasn't fatal."

Simon turned his attention to the extraordinary peryton. The beast folded its wings tightly against its sides and bent its forelegs, making it easier for Matt to slip off. The boys grinned at each other through their pain.

"I think because we animated the peryton in such an unusual way, it stayed animated. Somehow it sensed where we were," explained Em, climbing down behind Matt. "Thank you," she whispered to the beast, resting her cheek on the peryton's massive chest. Then she rushed over to hug Zach.

Despite his worsening breathing, Vaughn picked up the rest of the explanation. "After he vanquished Tanan, Zach saw the peryton up on the hillside, digging its antlers into the rock up there. It knew there was a way inside the island at that very spot. I managed to make it up the hill and found the opening, but I couldn't do anything else."

Em finished the story. "The peryton seemed to know there was a wider opening in the rock. It charged its way in, and I was able to get Matt onto its back." She grinned at Zach. "And here we are!"

Simon stroked the peryton's massive white head, running his fingers over its impressive, mottled, ivory antlers. Standing at full height, the beast had to be as big as two stags, and its thick hide shimmered like silver in the moonlight. Awed by its presence, Simon bowed.

"Thank you, indeed," he said.

The peryton shook its antlers, snorting as if in reply. And Simon realized that he could no longer sense Mara's pain.

The peryton scuffed its hooves on the rocks, forcing Em and Simon to step away. When they did, it leaped from the rocks and galloped across the sand, its wings spreading out from its sides. After a few more bounding strides, it rose up into the starry night sky. It hovered for a moment; then, in a sudden flare of pure white light, it was gone.

* * *

Chief Constable Clarissa Bond landed in an RAF helicopter just minutes later, a coastguard rescue boat following quickly behind. In no time at all, Matt, Zach, and Vaughn were en route to the hospital in the helicopter, while Simon and Em returned the abbey's speedboat to the boathouse. The chief constable followed them across to the abbey in the rescue boat.

"Can't we go straight to the hospital in this?" Em pleaded, as Simon steered the boat into the dock. "I don't want to go home."

Simon docked the boat. "The chief will take us to the hospital in a few minutes," he said, "but Mara needs us first."

Not keen to see Mara again anytime soon, Em reluctantly followed Simon across the lawn.

The studio was in the same state of chaos as when Matt and Em had left it earlier that night. Em hovered at the door. She wasn't sure she wanted to help Mara at all.

"Em, you must." Simon seemed able to read her mind. He took her hand. "Your grandfather would expect nothing less."

Behind the kiln, *Witch with Changeling Child* had returned to its original form, the horrible hag clutching the demon on her lap. Mara was nowhere to be seen.

Em shivered. "That picture is full of evil," she said.

"Yes," said Simon. "Yes, it is."

Fishing his Swiss Army knife from his pocket, he flicked open the blade. In four swift strokes, he had sliced the canvas from its frame. Em pressed the button to open the heavy doors of the kiln, and Simon fed the painting into the flames.

SEVENTY-FOUR

Jeannie was more than ready for them when they returned from the hospital in the small hours of the morning. She hadn't made it home until past ten, after the ferry's jellyfish-clogged engines had been cleared. Walking into the compound, she'd found the abbey and the grounds deserted, the kitchen doors flung open, and Mara's studio looking as if a gale-force wind had swept through it. She didn't know what had happened, and had been sick with worry. After a frantic couple of hours, she'd reached Simon on his mobile at the hospital. He'd apologized for not letting her know sooner, doing his best to fill her in on the night's incredible events.

"And she's not happy we all left her in the dark," Simon said, as they docked at the abbey in the boat the chief constable had left at their disposal. "So be warned!"

Hobbling on crutches, Zach walked into the kitchen first. Matt came in right behind him, his arm in a sling. Em, her hip bruised but nothing broken, helped Simon guide Vaughn across the threshold, his fractured ribs wrapped tightly, the cuts and gashes from his fall cleaned and stitched.

Jeannie stood blocking their view of the kitchen table, hands on her hips.

"Ye all are in big trouble," she said. She drilled Vaughn with her stare. "And you! Hardly a peep in years. Why did ye not get here sooner tae help? It's porridge for ye all for a week." Then she stepped aside. "But birthday cake first!"

A three-tiered coconut cake on the table blazed with twenty-six candles—thirteen for Em, thirteen for Matt. Pulling the twins into a hug the likes of which they'd never experienced in their lives, she kissed them hard. "Did ye think I'd let a couple of demented Animare get in the way of cake? Happy birthday, bairns."

Em and Matt grinned at each other, as Jeannie scooped Zach into a similar chokehold of a cuddle, kissing and pecking at the top of his head like a mother hen. Vaughn could see he was next. He figured his best bet was to remind Jeannie of his ribs, and then relax and enjoy the moment, because there was just one thing on his mind—he was glad to be back.

After devouring most of the cake, they gathered around the kitchen hearth, where Jeannie served them steaming mugs of hot chocolate.

"Oh, I almost forgot," she said, heading over to the pantry and returning with a plastic carrier bag. "One of the chief constable's men dropped this off right after I got home. They found it in the cave."

Simon reached in and pulled out Sandie's satchel. He looked at Em, then at Matt. "Which one of you wants to do the honors?"

"Together," said Em.

Mom should be here. We've never had a birthday without her.

I know. Maybe this will help us find her.

Taking the satchel from Simon, Em squeezed in between Zach and Matt on the other couch.

"Hey, watch the arm," yelped Matt.

"Oh, don't be such a baby." Em set the satchel on the coffee table in front of them. She fiddled with the catch, but it wouldn't open. "It's still locked!"

Vaughn took a small gold key off his key ring. "The day you left London, your mom asked me to get that bag out of her safety deposit box at the bank and bring it to her at Covent Garden. I've always carried a spare key for it."

"Do you know what's inside?" asked Matt.

"No," Vaughn said. "I don't. All I know is that your mom considered whatever was inside to be a kind of insurance policy—leverage was her exact word—against anything happening to her or to both of you. I always assumed she meant it was proof against the art forgery ring Sir Charles Wren had involved her in. I didn't know then that Arthur Summers was also blackmailing her. And it's only recently that I've learned that the rumors about the revival of the Hollow Earth Society are true. I'm not sure how much Wren knows about that."

With Matt and Zach leaning over her shoulder, Em opened the satchel. Reaching inside, she pulled out a rusty brass key bearing the crest of the abbey. She passed the key to Simon, who glanced at it, shrugged, and placed it on the table. Then she lifted out a thin metal case, half the size and thickness of a laptop.

An inscription etched on the front of it read:

> *May you never forget imagination is the real and the eternal.*
> *This is Hollow Earth.*

Simon picked up the slim metal case. "It looks like the kind of thing museums use to transport valuable books or pages from illuminated manuscripts."

He set the case on the coffee table in front of them, carefully breaking the seal and lifting the lid. Everyone leaned forward to look inside.

"It's just a page from an old book," said Matt, disappointed.

Under a protective shield of thin, clear Plexiglas was a page of vellum from an ancient illuminated manuscript. The page began:

> THIS Book is about the nature of beasts. Gaze
> upon these pages at your peril, for they may unleash
> Hollow Earth.

Shimmering gold leaf illuminated each of the first five capital letters. A trail of ink that had spilled from the scribe's quill looked like tiny teardrops across the page.

Em's expression was an odd combination of a smile and a frown. "It's weird," she said. "I can see these words in my head the way I can see an animation. It's as if they're glowing."

Zach sketched quickly in the air. "What's the page from?"

Simon went across the hall to the library, returning with a very old leather book. Flipping through, he found the place he was looking for and set the book down in front of them. It showed a picture of the page from Sandie's satchel.

"'*The Book of Beasts*,'" Matt read from the description. "'One of the last bestiaries produced by the ancient order of monks at the Monastery of Era Mina, and believed to have been destroyed in the nineteenth century.'"

"What's a bestiary?" asked Zach.

"A kind of alphabet book of imaginary beasts," said Vaughn.

"Now what?" asked Em, as Simon sealed the page back in its case.

"I don't know," Simon admitted.

Matt felt furious. "So after everything we've been through—even after discovering that our own mother is supposed to have bound our dad in a painting to stop him from hurting us—we've got no idea why this piece of paper is so important, and we're still no closer to finding our mom?"

Vaughn wheezed a little when he spoke. He picked up the

rusty brass key and dangled it thoughtfully. "Your mother clearly thought that page and this key were something worth keeping from you—from all of us. And knowing Sandie, whatever else she might have done for Sir Charles Wren and Arthur Summers to keep her secret about binding Malcolm in a painting, she would do anything to protect her children."

Jeannie gathered up the mugs, nudging Simon to look at the children. Zach was almost asleep, his head resting on the arm of the couch. The twins were pale, their eyes drooping as they fought to stay awake.

"I think," said Vaughn, carefully easing himself from the couch, "when we've all had some time to rest and heal, we'll just have to put our talents to finding out everything we can about this manuscript page and key.

"I'm convinced they have something to do with Hollow Earth, and *everything* to do with your mom's disappearance."

SEVENTY-FIVE

Matt and Zach were eating breakfast in the kitchen with Vaughn when Em wandered down the back stairs. Floating behind her was a version of herself dressed in white chain mail, wielding an impressive sword.

"My goodness," said Vaughn, almost spraying a mouthful of coffee across the table. "What is that?"

Neither Zach nor Matt looked up. They continued shoveling their breakfasts into their mouths. "You'll get used to living with a girl in the house," Matt said between mouthfuls. "Their dreams are pretty weird."

Jeannie snapped her fingers next to Em's head, and the dream Em dissolved in a cloud of white dust. Yawning, Em sat at the table next to Vaughn. Jeannie slid a bowl in front of her. Em stared at it.

"I thought you were kidding. Not porridge, Jeannie. It's still my birthday!"

"I don't joke about keeping me informed at all times of your whereabouts," Jeannie said pointedly.

"We had it too," said Matt.

"Eat up," Vaughn advised, scooping a spoonful of the white gruel from Em's bowl. "Simon's got plans for you this morning."

Two hours later, the twins were standing outside Renard's room at the hospital with Simon.

"There's been no change," said Renard's doctor, holding the door open. "But that can be a good thing when you're dealing with a traumatic brain injury like this one."

Em set her sketch pad and markers on the bedside table. Leaning over the bed, she kissed her grandfather's cheek. Matt pulled a chair up on the other side.

"Remember, only soft conversation," said the doctor, as Simon ushered her politely out of the door. "Your grandfather's brain needs peace and quiet to heal."

As soon as the doctor was gone, Simon closed the door and hurried around the room, shutting the blinds. While Em opened her sketch pad to a clean page, Matt perched van Gogh's *Poppy Fields*, the painting Em had brought to the hospital on their last visit, on the bed.

"Ready?" asked Simon. Em and Matt nodded in unison. They each took one of their grandfather's hands and began to draw.

Matt skillfully outlined the white-pebbled path running through the center of the painting, the thatched cottage, and the tall palm tree, before shading in the distant blue of the sea on the horizon. Em used her red, purple, and black markers to create the fields of lush poppies that filled the rest of the canvas. Together, the twins imagined van Gogh's blistering summer day in Saint-Rémy, France.

Em looked at Matt across the hospital bed. Matt turned to say something to Simon—and then Em was standing next to him on the pebbled path, their grandfather walking toward them through the field of thick, lush poppies.

Renard embraced them both. *I've always loved this painting. Thank you for bringing it to my room, Em.*

Grandpa, we might not have much time. We need to ask you something about our dad.

Let's walk toward the sea, shall we?

Hand in hand, they went toward the horizon, the poppies swishing in the summer breeze.

We need to know exactly what happened to him.

Renard sighed. *I had planned to have this conversation with you the day I took you to the vault. Your mother didn't want me to tell you, and after what happened to you down in the vault, Em, I fear she may have been correct.*

The sun was warm on Em's skin, yet she felt chilled.

It's my greatest regret, my dears, that I did not see what was happening to my own son. He was seduced by visions of great wealth and power.

The thick perfume of the poppies and the intensity of the hot sun were making Em feel sick.

Did he believe in Hollow Earth?

Yes. And so does your mother.

A green bench stood under a tall tree in front of the thatched cottage at the edge of the path. The three of them sat down.

That's why I agreed to help her. She and I bound your father in a copy of Fox's painting, so that he could never use your powers for his own gain.

The twins were speechless. Em snuggled close to her grandfather.

As you know, only an Animare and a Guardian together can fully bind another person. We both knew your dad was becoming dangerous and reckless. He knew that one day your powers might become the key to opening Hollow Earth.

The conversation was draining Renard's powers too. Matt looked ill.

Your mother and I bound Malcolm together. Then she fled with you both to London, telling everyone he had abandoned you there.

But why not just stay with you at the abbey?

Your mother couldn't bear to have you anywhere near your dad, bound or not. You see, your father is locked in a painting in the abbey's vault. The very one that caused you so much distress when you entered the vault that day, Em.

The twins were so startled at this extraordinary piece of information that they started to lose control of their animation. The scene around them began to bleed, as if someone had poured water on the canvas. The red of the poppies was seeping into the white pebbles of the path, a river of blue from the horizon was running past the bench. Em could hear her grandfather's heart monitor beeping loud in her head. Through the slipping colors, she looked at Matt.

Tanan must have assumed that Mom would carry the picture with her wherever she went, to keep it out of the wrong hands.

Matt reached down and picked up a handful of dissolving pebbles from the path, rolling them nervously in his hands, trying to process what he was hearing.

Sir Charles Wren and Arthur Summers knew your mother had bound your father illegally. Binding a person requires the Council's full knowledge and consent. Binding anyone other than an Animare is a grievous violation of Council rules—and even more so if the person in question is a Guardian.

I thought Sir Charles was head of the Council?

He is, Em. But there is money to be made from talents like your mother's, and Sandie was blackmailed. In order to keep you both safe and to keep herself free, I fear that she has done many things that only she can and should tell you about.

The beeping was much louder, the monitors screaming in the twins' heads. The edges of the cottage were softening now, the brown and yellow thatch oozing into the white walls.

Reaching into the poppy field, Renard scooped an armful of fading blossoms into his arms, tucking one in Matt's T-shirt pocket, before handing the bouquet to Em. Then he hugged them both.

Happy birthday. Be brave, both of you. I will be back with you soon.

Em was no longer sitting on the bench. Matt couldn't smell the poppies anymore. All he could smell was antiseptic. The painting faded just as the doctor barged into Renard's room, a nurse right behind her, to silence the high-pitched alarms of the monitors.

"What on earth is going on in here?" demanded the doctor crossly, checking the screens. "Every monitor is registering extremely high levels of brain activity."

She turned to admonish Simon and the twins. But instead, she was confronted with a speechless nurse and Renard's hospital bed covered in bright red poppies.

Outside the main entrance of the hospital, Simon turned toward Largs pier, the children beside him, the painting tucked under his arm.

"Don't you want to know what we learned?" asked Matt, walking a little way ahead.

"I'm guessing your grandfather told you he helped bind your dad in a painting," answered Simon, guiding the twins across Main Street and out onto the busy pier.

Em was jogging a little so she could keep up with Matt and Simon's long strides. "But how did you know that?"

"After you all went to bed last night," explained Simon, "Vaughn and I talked about everything that happened yesterday. We realized that although your mom is a powerful Animare, she wasn't capable of binding another person on her own. If Tanan was right, and your mom had done what he claimed she had, then we knew a Guardian must have helped her. And the only one it could have been was your grandfather."

"Do you think Mara's okay, wherever she is?"

"I can feel that she is," said Simon, squeezing Em's hand. "I think Tanan managed to get back over to the abbey as soon as the peryton appeared. It's likely he freed Mara from the painting before we got there, and I have a feeling they both escaped from Auchinmurn together." He sighed, adding, "I hope she'll get away from him and come back to us someday."

The pier was packed with tourists buying ice-cream cones, sausage rolls, and sandwiches and carrying them down to the beach. Fishermen were casting off the edge of the pier, bags and buckets filled with ice next to them, seagulls circling hopefully above. Simon pointed the twins to the picnic tables set up at the end of the pier, where Zach and Vaughn were unpacking one of Jeannie's famous picnic lunches.

"Do you think Grandpa's going to get better soon?" Em asked, slipping her hand into Simon's.

"Yes," he replied. "I think what you and Matt did this morning might have been just the jolt his system needed."

"How did you know that we would be able to bring Grandpa

into a painting with us?" asked Matt, one eye on Simon and the other on Zach and Vaughn lifting treats out of the picnic basket.

"It was Vaughn who suggested it," said Simon. "He figured that since you could imagine yourselves into a painting when you'd had very little training, there was the distinct possibility that now you would be able to take another person along with you."

The lure of lunch was finally too much for Matt. Keeping his broken arm tight against his body, so it wouldn't bounce against him, he ran on ahead to Vaughn and Zach and the food.

"I like Vaughn," said Em. "And I think he really likes my mom."

"I know he does." Simon smiled. "And I'm glad to hear that you like him too." They had reached the picnic table. Simon mussed his son's hair in greeting. "Because until Renard fully recovers, Vaughn will be your new tutor."

Vaughn handed each of them one of Jeannie's sandwiches. "And despite all the intriguing revelations of the past few days," he said, ignoring the children's groans of horror, "real lessons begin again tomorrow morning."

After lunch, while Zach helped Vaughn pack up the picnic basket, and Simon went to fetch the Range Rover, Matt and Em sat at the end of the pier, feeding the seagulls with the leftovers.

"Where do you think Mom is now?" asked Em, lobbing a crust high into the air and watching a gull snap it up. "Do you think she can feel us? And do you think we'll ever see her again?"

There was a catch in her voice, and she stared hard out to sea.

"I don't know where she is, but we'll find her, Em. I know we will." Matt mashed a piece of a sausage roll between his fingers. "Simon and Vaughn have promised to help us, and when Grandpa's better, he'll teach us everything we need to know about Hollow Earth. The next time anyone comes after us, we'll be ready for them."

"How can you be so sure?"

"Because we've survived amazing things these past couple of days. If we can get through that, we can get through anything." He turned to smile at his sister. "Mom always said we were special, you know."

Em knew Matt was right. She felt excited about their growing powers. She was part of a fantastic world that was as old as the islands themselves. But she was a little nervous, too. Despite how well she was controlling her fears, she was still anxious about what the future might hold.

Lobbing a handful of crusts into the bay, Em laughed as the gulls dive-bombed the water. "Next time we go into a painting, let's take Zach with us," she said. "We owe him. After all, he saved us from Tanan's demon with his amazing archery skills."

"How about we go into something wild—like by that Dalí guy or maybe some computer art?" said Matt with enthusiasm. Em rolled her eyes. "Oh, yeah, that's all we need. To take Zach inside computer art and let him loose! Can you imagine it?"

They looked at each other, then burst out laughing.

"Yeah," Matt grinned. "I can."

Vaughn whistled from the other end of the pier, waving at them as Simon pulled up to the curb in the Range Rover. Without warning, Matt scooped up all his crusts and crushed them into Em's hair. Then he scrambled onto his feet and darted down the pier toward Vaughn and Zach.

Shaking crumbs from her hair, Em leaped to her feet. "You'd better run, Matt Calder, 'cos special or not, I'm going to kill you!"

ACKNOWLEDGMENTS

We first imagined this book while driving from London to Cardiff. The traffic was heavy, so the trip took ages. When we finally crossed the bridge into Wales, we already knew who the main characters would be and we had the beginnings of the plot. The journey since then has been an exciting one, so we have people to thank who helped us to reach this place.

Thank you to everyone at Michael O'Mara Books Ltd. and Buster Books—Alison Parker, Philippa Wingate, and Liz Scoggins. Philippa shepherded us along with a healthy balance of nurturing and nudging, and editors Michelle Misra and Lucy Courtenay deserve an exploding fist bump or two.

As always, Gavin Barker of Gavin Barker Associates Ltd. continues to be the best backseat driver (thanks, G), and a warm welcome to Team Barrowman, Georgina Capel of Capel and Land Ltd.

To suit our story, we've taken some liberties with geography, renaming and repositioning a few places, and although we hope the book will encourage you to visit your nearest art gallery, you won't find *Witch with Changeling Child* or the Scottish artist Duncan Fox on display in any of them. The painting *Witch with Changeling Child* was inspired by the horrible creatures in the corner of Henri Fuseli's *Titania and Bottom* (1790), and William Blake's *The Ghost of a Flea* (1819–20) inspired Fox's *The Demon Within*. Both of the real paintings can be viewed at Tate Britain in London.

One of the most famous medieval manuscripts is *The Aberdeen Bestiary*, which inspired our *The Book of Beasts*. Also, part of an inscription attributed to Duncan Fox—"Imagination is the real and the eternal"—comes from the poet William Blake, who believed that a place like Hollow Earth was possible.

For more information about the art that you'll find in these pages (and lots of other creative stuff), visit our website at hollow-earth.co.uk.

Finally, Auchinmurn Isle, the abbey, and all its inhabitants have existed only in our imaginations. We're thrilled that now they'll come alive in yours.

WHAT LIES AHEAD FOR MATT AND EM?
FIND OUT IN *BONE QUILL*.

The battle for control of the Calder twins' imaginations began on the afternoon of their third birthday. Sandie was enjoying the last slice of Jeannie's double-decker chocolate cake when Malcolm raced into the kitchen.

"I've found it!" he said, waving a red leather journal in front of Sandie in feverish excitement. "Proof that Hollow Earth is real!"

Sandie's fork clattered to her plate. "What?"

"It's all in this diary! 'The key must not be found'—but this is the exciting part. Listen to this." Malcolm flipped to another. "'After all that I have witnessed, after the horrors that have been revealed to me in Hollow Earth, I know this. The powers within are too terrible for man to control.'"

"All these months of searching, and finally this!" He began to

pace in front of the French doors. "With Matt and Em's help, I—"
He stopped, then turned and smiled at Sandie. "We will control
Hollow Earth and then . . . everything will be ours."

"You're mad, Malcolm," sputtered Sandie, dread creeping up
her spine. "I don't want everything."

A part of Malcolm had always been wild—so focused on his
own obsessions that he ignored the feelings and opinions of others. Sandie had hoped marriage would calm him, but since the
birth of the twins, this obsession with Hollow Earth had been
eating away the Malcolm she'd fallen in love with.

"I don't care how you squander your powers or your life, but
you can't use the twins to further this madness!" she went on, her
pulse quickening. "They're too young, practically babies. Their
powers are not yours to control."

Malcolm gripped Sandie's shoulders. She flinched. "I won't be
stopped by you or anyone else," he said coldly. "To master Hollow
Earth is my destiny."

The next morning Sandie was glad of the chance to breakfast
quietly with Renard while Malcolm played with the twins outside. But as she gazed out the window at the great glass sculpture
in the abbey grounds, she noticed something strange.

The sculpture was a massive mobile of mirrors suspended
from the trees at the western point of the grounds, shimmering
and spinning in the changeable winds that ran along the island's
coastline. Matt and Em were sprawled under the installation on

a blanket with their dad, painting. But what was reflected in the mirrors was not the cozy scene that it should have been.

Instead, each shard was reflecting the swirling greens, browns, and yellows of a mysterious cave mouth.

When the wind caught the mobile, the mirrored glass spun and Sandie saw the telltale glow of an animation. A stabbing awareness pierced her mind.

She recognized the image.

Lasers of light suddenly shot from the cave mouth, every fragment of mirror multiplying the effects, creating a crisscrossing grid of light encasing the trees, trapping Malcolm and the twins inside.

"Renard!" Sandie screamed. "Stop him!"

Renard Calder appeared at his daughter-in-law's side. He stared in shock at the scene unfolding on the lawn.

"My God, what's he doing?"

"I think he's using the mirrors to increase the twins' powers," replied Sandie, her voice seared with panic. "Malcolm has Duncan Fox's painting of the entrance to Hollow Earth, and the twins are animating it!"

"Impossible!" gasped Renard. "That painting is locked in the vault!"

"When have locks—or even you—managed to stop your son?"

She raced through the French doors and across the wide lawn toward the trees that had lit up as if candles burned from their branches. Renard was close behind her.

"Stop!" Sandie screamed at the grid of light surrounding her children. She jabbed her finger into one of the light beams, yelping and drawing back when a shock shot up her arm and exploded in a million red dots in her head.

Desperately searching for a way through the grid to reach the twins, she called out: "Mattie, Emmie! Come over here to Mummy!" Once. Twice. Each time louder and more insistently.

The twins never budged, never looked up, never stopped painting.

Malcolm was crouching next to them with his hands resting on their shoulders, his head close to their ears, whispering to them.

Renard pinched the bridge of his nose. "He's inspiriting them. I can feel him . . ."

"How could he?" Sandie raced up and down, frantically scanning the neon cage, searching for a way inside. "It's against everything we stand for. Everything!"

Matt's and Em's tiny fingers were flying across their shared sketch pad. The gilt-framed painting of the cave mouth was propped next to them, beside another Fox painting of a scaly, hairless demon. Malcolm's knuckles were turning white, his fists clenched on the twins' slumped shoulders, holding them in place.

"What will his inspiriting do to them?" cried Sandie.

"I don't know." Renard's face was white.

"Malcolm! Stop!" Sandie was crouching at the tree line, trying to catch Matt's or Em's attention, to break Malcolm's spell. "Please! They're too young. You'll hurt them!"

The twins painted on, oblivious to the danger looming over them.

Malcolm slowly lifted his head. With eyes blazing, he looked over at Sandie, his handsome face contorted, his skin pale. Lifting his hand from Em's shoulder, he held a finger to his lips.

For Sandie the next seconds unfolded in horrifying slow motion. Matt and Em put down their paintbrushes and took each other's hands. They clambered to their feet, watching excitedly as the painting they'd been copying projected itself around them like a 3-D movie, wrapping them in thick, swirling brushstrokes of green, brown, and yellow. At first the twins giggled at the lines of color. But then the painting began to close in on them. They clung to each other, their expressions quickly transforming from delight to apprehension.

"Daddy! I don't want to do this," wailed Em.

"Make it stop," cried Matt.

Fading into the churning colors, the twins disappeared completely.

Sandie screamed and charged toward the grid. On the shards of mirrors shifting in the wind, Matt's and Em's reflections appeared at the mouth of the animated cave.

"Go in! The key will be inside the cave. Bring it to me!" Malcolm shouted, shooing them inside with his hands.

"No!" Sandie shrieked.

She watched helplessly as the twins, tightly holding hands, vanished inside the cave. Malcolm's eyes blazed in triumph.

Sandie collapsed to the grass. Renard was frozen to the spot.

After five agonizing minutes, the twins scrambled empty-handed from the cave. They were both crying.

With a roar of frustration, Malcolm tore up the twins' painting. The air seemed to open above the blanket, and the twins tumbled onto the grass among the fading lines of light.

Frantically gathering them up, Sandie wrapped her children in the blanket, cooing softly to them. Blood trickled from Matt's nose. Em's eyes were red-rimmed and unfocused. Neither of them spoke. They seemed to be in a trance.

"They'll be fine in the morning," said Malcolm, mussing Matt's hair. "Disappointing, though. I was sure that painting was where he'd hidden the key. Maybe it's in the other one."

Renard pulled Sandie and the twins into his arms to comfort them. Malcolm began to laugh.

"You will eventually see things my way, Sandie," he said. "Our children will be capable of extraordinary things when they fully come into their powers. We will find Hollow Earth together!"

Renard stared at the expression on his son's face, and then at the still-blank faces of his grandchildren. "You will never inspirit or harm these children again as long as I live, Malcolm," he said.

"You're an old man, Dad." Malcolm grinned. "I may not have long to wait."

Renard dropped his hands to his sides, sending a wave of energy toward his son and knocking Malcolm off his feet. Malcolm crashed to the ground, cutting his head, and let out a feral howl as Renard sliced into his thoughts. The older man's eyes opened wide in anguish—and Malcolm pounced.

Renard pivoted in time to catch his son's arm, twisting him into a headlock and bringing him to his knees. Snarling, Malcolm sank his teeth into Renard's forearm, tearing at his flesh. The pain broke Renard's concentration, allowing Malcolm to pull away from his father's grip.

"These are my children," screamed Malcolm. He wiped at the blood flowing from the cut on his head. "I will decide their fate. Not you and not her!"

"No, you will not!" said Renard, slamming into Malcolm's chest, knocking him against a tree. Malcolm's eyes slid shut at the impact.

The exhausted twins were asleep, huddled in their mother's arms. Renard lunged for the sketchbook. Holding his bloody arm over a blank page, he let his blood pool onto it.

"What are you doing?" cried Sandie.

"We must bind him. Right now," said Renard, pushing the unconscious Malcolm's hair from his forehead and letting the blood from the gash mingle with his own on the page.

Sandie laid the sleeping twins down and knelt in front of Renard, her hand on his. "We can't. . . . The consequences if we're discovered . . . They don't bear thinking about."

Renard lifted his eyes to Sandie's. His shame and sadness for what he was about to do robbed Sandie of her breath.

"We must . . . we must . . ." Renard struggled for words. "When

I tried to get into Malcolm's head to calm him, I saw the most awful things. Demonic beings clawing up from the bowels of the earth, an army of rotting corpses lurching behind them. I saw beasts battling above the sea, their massive wings churning tidal waves beneath them. . . ." He paused, handing the page to Sandie. "And I saw Matt and Em awash in their own blood. My son is a monster. He must be stopped. Do it before he wakes up!"

Malcolm groaned; his eyes fluttered. Sandie stared at the other Fox painting Malcolm had left on the blanket. The monster Malcolm had become deserved to be bound in a painting of a horrible, scaly demon. Seizing one of the twin's paintbrushes, she cleaned it with shaking fingers, dipped it into the blood on the page, and began to copy the skinless monster.

Renard put his hand on her shoulder and closed his eyes. The wind picked up. The air smelled of seaweed and a hint of pine tar. The paintbrush felt hot. Sandie's skin began to blister as she outlined the demon in Malcolm's and Renard's blood. Keeping the brush at the heart of the canvas, Sandie let Renard's power surge through her animation.

The trees rustled. The waves slapped the shore. A ghostly silhouette coiled up from the page. It hovered above Malcolm's head, tendrils snaking over him, embracing him, coating him in darkness. Malcolm slowly began to fade, his being absorbed into the animation, binding him in its form.

JOHN BARROWMAN & CAROLE E. BARROWMAN

John is an actor, a recording artist, and Carole's wee brother. He's starred in West End and Broadway shows, and hosted and coproduced his own BBC entertainment show, *Tonight's the Night*. He has guest-starred on many TV shows, including *Desperate Housewives*. His most popular role is that of sci-fi hero Captain Jack Harkness, whose first appearance in the revamped *Doctor Who* resulted in the spin-off series *Torchwood*.

Carole is an English professor at Alverno College in Milwaukee, Wisconsin, and John's big sister. She also directs Alverno's Creative Studies in Writing program, writes a monthly column on crime fiction for the *Milwaukee Journal Sentinel*, and writes articles and reviews for the *Minneapolis Star Tribune*.

Born and raised in Scotland, Carole and John have been making up stories together since they were kids. They love art—looking at it and creating it—and whenever they travel to a new city, they always visit its art museum.

"*Keeper of the Lost Cities* is a little bit *Alice's Adventures in Wonderland*, a little bit *Lord of the Rings*, and a little bit *Harry Potter*. And it's all fun!"

—MICHAEL BUCKLEY,
New York Times bestselling author of the Sisters Grimm and NERDS series

"A delightful and dangerous adventure with complex characters and relationships you'll root for to the end of time."

—LISA McMANN,
New York Times bestselling author of *The Unwanteds*, on *Keeper of the Lost Cities*

"DO I HAVE FAMILY IN THE IMAGINE NATION?" JACK ASKED. "ARE THEY SUPERHEROES?"

"YOU'RE A MYSTERY, JACK. BUT THAT'S ALL ABOUT TO CHANGE."

DON'T MISS THE THRILLING ADVENTURES of Jack Blank, who could be either the savior of the Imagine Nation and the world beyond, or the biggest threat they've ever faced. And even Jack himself doesn't know which it will be. . . .

EBOOK EDITIONS ALSO AVAILABLE

From Aladdin
KIDS.SimonandSchuster.com

Did you **LOVE** this book?

Want to get access to great books for FREE?

Join

Simon & Schuster IN THE book loop